A Daughter's Guide to Mothers and Murder

Books by Dianne Freeman

Countess of Harleigh Mysteries

A LADY'S GUIDE TO ETIQUETTE AND MURDER

A LADY'S GUIDE TO GOSSIP AND MURDER

A LADY'S GUIDE TO MISCHIEF AND MURDER

A FIANCEE'S GUIDE TO FIRST WIVES AND MURDER

A BRIDE'S GUIDE TO MARRIAGE AND MURDER

A NEWLYWED'S GUIDE TO FORTUNE AND MURDER

AN ART LOVER'S GUIDE TO PARIS AND MURDER

A DAUGHTER'S GUIDE TO MOTHERS AND MURDER

Countess of Harleigh Novellas

GEORGE AND FRANCES ROLL THE DICE

Published by Kensington Publishing Corp.

A Daughter's Guide to Mothers and Murder

Dianne Freeman

KENSINGTON PUBLISHING CORP.
kensingtonbooks.com

This book is a work of fiction. Names, characters, businesses, organizations, places, events, and incidents either are the product of the author's imagination or are used fictitiously. Any resemblance to actual persons, living or dead, events, or locales is entirely coincidental.

To the extent that the image or images on the cover of this book depict a person or persons, such person or persons are merely models, and are not intended to portray any character or characters featured in the book.

KENSINGTON BOOKS are published by

Kensington Publishing Corp.
900 Third Avenue
New York, NY 10022

Copyright © 2025 by Dianne Freeman

All rights reserved. No part of this book may be reproduced in any form or by any means without the prior written consent of the Publisher, excepting brief quotes used in reviews.

All Kensington titles, imprints and distributed lines are available at special quantity discounts for bulk purchases for sales promotion, premiums, fund-raising, educational or institutional use.

Special book excerpts or customized printings can also be created to fit specific needs. For details, write or phone the office of the Kensington Special Sales Manager: Kensington Publishing Corp., 900 Third Avenue, New York, NY, 10022. Attn. Special Sales Department. Phone: 1-800-221-2647.

KENSINGTON and the K with book logo Reg. US Pat. & TM Off.

Library of Congress Control Number: 2025932702

ISBN-13: 978-1-4967-4514-9
First Kensington Hardcover Edition: July 2025

ISBN-13: 978-1-4967-4516-3 (e-book)

10 9 8 7 6 5 4 3 2 1

Printed in the United States of America

The authorized representative in the EU for product safety and compliance
is eucomply OU, Parnu mnt 139b-14, Apt 123
Tallinn, Berlin 11317, hello@eucompliancepartner.com

A Daughter's Guide to Mothers and Murder

Chapter One

Paris, September 23, 1900

"If this isn't the good life, then I don't know what is." Patricia Kendrick, the hostess of our picnic, raised her wine glass as if toasting everyone in the park. "What an exquisite day to be out enjoying nature!"

"Indeed, it's hard to believe we are still in Paris," I said. Our picnic site was an open meadow alongside Lac Inferieur in the midst of the natural beauty of the Bois de Boulogne, one of the largest parks in Paris. I was half turned away from our table so I could watch the rowers work their way out to the two tiny islands in the middle of the lake. Now that I thought about it, those islands were man-made. In fact, if I was not mistaken, so were the lakes. Both Inferieur and Superieur and their charming little brooks were constructed in the middle of the last century, with water piped in from an artesian well at the southernmost end of the park.

Natural or not, it was impossible to argue against the beauty of this lovely park.

The day was warm for so late in September, which likely

sparked the idea for this picnic. Impromptu, my sister had called it, but our table was covered with white linen, we had the requisite china, silver, and crystal. Two footmen were carrying the hampers, packed with sweet and savory delights, from the carriage parked around the other side of the hedge. It would be far too much food for the four of us, my sister, Lily, her mother-in-law, Patricia, and Patricia's daughter, Anne. And of course, Lily's four-month-old daughter, Amelia, who was perfectly content to gnaw on her own fingers.

"When did you return from Deauville, Frances?"

I turned my attention to Patricia. She was in her mid-forties with deep brown eyes and golden-brown hair that she wore parted in the center and woven into intricate twists behind her head.

"Just yesterday," I replied. My husband and I had been on something of a belated honeymoon for the past three weeks. We had come to France a month ago on behalf of his young ward and her half-sister. We had to settle some issues pertaining to their late father's estate, part of which involved a villa in the seaside town of Deauville—a villa neither girl wanted to keep or even see.

The girls had refused to go with us, so George and I traveled to Deauville on our own, and once our business was finished—we ended up buying the villa ourselves—we finally enjoyed a honeymoon. The two of us. All alone. My expression turned dreamy at the thought of it. "It was wonderful," I told Patricia, who nodded in understanding.

"Once you have a houseful of young people, it's almost impossible to find time for each other," she said. "And Deauville is such a pretty town—there's nothing to do but relax."

We had managed to find plenty to do—not all of it relaxing and some quite terrifying, but I couldn't discuss that with Patricia. "It was a lovely holiday, but I can't wait to get home to Rose." Rose was my nine-year-old daughter.

"I completely understand," Patricia said. "I've truly enjoyed all my work for the Exposition commission, but I'm also eager for it to end so that I can go back home to my family."

Patricia was involved with the British commission for exhibits at the Paris Exposition, the world's fair that had been running since April and would end in November. Of course she was looking forward to some time with her husband. He had remained in England to mind his business ventures, while Patricia had leased an apartment here in Paris, and except for a month during the summer, when she returned to England and George and I had used her apartment, Patricia and her husband had been apart.

"You and Father should plan a holiday for yourselves as George and Frances did," Anne suggested. She and Lily were seated across the table from us, trying to entertain Amelia, who seemed less than delighted with her surroundings.

"If you wait until November, I'd advise going somewhere farther south and warmer than Deauville," I said. "In the meantime, it must be nice to have Anne here to visit."

"It is, of course. I only wish I had more time for her." Patricia tipped her head and narrowed her eyes at me. "Did you golf on your holiday?"

"You might call it that," I said. "I'm still learning the game and have yet to develop any expertise." In truth, I was awful, which both bothered and surprised me. I'd always been good at physical activities.

Patricia barely waited for me to finish speaking before gesturing to Anne. "Did you hear that?" she said. "Frances also plays golf. The two of you must have a round together."

Anne glanced up with a grin. She looked like a younger version of her mother, but where Patricia's choice of hairstyle made her features severe, Anne's brown eyes winged with delicate brows were surrounded by waves of brown hair that softened the angles of her face. She had little Amelia on her lap and was fending off the wet fingers the baby had just pulled from her mouth and seemed determined to wipe on Anne's face. "No, darling," Anne said. Pushing the small fist away, she glanced at me. "I did hear that. I'd love the chance to practice if you can find the time, Frances. Did Mother tell you I'm here for the big tournament next week?"

Lily took custody of the baby, and I handed Anne a napkin to wipe her cheek. "I wasn't even aware there was a big tournament coming up."

Anne sighed. "That doesn't surprise me. The tournament is part of the Olympic Games." She gave me a close look. "Have you heard that the second Olympic Games are here in Paris?"

"No, I had no idea. All the events I have heard of this summer were part of the Exposition. Have the games just begun?"

She chuckled and glanced at her mother, who shook her head. "I didn't know about the games, either," Patricia said. "Apparently, they have been taking place all summer right under our noses."

"The competitions were all over the city," Anne said. "There was fencing in the Tuileries Garden, croquet and polo right here in the Bois de Boulogne, and rowing and swimming in the Seine."

I nearly laughed before I realized she was serious. "People were swimming in the Seine? George and I have been back and forth between London and Paris. Apparently, our absence led to our ignorance of these events, but I am very sorry to have missed that one."

"I don't think your lack of knowledge was due to your absence," Patricia said with a quirk of her lips. "I was here most of the summer and had no idea. Have you heard anything about the Olympics, Lily?"

My sister had stepped away from the table to bounce Amelia in her arms while she fussed. She shook her head. "I don't hear anything these days."

"The officials are not promoting the sporting events as much as they are the Exposition," Anne said. "Therefore, most of the competitors have been French, and some of them didn't even realize they were competing in the Olympic games. They thought it was just another match or tournament."

"Heavens," I said. "Does that mean you are competing for England?" I grasped Patricia by the arm. "You must be so proud."

"Why, yes, of course," she said. "I'm always proud of my children." She gave Anne a bemused look. "I hadn't really thought of it as competing for England."

Anne laughed and patted her mother's hand. "I sincerely doubt that England even knows about it, Mother, so you needn't feel badly."

"If you are proficient enough to play in the Olympics," I said, "you could have no wish to partner with me. My skill is sadly lacking. George is far better. He is currently having a game with a friend of ours. Perhaps all four of us can go out and I'll try to keep up."

"That would be perfect," Anne agreed. "The tournament is little more than a week away. I would love to have a practice game or two before then."

"I wish I had time for a little exercise," Lily said, joining us at the table. "Amelia keeps me too occupied."

A passerby, glancing at our group would never have guessed Lily and I were sisters. Like the way Anne and Patricia were clearly mother and daughter, Lily looked the image of our mother. Both of them were blond, petite, and blue-eyed, with curvaceous figures. I inherited Mother's blue eyes, but everything else came from my father. My dark hair, spare figure, and my height. Where Lily was barely five feet tall, I was much closer to six—and I refuse to say just how close that was.

"Have you not hired a nurse?" I asked her. Lily and her husband lived in the north of France, but she was in Paris until

November so that Patricia could enjoy some time with the baby before returning to England. Leo, who had stayed at home, managed one of his father's factories, which had him at his office all day and often entertaining customers in the evening. Without a nurse, Lily was on her own.

Patricia chuckled. "We are not the aristocracy, Frances. I know you had to raise your daughter according to the Wynn family traditions, but they are babies for so short a time, what mother would want to miss one moment of it?"

Lily smiled, but based on the dark circles under her eyes, I'd wager she wouldn't mind missing a few moments. Perhaps even one full night. My daughter was from my previous marriage to Reginald Wynn, the Earl of Harleigh. It's true that Rose began life under the loving gaze of the same nurse who had cared for Reggie. It was a family tradition, and I had no argument with it. When the older nurse moved on, I engaged another. I was still Rose's mother and could spend all the time I wished with her, but having the nurse meant Rose and I were not forced to spend twenty-four hours of every day in each other's company, regardless of our desire to do so.

"I see your point, Patricia," I said. "Babies can be such a delight, but Lily is also managing a household, taking care of Leo, and entertaining his business associates. I'd hate to see her neglect her own health for lack of time."

Patricia gave me a look of incredulity. "Come now, Frances, I managed to raise four children on my own while at the same time caring for my husband, and my health never failed." She tipped her head to look past me to Lily. "I'm sure if Lily needs help, she will ask for it."

Lily ducked her head. "Of course, I would."

I wasn't so sure of that. Lily looked exhausted and unhappy, but perhaps I was seeing her at an inopportune moment. I'd drop the issue for now—perhaps forever. My mother was arriving in Paris the next day for her first glimpse of her new granddaughter. I'm sure the woman who had arranged for an endless string of nurses, governesses, tutors, and instructors on every conceivable subject or skill for her own children would have an opinion about her newest granddaughter's present situation.

Once the food was unpacked and we began our feast, I asked Lily if she knew Mother was about to arrive in Paris.

Her eyes rounded. "Tomorrow? I had no idea. She'd told me in her last letter she'd stop in Paris for a visit on her way home, but she never mentioned a date. Will she be staying with you?"

"Oh, yes," I said. "Between you and Anne, I thought Patricia had enough guests. Father is continuing on to New York." I paused to observe Lily's reaction to this news. "I hope you weren't planning to see him."

She waved a hand. "I can't believe he stayed away from his office for all these months while they were in Egypt, I doubt he'd find one small baby as interesting as the pyramids or the stock market, but I am glad Mother is staying for a visit." She glanced around me to note that Anne and Patricia were involved in their own conversation, then returned her attention to me. "You may find this difficult to believe, but I actually miss her."

"I confess to the same sentiment. Sometimes I wonder if there's a twisted part of us that wants to be corrected and critiqued all the time." We both shuddered in remembrance. "But beneath all her bluster is a mother who loves us."

Lily grinned. "Perhaps I needed to become a mother to recognize that. I hope you'll bring her to see me soon after she arrives."

"I doubt I'd be able to keep her away. You should expect us tomorrow afternoon."

As the day wore on, the four of us lapsed into a companionable silence, while birds sang in the trees and other picnickers chatted and laughed in the distance. We were situated with a view of the two lakes and the woods behind them, but one of the main roads stretched along beside us as did a walking path.

"There must be a race this afternoon," Lily mused. "The road seems much busier than when we first arrived."

"I think you are right," Patricia said. "The Hippodrome Auteuil is right beyond the trees across the road."

"Look, I think that's Sarah Bernhardt arriving right now." Lily pointed unnecessarily to the open carriage that had just pulled into view. All of us would have recognized the renowned actress without the prompt. Seen from across the meadow, she was a slender figure wrapped in white fur wearing a large white hat, but even seated in the carriage, she was animated, her motions quick and constant. It could only be the Divine Sarah.

When the few pedestrians alongside the road waved to her, she laughed and waved back with enthusiasm.

"George and I will be here for another two weeks," I said. "We must try to attend one of her performances. Who knows when we'll have another chance? With her own theater here, I doubt very much that she'll ever return to London."

"Or America," Lily added. "You should take Mother."

"I'll certainly ask her." I said, noting a few more picnickers settling into our area and even more out enjoying an afternoon stroll.

"Frances." Lily touched my arm to draw my attention then spoke in a whisper. "I believe I know that woman walking toward us. Isn't that Alicia Stoke-Whitney?"

She was correct. The petite redhead in a yellow walking gown, holding a parasol aloft, had separated herself from a group of merry-makers near the lake and was headed our way. The last time my sister had seen Alicia she learned—well, there is no graceful way of saying this—that my first husband had died in Alicia's bed.

After that little incident, I had managed to keep my distance from Alicia until she forced the issue by inviting me, publicly, to a party she was hosting. My sister was there, so I had to explain my reticence to associate with Alicia. Though Lily urged me to send my regrets, I had no choice but to accept. My refusal would have given credence to the rumors that Alicia and my late husband had been lovers. The fact that they had been was an irrelevant bit of truth society did not need to know.

From that point on, Alicia considered me a friend. Initially, I continued to avoid her, tolerating her only when avoidance was impossible. But over time she began to grow on me. Alicia was completely self-centered, untrustworthy, and irresponsible, but something about her made me—well, I suppose the word would be *care*.

Her irreverence toward everything was both shocking and refreshing. I'd come to believe it was her way of coping with life, which had not always been kind to her. Many of her problems, however, were of her own making.

My sister had no knowledge that so much water had passed under the bridge since she'd last seen Alicia, and there was no time to explain since the woman was nearly upon us. I could sense Lily puffing up in moral outrage, but all I could do was take her hand and keep her in her seat, while I rose to my feet, whispering, "It's fine. I'll explain later."

Alicia shared her brilliant smile with the four of us, then held out both hands to me. "Frances, my dear friend. It's been an age since I've seen you. You are looking well."

Lily stared in astonishment while I greeted Alicia and introduced her to my companions. She and Patricia exchanged a few pleasantries about the Exposition. Alicia was also a member of the British commission, though not on the same committees as Patricia.

After a few minutes of conversation, Alicia turned back to me. "I am meant to be chaperoning my daughter, Harriet, and her friends."

"Chaperone?" I nearly choked on the word. Alicia? I followed her glance to the group of young people gathered near the water. Whoever set Alicia to the task of being a chaperone must either have been completely desperate or had no acquaintance with her.

"I must get back to them soon, but I wonder if you'd mind taking a short walk with me first."

I was curious enough to agree, and we set off toward the footpath near the road that led to a wooded area. "How is Harriet finding Paris?" I asked.

"Quite enjoyable, I think. She has settled in with a group of young people, both English and French." Alicia paused and two tiny lines formed between her delicate brows. "There's also a certain gentleman who has shown quite a bit of interest in her. That is what I wanted to ask you about."

I looked at her, intrigued.

"He's an American. I wondered if you know him."

I chuckled. "It's a very large country, Alicia, and I've been away from it for over ten years. I doubt very much—"

"His name is Carlson Deaver."

"Oh! Well, I suppose I do know him—not personally, but as I'm sure you know, his sister, Lottie, and I are friends. I believe I heard he was living in Paris, as is their mother."

"Yes." She drew out the word. "Mrs. Deaver is another subject I'd like to discuss, but that must wait for another time. First, what can you tell me about Carlson?"

"Almost nothing. His sister, Lottie, is married to my late husband's cousin, Charles."

"That's right, I've met her." She poked the air with her index finger, then actually bit her lip when I glared at her. I waited for some comment about Lottie's clumsiness or Charles's lack of wit. To her credit, she chose not to insult my relatives, folded her finger back into her fist, and said, "Please, go on."

Surprise, surprise, the woman was learning.

"As you already know, Mimi Deaver is Carlson's mother.

His father, I believe, passed away last autumn. Shortly after Lottie and Charles's wedding. Mr. Deaver was involved in railroads, if I'm not mistaken, and left quite a fortune to his children and widow."

Alicia continued to stare at me with an expectant gaze.

"And they are from New York City," I continued, "and that is all I know."

"That's all?" She looped her arm through mine and dragged me off the path and across the grass toward the lake where we could still see her charges but were out of their hearing. "Can you tell me nothing of his character? No exploits from his past?"

"Alicia, he was part of New York society. I was not. Then after several months of not being acquainted with him in that city, I moved to England, where I had no way of becoming any more familiar with him. I'm sorry, but I can't provide insight to a man I simply do not know."

She studied me through narrowed eyes for a moment, then gave her head a firm nod. "Then I'd like to have you investigate him for me."

"What?"

"Must you shriek so?" she asked. Taking my arm, she pulled me closer to the spray and burble of the waterfall. "Investigate him," she repeated. "You've done that before. You investigated your sister's suitors."

We came to a stop at the lake's edge and pretended to watch the water cascading over the rocks. "That is not exactly true. I had a police officer investigate my sister's suitors. There is quite a difference. I didn't do it myself—well, I didn't do much of it. If you want to look into the man's background, you should hire someone."

She spread her arms wide. "Who? I don't know anyone in Paris who does such things. Only you. I want to hire you, but for some reason, you are playing hard to get."

"I am simply saying you can do better than me," I said.

Heavens, one would think we were speaking of matrimony. "What are you trying to find out? If he truly has a fortune?"

"I wish to assure myself that he's not a murderer." Alicia held up a hand as I gasped. "Don't you dare shriek again," she said. "I don't want everyone around us to wonder what we're talking about."

I took a glance at the grassy picnic area behind us and saw that no one was paying us any attention. The flowing water was effectively covering our conversation. I noticed a bench nearby, facing the lake, and drew Alicia to it. Once we were settled on the bench, I began my questions.

"What possible reason do you have to even wonder such a thing about the man?"

Alicia tossed a dangling cluster of red curls behind her shoulder. "His first wife was murdered."

"By him?" I asked.

"I suspect you are jesting," she said, shaking a finger in my face. "But the truth is nobody knows. It remains an unsolved case. I would like to know beyond any doubt that Mr. Deaver had nothing to do with his wife's murder before I allow him to court my daughter. I'm sure you can understand my position."

Indeed, I did. Alicia's late husband had been the soul of propriety on the surface but, beneath that veneer, was a man with criminal tendencies. Even Alicia had not seen his true self until it was almost too late. After his deception, it was hardly a surprise that Alicia's trust would be hard won. I couldn't help but grimace as the memory invaded my thoughts.

"Yes," she said. "I see you do understand. If my daughter is going to become involved with this man, I must at least know that she will be safe in his company."

"At the very least," I agreed. "I didn't know Mr. Deaver had been married. What can you tell me about his wife and her death?"

"Only what the newspapers had to say. It happened in January, so, not long after Harriet and I came to stay in Paris. I was still scrambling to get the two of us settled and hadn't become involved in Paris society yet."

"His wife hasn't been dead a year and he is showing interest in Harriet?" Though it hadn't been a full year since Harriet's father, Alicia's husband, had passed, either. Perhaps observing the proprieties wasn't important to Alicia.

"The timing was what first had me wondering," she said. "It seems to me that most men would mourn their wives for a year. Mr. and Mrs. Deaver were relative newlyweds, married barely a year at the time of her death. They ought to have still been in the honeymoon phase of the marriage. Yet he is already looking for a new wife."

Apparently, the proprieties did mean something to her. "You could always ask him to defer his attentions to Harriet until a proper mourning period has been observed," I suggested.

She looked pained. "He is a very wealthy man. If Harriet puts him off, someone else will snap him up."

"You and I both know that an advantageous match does not necessarily make for a good marriage."

"Yes, experience has taught me that much." She failed to repress a tiny shudder. "If Harriet wasn't fond of him, I wouldn't go through this much trouble."

"I see. What else did the papers report?"

"Carlson's wife, I believe her given name was Isabelle, was home alone. The police say someone broke into the house in an attempt at burglary, unaware that Mrs. Deaver was still at home. Their suspicion is that the burglars killed her."

That sounded rather cut and dried to me. "Then why do you think it possible that Mr. Deaver had something to do with his wife's murder?"

She raised her brows. "Because the police never found the supposed burglars nor any of the stolen loot."

I laughed at the use of the word. "Loot?"

"Mostly jewelry, if I remember correctly. But the important part is that no one was ever brought to justice. That leaves too much room for suspicion for my comfort."

"I don't know if I can do enough to put your mind at ease," I said. "However, my mother will arrive in Paris tomorrow. I know she had an acquaintance with Carlson's father and mother. She may be able to provide more information about Carlson, but without assistance from the French police or the newspapers, I may not be able to go any further than that."

"Even a little information is better than none," she said.

"Then I will see what I can do."

Chapter Two

Patrica had rented an open carriage to transport us to and from the park. On the ride home, she pointed out various landmarks to Anne, while Lily and I amused Amelia who was nestled between us in her basket, shaded by our parasols.

I could practically feel the curiosity bubbling up inside my sister, but I managed to stop her from interrogating me about my friendship with Alicia by turning the tables and questioning her about Carlson Deaver.

She blinked in surprise, then frowned as she thought about it. "I may have been seated next to Carlson at someone's dinner once, but I wouldn't say I know him at all," she said. "Why do you ask?"

"Well, no doubt you were wondering what Alicia and I were discussing—"

"I was, indeed." Lily's eyes sparkled with interest.

"Alicia has a daughter—"

Her expression soured and she leaned in close to me. "That notorious woman has the nerve to raise a daughter?"

"Lily, don't be unkind. Alicia may be free with her affections, but she has many good qualities."

"Does she? Name one."

A difficult task, since in the length of our acquaintance, Alicia had never exhibited any. "I have yet to uncover them, but—"

"If you keep digging, you'll find she has a heart of gold?"

"I sincerely doubt that, but if you'll cease interrupting me, I might be able to explain myself more succinctly." I'd spoken with a little more heat than I'd intended and glancing up, I could see we'd drawn the attention of the Kendrick ladies seated across from us.

Patricia favored us with an indulgent smile and a wave of her hand. "You needn't concern yourselves. I completely understand how it is with sisters."

Anne's expression was more mischievous. "With the three of us at home, Mother never had a quiet moment."

"Don't mind us," Patricia said. "Carry on as if we weren't here."

That was impossible now, at least not without being terribly rude. "I was simply trying to explain to my sister that Harriet Stoke-Whitney, a sweet and delightful young woman, seems to have caught the attention of Carlson Deaver. Since he's an American, Mrs. Stoke-Whitney was inquiring about my knowledge of the gentleman—as any concerned mother would."

Aha, a good quality! I turned back to Lily. "Alicia is a concerned mother."

Lily pursed her lips and glanced at me through the corner of her eye. Clearly, she wasn't convinced.

Anne frowned. "Carlson Deaver? I believe he is competing in the men's golf tournament next week." She laughed and spread her hands. "And now you know everything I know of the man."

"If I remember correctly, Carlson should be older than you,

Frannie. Somewhere in his early thirties. How old is Miss Stoke-Whitney?" Lily asked.

"I believe she's eighteen. It does seem a large age difference, but it is hardly unusual for a gentleman, particularly a wealthy gentleman, to be a decade or so older than the woman he is courting. I don't think that troubles her mother as much as the fact that she knows nothing of him."

"Is he related to Mimi Deaver?" Patricia had a wary look on her face.

"Yes." Lily answered before I could part my lips. "She's his mother, and she had a less than glowing reputation in New York. I don't know how Paris society feels about her relationship with the Comte de Beaulieu." She tipped her head to the side. "Is it *comte* or count in France?"

"It's *comte*," Patricia said. "And his status is impeccable. Republic or not, Parisians still esteem their nobility. He also dedicates his time to a number of worthy associations, including the Exposition, so he's well connected. And he's charming. If the *comte* champions her, society accepts her." She shrugged. "I believe she is quite devoted to him."

When a married woman leaves her husband in New York and moves to France to be with another man, I'd say devotion to that man is a given. On her way to Paris, Mimi had dropped off her daughter, Lottie, at my house in London as if she were a parcel. She had also handed over a large bank draft, so I could hardly complain. Her intent had been for me to help Lottie find a titled husband, and though I had little to do with it, she did. Lottie had fallen in love with my late husband's cousin, Charles. I couldn't imagine a more perfect match, other than my own, of course.

"Devoted is most certainly the word. She's only left his side twice. Once for her daughter's wedding and, perhaps a month later, for her husband's funeral," Lily said.

At least she attended his funeral, I thought.

"I believe the elder Mr. Deaver's death left Mimi, Lottie, and Carlson quite wealthy," Lily continued. "If that is Mrs. Stoke-Whitney's concern, you may ease her mind."

No, that wasn't exactly Alicia's concern. Money may make up for a multitude of sins, but not murder. "Do any of you know anything of Carlson Deaver's late wife?"

"I wasn't aware he'd been married," Lily said with some surprise. "It must have been before Leo and I came to live in France. We didn't stay long in Paris before moving on to Lille, but I do think Carlson was living here even before Mimi arrived." She snapped her fingers as if a thought had just occurred to her. "Mother keeps up with society news. You should ask her when she arrives."

"Mother has been in Egypt for at least six months now."

"Nevertheless, society is very important to her," Lily said. "I'd still ask her. And of course, you could always ask Lottie."

Patricia had the driver drop me off at the apartment we leased in the sixth arrondissement. George and I had stayed at Patricia Kendrick's apartment when we were here in July, but when we returned to Paris last month, we felt that we couldn't impose on her again.

Fortunately, as the Exposition wound down, more accommodations became available. We were able to lease our current apartment until the second week of October. The apartment suited us well enough, but the staff had been more than we could hope for. The owner was a lawyer, or *avocat*, as the French call them. He was also a bachelor who worked late and traveled a great deal, which meant his staff never knew when he'd be home for dinner, pop in for lunch, or suddenly be out of town for several days. Therefore, when we packed up after only a few days in Paris, and left for Deauville, they thought nothing of it.

I thanked the concierge who opened the gate to the courtyard. Though he was a pleasant young man, I rather missed the crotchety couple who served that role at Patricia's apartment. I climbed the steps to the first floor and let myself in. Conversation from the salon told me that George had returned ahead of me. And he had company.

I stopped in the foyer to remove my hat and gloves. Leaving them on the entry table, I used the mirror over the table to tidy my hair before joining them.

Our guest was Inspector Daniel Cadieux, a detective inspector with the Sûreté, the criminal investigative branch of the French police. Both he and George stood as I entered the salon. My gaze was immediately drawn to George, my husband and the taller of the two. With his green eyes, aristocratic nose, and dark beard, simply looking at him made my heart beat faster. Handsome in his own way, Cadieux was a hair shorter than me, cleanshaven, with dark eyes and thick dark hair that he wore combed back from a smooth forehead.

Both men were fashionably lean and dressed for golf— George in loose trousers, Cadieux in knickerbockers, and both in tweed jackets. Standing side by side, they looked like the type of men mothers warned their young daughters about. Devilishly handsome, with mischief glinting in their eyes, any mother would think they were trouble.

"*Bonjour*, Madame Hazelton," Cadieux said with a smile.

"*Bonjour*, inspector, George. I trust you both enjoyed your time on the links?"

"An excellent way to spend the morning," Cadieux said. "Next time perhaps you will join us?"

Oddly enough, it seemed quite normal to have the French policeman in our home socially. We'd met Inspector Cadieux on our first case in Paris, back in July, when George's aunt asked him to investigate the death of her friend. Though George is the son of an earl, he's the third son, and as such he couldn't expect the earldom to support him. George studied law and went to work for the Home Office, where he honed his investigative skills. At one point, he helped me out of a pinch, and we've been sleuthing together ever since.

In Paris, we'd gotten under Inspector Cadieux's skin, an action he returned in kind, but ultimately, we found a way to work together and became friends. When Cadieux learned that George enjoyed a round of golf, he insisted the two of them do just that the next time we visited the city. They both looked as though the fresh air, if not the golf itself, had done them good.

"How was your game?" I asked, as I settled into my favorite arm chair, upholstered in emerald green and fashioned in the art nouveau style, with delicate embellishments in the wood. Cadieux returned to the matching chair across from mine and George took the sofa. Each of them had a glass of brandy in hand. George offered to pour one for me, but I declined. The fresh air I'd enjoyed at the picnic in the park today had already relaxed me. Alcohol would put me to sleep in no time.

Over the course of the following thirty minutes, I had cause to reconsider. Sleep might be a better alternative to the hole-by-hole retelling of their day. Between the two of them, George and Cadieux accounted for every stroke taken on each hole until I felt as if I knew every bunker and blade of grass on the course well enough to have played it myself. That was a much greater familiarity than I desired.

George had just finished describing a particularly tricky shot he'd made over a pond and onto the green, when I remembered Inspector Cadieux's profession.

"Inspector, do you recall anything about the murder of Mrs. Carlson Deaver in January of this year?"

Cadieux had been about to take a sip of brandy. He stopped in mid-motion and lowered his glass while staring at me as if I had sprouted a second head. George also looked taken aback, but he recovered first. "What makes you ask? Did someone bring up that topic with you?"

Surprised by their reactions, I told them about Alicia's request that I learn something of Carlson Deaver for her. "She was troubled by the fact that his wife's murder was never solved. Actually," I lifted my fingers to my lips as I chuckled, "she's a bit concerned that Carlson might have done her in himself."

Cadieux's sharp glance stopped me mid-chortle. A moment later I remembered to close my mouth.

"Why would she think that?" George asked.

I held up my hand in a cautionary gesture. "She has no evidence to that effect. It's only an idea that developed in her own mind. Some sort of resolution of the case would put her more at ease."

Cadieux studied his drink, while George observed him.

"Tit for tat, gentlemen," I said. "I've explained how the subject came up. Now you ought to explain why you were so alarmed when I mentioned her name."

They exchanged a look.

Cadieux shrugged.

I sighed. "You know I'll find out."

"As it happens, we were discussing that very case during our round today," George said.

"Then the case isn't closed?"

"Not officially," Cadieux said. "But we haven't had a new lead for six months."

I decided to have that brandy after all. George kept it in a cabinet that backed up to the sofa. "What can you tell me about the case?" I asked. After pouring a glass for myself, I held up the bottle as an offer. When they both refused another pour, I returned to my seat.

"Did you know the couple?" Cadieux asked.

"Because they were part of New York society," I said, "I know the Deaver family. Carlson's sister happens to be married to my cousin, so I am well acquainted with her, but I don't know Carlson and never even met his late wife."

The inspector leaned forward in his chair, resting his elbows on the arms. "Monsieur Deaver arrived in Paris early in '98 for an extended visit with several friends. Other Americans. After a few months, those friends decided to move on, but instead of traveling with them, Deaver took a lease on an apartment. Over time he made some Parisian friends, and he took up with an actress named Isabelle Rousseau. In January of '99, much to the surprise of friends on both sides, the two married."

"I suppose that is a little surprising," I said.

"Indeed. There was a great deal of debate over how an actress managed to marry such a wealthy gentleman, but then it was put down to him being an American." Cadieux tapped his head. "Everyone knows they are a little odd."

When he caught my scowl, he held out a conciliatory hand. "Present company excepted, of course, *madame*."

"Of course." I was confident Cadieux considered me a little odd regardless of his statement, but no matter. It really wasn't that unusual for a wealthy American to marry a beautiful actress. In fact, it happened frequently. But not so frequently when the family was part of society. "I assume she gave up the stage when they married."

"She did, though she kept in touch with at least some of her theater friends. If she had any family, she had long since lost touch with them."

I glanced between the two men. "Nothing you've said so far, would lead me to expect her murder. What happened?"

George held up a hand. "Why don't I do the honors?" he suggested to Cadieux. "You may correct me where I'm in error."

Cadieux gestured for him to proceed and sat back.

George turned to me. "On the night of January 26th, Isabelle Deaver was alone in their apartment when someone broke into the house, apparently with the intent of robbery. Her husband was away from home, and she had plans for the evening as well, so even their servants were enjoying a night off. The thieves were probably as surprised to see her as she was to see them.

"The police don't know exactly what transpired except that the thieves didn't kill her there. The apartment looked to have been ransacked, but they found no traces of blood. The criminals abducted her, perhaps with the intent of demanding a ransom, but ultimately, they killed her—quite violently several hours later. Madame Deaver had been battered then strangled. Her body was found the next morning in the Marais, near the place des Vosges."

"The next morning?" I turned to Cadieux. "Carlson must have been wild with anxiety for her."

"Monsieur Deaver returned home not long before she was found," Cadieux said. "The police had been called to the apartment the night before, so they had already been and gone. When he came home, he would have seen signs of the break-in and no sign of his wife. We had left an officer at his residence to explain the situation to him. He said that Deaver had clearly consumed a fair amount of spirits throughout the evening, and the first thing he did upon hearing his wife was missing was to pour himself another drink."

"But was he more concerned for his wife or the stolen property?" George asked.

"The officer believed Deaver was quite distraught about his wife," Cadieux said. "But you must understand, the man was drunk. He'd been drinking all night with friends and continued once he came home. Fortunately, his mother arrived about that time. The officer left and she took over his care."

"Yes, by that time, Mimi would have been living in Paris, too," I said. "So when Carlson came home, the police didn't know his wife was dead."

Cadieux shook his head. "Not yet. We had found a body near the place where Isabelle Deaver worked. The woman was young and matched the description of Isabelle Deaver as far as height, age, and hair color, but we still needed an identification to be sure it was her. We telephoned the Deaver apartment and spoke to Mimi Deaver. It was she who came in to identify the body. An investigation was launched, but stalled after the interview stage. There has never been enough evidence to send us in any one direction—until a few days ago, that is."

"Amazing. After all this time, you have a new lead." I leaned forward, eager for the details.

If I were to describe Inspector Cadieux in one word, it would have to be unflappable. Nothing surprised him. Nothing shocked him. Nothing ruffled his calm demeanor. At least not under any circumstance in which I'd seen him—until that moment.

He fidgeted, smoothing back his perfectly tidy hair, blowing out puffs of breath, and rubbing the back of his neck as if it truly pained him to continue the story. Finally, he released a sigh. "Three days ago, someone received a blackmail note—or rather what looks like a prelude to blackmail."

I glanced from Cadieux to George, wordlessly urging him to fill in the details that the inspector seemed reluctant to reveal.

"The recipient," George said, "received a piece of jewelry, an earring, that she recognized as having belonged to Isabelle Deaver, along with a note that read 'I know what you did.' "

I grimaced. "Heavens, that is rather damning. And you said 'she.' Apparently, you know who it is. How did you find out?"

George turned to Cadieux and raised a brow. "Frances might be able to help us," he said.

Cadieux leaned forward. "The recipient is Sarah Bernhardt."

"No!" I could not have been more astonished. Sarah Bernhardt in receipt of a blackmail note, accusing her of murder? I would never have guessed it. "Sarah Bernhardt, the actress?" I asked, in case there was any confusion.

"The very one," George confirmed.

"Do you think she did it?"

"Of course not!" Cadieux was adamant. And still agitated.

George cast a glance at the other man before coming to his

feet, removing the glass from Cadieux's hand, and topping it off from the bottle atop the cabinet. "You asked how the police found out about this—let's call it a threatening note for now." He handed the glass back to the inspector. "Madame Bernhardt contacted the police herself."

"An officer called on her to take her statement," Cadieux added. "He was inclined to bury this information. Madame Bernhardt noticed his inclination and contacted some friends of hers, very high up in the prefecture. While most people might use such a connection to protect themselves, she used it to insist that we look into this case again. She wanted a thorough investigation to be done. She wanted justice for her friend."

"That's very admirable," I offered. "Yet you sound less than pleased. If the case wasn't closed, why is that a problem?"

"No one wants to take it," George replied.

"This is the only new lead we've had for months, and no matter how you look at it, it implicates Sarah Bernhardt." Cadieux pronounced the name with solemn reverence. "Of all people. And yet, how can we ignore this evidence?"

George shrugged. "By continuing to hand it up and down the line like the proverbial hot potato."

Cadieux dropped his head into his hands.

"Come now," I said. "I understand she's a beloved figure, but surely—"

The inspector swiped a hand in front of him as if pushing my words aside. "If you can say that, then clearly, you do not understand. No officer wants to be known as the man who arrested Sarah Bernhardt. Imagine the ignominy!"

George gave me a look of sympathy, but Cadieux scowled at me as if I were quite obtuse. "And because the evidence points to her," he continued, "no officer is willing to take on this case. I have never seen so many men suddenly become ill. Some have even threatened to resign."

Well, that was simply absurd. "What if she did murder Isabelle Deaver? Are you saying you'd let her get away with it?"

Cadieux shook his head in disgust. "She would never lower herself to do such a thing. There is no chance she is guilty of the crime."

Somehow, it didn't sound as though Cadieux had come to that conclusion through diligent police work. "Fine, she's not guilty," I said. "Then what is the risk of investigating?"

George cleared his throat. "It seems Madame Bernhardt wishes to take part in the investigation."

"Does she?" I said. "I have heard she is not one to remain idle."

"Since she received the note, she sees it as her duty," Cadieux said. "With her fearless nature, it would be difficult to keep her safe."

"Aside from the fact that no one believes she committed the crime," I began, parsing my words as I spoke, "she did receive the note, so she must be considered a suspect, must she not?" Surely, Cadieux wasn't considering allowing the woman to participate in the investigation.

"Not only a suspect," George said. "But one who is unwilling to state where she was at the time of the murder, and with whom. Even if following this evidence leads the police to a standstill, she will look very guilty indeed. There may be pressure from above to arrest her."

Cadieux lowered his head, massaging his temples. "My superior dropped this case on my desk as I was leaving yesterday. I have very specific instructions to find the culprit who wrote this note and then find Isabelle Deaver's murderer. And that person had better not be Sarah Bernhardt. In fact, he specifically said I was to keep her safe."

He sat back in his seat with a sigh. "I'm not entirely certain, but my job may depend on this." His expression brightened as he held up a finger. "But I have one avenue open that may help me to accomplish this task, keep my job, and not be run out of Paris as blot on the honor of all Frenchmen."

"Well, that must give you great relief," I said with a slight tinge of sarcasm. "What is it?"

George lifted his hand. "Me."

"Ah, now I understand why the two of you were discussing this case. And I can see the genius of this plan."

"Hazelton is not a Frenchman, nor a policeman. He can turn over every stone without worry." The inspector turned to George. "If the evidence leads you to Madame Bernhardt, then it can be on your head, *mon ami*."

Chapter Three

Once Inspector Cadieux left, George and I changed for dinner—possibly the last peaceful meal we'd enjoy before my mother arrived. I honestly didn't know what to expect from her. When she visited me in London last October, she stayed for four months, complaining about me, my staff, and even the weather in England. Though I was confident she could still find something to criticize about me, I knew she loved Paris, and there was absolutely no fault she could find with our accommodations here.

The apartment was spacious and bright. The housekeeper could have a meal ready with only a moment's notice or cheerfully keep it warm for hours if necessary. Miraculously, it was always superb, and if I had any suspicion this skill had something to do with the restaurant around the corner, well, I'd just keep that to myself. For temporary housing, we could hardly ask for more.

Which reminded me . . .

I took the arm George held out for me and let him lead me down to the dining room. "I wonder if my mother plans to return with us to London when we leave."

George gave me a look of horror and tripped down the last step, grasping the banister to avoid a fall. "Egad, you don't mean return to our home, do you?"

"I suppose she'd stay with Aunt Hetty, now that I think about it. We do have rather a full house at the moment."

That full house consisted of Rose, my nine-year-old daughter, Lissette, George's fifteen-year-old cousin and ward, and Christine, her twenty-year-old half-sister. They were currently staying with my Aunt Hetty while George and I were in France, but they'd be back under our roof upon our return to London. Though we did have one more guest room, my mother moving in with us would be a declaration that the honeymoon was well and truly over. I wasn't ready for that yet.

The moment we seated ourselves at the dining table, the housekeeper, Madame Auclair, and one of the maids brought out steaming bowls of soup and crusty bread. Though I'd had plenty to eat at the picnic, the aroma tempted me to dip into the soup before the door had even swung closed behind them.

"I thought your mother was simply stopping in France to get a look at her new granddaughter before following your father back to New York," George said between bites.

"She wasn't clear about her plans. Though that may be the case, she has other options. She could go with Lily when she and the baby return to Lille, or she could come to London with us. She hasn't seen Rose for months and you know how Mother adores her."

It wasn't long before that due to a misunderstanding, my mother was determined to put some distance between herself and my father. Once they'd worked things out, however, they embarked on an excursion to Egypt that had them spending more than five months in close company with each other.

This would be the first I'd seen of her since they set off. I hoped they were still speaking to one another and that my father's decision not to stop in France was only indicative of his eagerness to return to his work. But typical of Mother's correspondence, her letter had been short and vague. I suppose I'd find out when she arrived.

"I dare say her plans depend upon how eager she is to return to New York." I glanced up to see George gazing wistfully at me from across the table. I reached out and placed a hand atop his. "Our time alone was lovely, but we had to return to the rest of the world at some point, dearest."

He arched a brow. "How did you know what I was thinking? I'm not sure I approve of a wife who can read my mind."

"It was only because I had the same thought. Though I have to admit I keep wondering what Rose and her cousins are doing. Even though the world of you and I alone is a wonderful place, I miss them. And starting tomorrow, our world includes my mother."

George grimaced and released my hand. I couldn't blame him. Though George was charming and found a way to get on with nearly anyone, Mother could be equally determined to be contrary. George had some experience with that side of her, so he tended to approach her as one might an unexploded shell. If he could avoid her completely, all the better.

Madame Auclair returned for our soup bowls, the second course in hand. We finished our meal conversing about places we'd like to see before leaving Paris in two weeks and what we might buy to take home to the girls.

"I must find something else to call them as a group," I said. "They range in age from nine to twenty, and only Rose is truly young enough to be considered a girl."

"The fearsome threesome?" George suggested. "The terrible trio?"

I scoffed. "There is nothing terrible about any of them. And fearsome?"

"I am completely surrounded by females, Frances." He gave me a wink. "Fearsome is indeed appropriate. Thank heaven for the staff or I'd have no one to sympathize with me."

Before our marriage, George had lived in a household of

men—butler, chef, valet, and footman. Then Rose and I moved in and of course I brought my maid, Bridget. Last month we added Lisette and Christine. That was quite a change for him.

"I hadn't looked at it from your point of view," I said, trying not to laugh. "The trio, might not be bad—without the modifier, of course."

When Madame Auclair returned for our plates, I suggested we take our coffee in the salon. George agreed, and we headed down the hall. "I suspect you are eager to discuss the new case," he said as we entered the room. He moved around the back of the sofa and picked up a large file that had been waiting on the table.

"Is that from Cadieux?" I asked, settling in to the sofa. "He must have been very sure of your agreement to have brought that with him to the golf course. Was he carrying it in his bag for eighteen holes?"

"No, he brought it here this morning, and we left for the course together. The thought of this file waiting here has been tantalizing me ever since." He paused and gave me a crooked smile. "I suppose the inspector knows me well enough to have known I'd be interested."

"Is it the record of their investigation?"

George sat down beside me and opened the file on the coffee table in front of us. "Yes, I'm eager to see what we have here."

I cleared off a space on the table for the coffee tray and eyed the substantial file. "I'm surprised Cadieux had so much information to give you. It didn't sound like the police want to find the guilty party."

George tipped his head back and glanced at me down the length of his nose. "*Au contraire*. They would love to find one—just not Sarah Bernhardt."

"I don't understand that. Whoever wrote the threatening letter thinks her guilty of murdering Isabelle Deaver. Don't you think it's quite possible that she is?"

The housekeeper brought in the coffee, along with a selection of cheeses, and left them on the table for us. George seemed lost in thought while I poured. "Tell me this, Frances, how do you think the good citizens of London, or all of England, for that matter, would feel if the detectives at Scotland Yard were investigating the Queen for murder?" He lifted his brows as he took the cup I offered. "Do you suppose they would consider that an outrage?"

"I suspect any English policeman worthy of the name would shy away from that investigation, but surely you don't consider that a fair comparison? Victoria is the queen, after all."

"To be honest, I was trying to think of someone who is iconic to the British, yet isn't political. Sarah Bernhardt is exactly that to France—a beloved icon. I daresay some of my fellow Brits might well object to the prosecution of Madame Bernhardt."

I gave his claim some consideration. "You are probably correct. She is quite idolized in America, too, now that I think of it."

"America, too," George mused. "So the person responsible for her arrest could be reviled the world over."

"Yet, the threat of such a fate doesn't seem to bother you."

"Actually, I rather like the idea. If I am reviled the world over, then I can all the more easily hide away with you." He leaned in and gave me a kiss.

I placed a hand on his cheek. "That's a lovely ulterior motive, but if we are to make you the most hated man in the world, we had better dig into this file, don't you think?"

"All right, then, Madame Killjoy. I suppose we do have our work cut out for us."

I retrieved paper and pen from the desk in the corner while George sorted through the file. "I'll make note of anything we need to inquire about further as we go. That way we can make a plan of attack," he said.

"The first item in our plan ought to be how we might avoid including Madame Bernhardt in the investigation," I said.

"Any information we uncover will be questionable if one of the suspects is involved in uncovering it."

George looked bewildered. "I propose we simply tell her no."

I gazed at him over my coffee. "What a splendid solution. I don't know why I didn't think of that."

He narrowed his eyes. "I sense that you are poking fun at me."

"Ah, you are a good detective." I placed my cup on the coffee table and leaned toward him. "Did you not hear Cadieux? It sounded as though she was determined to involve herself in this investigation. Do you know much about Sarah Bernhardt?"

"I thought I knew enough, but you appear to know something I don't, so my answer must be no."

I sat back and folded my hands in my lap. "Though I am shocked at the thought of the police dismissing Madame Bernhardt as a suspect, I do find much to admire in her. For one thing, when she decides to do something, she does it. She turned the Odéon Theater into a hospital ward during the troubles they had here thirty years ago. In fact, her stellar career could be chalked up to her own determination. If she says she wants to take part in this investigation, we had better have a plan to convince her otherwise."

"We'll have to emphasize the threat to her safety," he suggested.

"Pfft!"

He raised his brows. "I take it that won't do."

"I think she would see that as a challenge. To be honest, I'm not certain what will discourage her." I tapped my lips with my index finger as I considered our options. There weren't many. I glanced up at George. "Perhaps we could give her something to do—some task that makes her feel as though she is helping without being risky or involving her too much."

George's lips widened into a grin. "Why do I get the feeling you simply want to work with the lady?"

I felt my cheeks burn. Bother! "I'll admit I am rather excited to meet her, but what I've said about her is true: If she wants to investigate, it will be difficult to stop her."

"That might not be a bad thing," George said. "Perhaps we should meet with her first, see what she's like, and how determined she is. We may find that she could be of real assistance."

I did prefer a plan, but George was good at thinking on his feet, so I agreed. "Now, I suppose we had better take a look at Cadieux's reports."

George had sorted the contents of the file into two stacks, one of documents and another of photographs. I wasn't sure I was ready for the latter. Interviews were on top of the document stack. The first ones I found were from Carlson Deaver and his neighbors. "Mr. Deaver was at a club involved in a card game all night according to this."

George glanced up from another set of notes. "Cadieux told me the police had verified his alibi. You should find that information in the file, too."

"Yes, here it is. He arrived at the club at five in the evening and remained until almost six the following morning." I returned the report to the file. "That sounds rather convenient, unless he made a habit of gambling until dawn."

"He did not, so the fact that he was gone on that night, is indeed convenient. And a bit suspicious. We should definitely interview him ourselves."

"You ought to invite him for a round of golf."

"What makes you think he plays?"

"Anne Kendrick told me. Remember, I was looking into his background before this investigation fell into your lap."

George gave me a look of interest. "Tell me more."

"That about sums it up. He is meant to play in the tournament in Compiègne next week."

"Are you talking about the Olympic competition?"

"I am, indeed. Anne will be delighted to know you've heard of it. She is playing in the women's tournament. Shall I see if she will make up our foursome?"

"Certainly. If Mr. Deaver thinks this is merely a casual round of golf, he will be more relaxed and receptive to questions."

George proposed we plan the outing for two days hence and penned a quick note to send to Carlson Deaver inviting him to join us. Since I might well see Anne the following day, I could extend the invitation in person.

Having disposed of that matter, I returned to reading the police interviews. The next ones were of several people from the theater, including Madame Bernhardt. "Sarah Bernhardt denies having anything to do with Isabelle Deaver's death, but she refused to reveal where she was and with whom."

"The police didn't seem to think she had a motive," George noted.

"Well, they didn't look very hard. Did you see this?" I handed him two sheets of notes. "Two of the actors claim Madame Deaver paid a call on Madame Bernhardt in her dressing room. It ended with a heated argument."

George glanced with interest at the notes. "The day before the murder, too. The witnesses don't seem to know what they argued about, but report that the two of them normally got on quite well."

That coincided with the statement I was reading from another fellow actor. "Perhaps the police had it right. From what I see here, Isabelle worked with Sarah for several years before her marriage. They remained friends afterward, which indicates they had more than a working relationship. Isabelle visited almost weekly." I lowered the notes to my lap and looked at George.

"It's been my experience that friends do argue from time to time," I said.

"Of course they do," he agreed. "When one feels comfortable speaking one's mind it often happens that one's friends are equally comfortable pointing out when one is completely in error."

"Which is something that doesn't happen among casual acquaintance."

George's lips formed a grim line. "Neither does murder, at least not the murder of a woman. It's often someone she knows well."

I jotted down the first of our notes. "So, while the argument itself may not have led to murder, it indicates they had a close acquaintance. Their relationship means we must interview the icon. The Divine Sarah may be a suspect, but she may also be able to give us a better understanding of Isabelle."

"She may even provide us with her alibi," George suggested.

I gave him a sharp look. "That's true. We are not the police, after all. She could be perfectly happy telling us what she was doing that night. That reminds me," I shuffled through some pages I'd removed from the file. "I thought I saw a theater schedule in here. Yes, here it is." We checked the date of the murder against the schedule. "According to this, Sarah would have been on stage between eight and ten that evening."

"Isabelle was supposed to be going to the opera which would have begun at eight o'clock, about the same time as Sarah's play." George picked up the cheese knife and cut a slice of Camembert. "But she never left the house because someone broke in."

"Have the police estimated what time that happened?" I asked.

George gestured to the file. "We have much reading to do."

I frowned. "Remind me, why don't we believe those who broke in are the ones who murdered Isabelle?"

"The threatening letter."

"That's right. Where is it?"

"At the Sûreté," George said. "It's new evidence, still being processed. We'll have to go there to see it."

I added that task to my notes. "Didn't Cadieux describe it as a 'prelude to blackmail' note?"

George nodded. "There was no demand for money and no overt threat. It simply said, 'I know what you did.' It was accompanied by a piece of Isabelle's jewelry. Apparently, something distinctive, since Sarah recognized it."

"Now that is truly confusing," I said. "Someone sent Sarah a note implying they know she did something wrong, then included a recognizable piece of jewelry so that she'd be sure to know what they meant. But wouldn't you think that whoever had Isabelle's jewelry is also the person who robbed her home and murdered her?"

"Are you saying the blackmailer is also the murderer?"

Was I? "How else did they get Isabelle's jewelry?"

I waited while George took a sip of coffee and stared across the room before pointing his index finger at me. "They might have stolen it from the actual murderer."

"If so, then the blackmailer really would know who the murderer is, and they think it's Madame Bernhardt."

George raised his brows. "That is not irrefutable proof."

I returned my attention to the interviews. "Perhaps not, but I have a feeling you are well on your way to becoming the most hated man in Paris—possibly the world."

Chapter Four

The following morning, George left to pay a call on Cadieux, to see the letter sent to Sarah Bernhardt, and to find out what the police made of it. I knew George was eager to dig into this investigation, but I couldn't help wondering if it was simply a ploy to be away from the apartment when my mother arrived.

I wished I'd thought of it.

I anticipated her visit with a mixture of joy and dread. She was my mother, after all. I loved her, and I knew she loved me. But she had a way of showing that love with constant criticism. My plan was to keep her as busy as possible while she was here and do my best to ignore any complaints that I could do nothing about.

I jumped when the doorbell rang. Buck up, old girl, I told myself and headed to the door.

Madame Auclair had just taken mother's wrap when I joined them in the entry hall. With her free hand, she gestured to the footman to relieve the cab driver of mother's bags. As they made the exchange, Mother stepped out of the way and bumped into me.

"There you are, Frances," she said, sweeping me with a glance. "My, how good you look!"

I returned the compliment with all honesty. I considered my mother, at barely five feet, pocket-sized, and her blond hair, round blue eyes, and strawberries-and-cream complexion, made her seem like a living, breathing doll.

Her last comment was thrown over her shoulder as she picked out some coins from her purse to give the driver, who held up his hands and took a step back. "Madame, no. Your husband has already paid me enough."

Mother declared that to be nonsense. "You have been very generous with your time and assistance. Now allow me to be generous in my payment."

How could he argue with that? He bowed and thanked her while I stood staring in amazement. I had seen her harsh exterior soften when she and my father had first reconciled, but I hadn't let myself believe it could last this long. And never in my wildest dreams did I imagine she would become even more congenial.

While I recovered my bearings, Mother turned back to me with a smile—a smile! She gestured to the salon. "Shall we make ourselves comfortable?"

I shook off my surprise. "Yes, of course. Mother, please come in. Would you like coffee or tea?"

She followed me into the salon. "I'll always welcome a cup of coffee, but especially now. Nothing is as good as Parisian coffee."

Well, now she'd won a place in Madame Auclair's heart. The housekeeper might not speak a great deal of English, but she clearly understood this. She sent Mother a look of approval and fairly danced off to the kitchen to prepare a cup of coffee for someone who obviously knew how to appreciate it.

I observed Mother as she settled into one of the armchairs that bordered one half of the coffee table and took in her surroundings. "What a lovely place you and George have managed to find for yourselves, but I thought you'd said it was on the first floor?"

"You are in Europe, Mother. This is the first floor. The one below us is the ground floor." Our leased apartment was smaller than the one we'd borrowed from the Kendricks during the summer, but it was the perfect size for us. There were four bedchambers, a large salon, and a dining room, with kitchen and servants' rooms all on one floor.

I pointed that out to Mother, who flapped a hand in response. "Stairs are no trouble for me. After all the walking we've done on our trip, I may be more fit than ever."

"I believe you look better than I've ever seen you." Continuing with the doll analogy, Mother had always looked rather fragile to me, like the type of doll one must handle with care. Now, though her face and figure were as fine as ever, she looked—dare I say it? Robust.

I didn't say it. Mother had worked so hard for so many years to look perfect, at least as she perceived perfection. I wasn't sure she'd appreciate the word, though it suited her well. It made her look friendly and inviting. Goodness, perhaps she actually was friendly and inviting.

Time would tell.

Madame Auclair returned with the coffee and its accompaniments. When she dropped the tray off on the table, I took a seat opposite Mother and poured us each a cup. "It sounds like Frankie put you in a cab this morning, then boarded a ship for New York, is that right?"

"We were enjoying ourselves so much on our adventure I daresay we stayed far longer than he'd anticipated. Your father has been champing at the bit to return to his office for at least the past week. I hope Lily won't be upset that he didn't stay long enough to see her."

"Lily knows Frankie well enough to understand," I said. I

was named after my father, Franklin. At some point in my childhood, we both took to calling each other Frankie, though my siblings used the more traditional Father.

"Now tell me what the arrangements are," Mother said. "I take it Lily and the baby aren't staying with you or I'd have seen them by now."

"Lily and Amelia Jane are at Patricia Kendrick's apartment. Anne Kendrick is also staying there. I'm sure you remember her from Lily's wedding. She is Leo's middle sister. Since Patricia seemed to have a houseful, we thought you'd prefer to stay here with us."

Mother seemed satisfied with that answer. "Rose and your husband's ward are not with you in Paris?"

"They are in London with Aunt Hetty. We'll join them in about two weeks. Now that you are here, I wonder if you'd prefer to settle into your room or go directly to the Kendricks' apartment to see your new granddaughter? I'd love to hear about your trip, but I understand if you are eager to see the baby."

"Oh, yes. Let's do go this morning. Lily is a horrible correspondent. I asked her to send a photograph of Amelia, but I haven't even seen that."

"Then we shall go immediately." I rang for the housekeeper. "Lily is half expecting us, anyway."

When Madame Auclair entered the room, I asked her to send someone for a cab. "I hope you don't mind that I have made luncheon plans for us as well, Mother."

"Frances, don't fuss. After all these months touring, I have built up quite a bit of stamina—enough, I am sure, for a morning visit and a luncheon."

"I just want you to be comfortable," I said.

"I will let you know when I am not."

Of that, I could be certain. With a quick stop in our rooms

for hats and wraps, we were out the door, in the cab, and at the Kendrick apartment in no time.

The cab set us down at the gate, and *madame la concierge* let us into the courtyard. I greeted her and dropped a coin into her arthritic hand, then we crossed the open area to the steps leading to the Kendricks' apartment.

"I rather like the idea of leasing an apartment for one's stay in Paris," Mother remarked, taking in the center garden, where the hydrangeas still flourished. "A place and staff of one's own has a definite advantage over a hotel, however elegant it may be."

"It does make one feel more comfortable," I said, watching her step quickly up the stairs. Heavens, I might have a difficult time keeping up with her.

I had barely applied the knocker when the door was thrown open by my sister. I was struck once again by how much she and our mother resembled each other.

"Mama!" Lily cried. She threw her arms wide, which was all the invitation Mother needed to step into them. "Oh, my dear child," she said patting Lily on the back. I stood back a step. Neither of them had ever greeted me with such enthusiasm, but then I recalled that Mother and Lily hadn't seen each other since Lily's wedding almost a year ago.

After a closer look, I saw that Lily was crying. It wasn't a happy, joyous crying. Nor was it the wailing type. It was just a forlorn sort of leaking of tears.

When they released each other, I took Lily's arm, led them both into the salon, and sat my sister on the sofa. "Whatever is wrong, dear?"

Lily pulled a handkerchief from her pocket and wiped at the dampness on her cheeks. "It's nothing, Frances." She gestured for Mother to sit next to her, which Mother did while watching Lily cautiously. "Everything is fine," Lily said. "I'm rather short on sleep with the baby keeping me up at night. It tends to make me emotional. I'm sure you remember those days, don't you, Frances?"

The way she looked up at me, made me think she was desperate to hear that she wasn't alone in whatever it was she was going through. I took a seat on her other side. "I do not recall anything like that, Lily, because I had a nurse looking after Rose." Now that I was so close to her, I could see the exhaustion and tension in her expression. This was not a matter of one night's loss of sleep.

"How long has Amelia not been sleeping?"

"Probably right from the beginning, if she's like any other child." Mother patted Lily's hand while she spoke. "Frances is right, you ought to hire someone to help you with her."

Lily shook her head. "No, no, no. I have a little help while I'm visiting Leo's mother. Anne is with Amelia right now, and when Patricia is home, she sometimes watches her so I can take a nap." She grimaced. "We will get past this stage and everything will be fine."

It seemed to me that everything was far from fine. From the look on Mother's face, she and I were in agreement, but before we could pursue the matter, Anne entered the salon with Amelia in her arms.

"Here we are," Anne said. "All neat, tidy, and rested for a visit with your grandmama." Anne presented the baby to Mother, who reached out eagerly for her.

Now her eyes filled with tears. "My goodness, Lily, she's absolutely beautiful!"

While grandmother and grandchild communed with each other and Lily looked on with a smile, Anne took a seat in a nearby chair. "I'm surprised to see you here," I said, leaning toward her. "I would have thought you'd be on the golf links, practicing for the big tournament."

"I ought to be," she replied. "Mother told me she would arrange for someone to train with me, but she forgot all about it when some other Exposition incident arose." She sighed. "I don't necessarily need a coach, but my French isn't really up to snuff, and I'm concerned that I won't find my way to a course, or be able to explain what I want once I get there."

"The fact that you would have a bag of clubs with you ought to be explanation enough, I should think, but if a translator would make you feel more comfortable, why not ask the housekeeper if she could spare one of the staff?"

"Why, I never thought of that. What an excellent idea."

"Before you implement that plan, George and I would like you to join us for a round tomorrow. He reserved a tee time with the club secretary at the course in Compiègne."

"The Olympic course," Anne said with surprise. "I'd be delighted to join you, but do you know the course is at least an hour away by train?"

"I'm told it is about the same by motorcar, and since we have access to one, we will happily transport you as well."

I could see the excitement in her expression. "Touring through the French countryside in a motorcar," she said, "then playing a round of golf at Compiègne. What could be better?"

"I should make you aware that you will be making up a foursome. George has asked Carlson Deaver, as well." I grinned at her. "Your fellow Olympian."

Anne laughed. "You make us sound larger than life."

"It is rather an important event, don't you think?"

"Not that anyone knows," she said. "France is keeping the Olympic games rather a secret."

"That is unfortunate. I believe France has a great deal more money invested in the Exposition and, thus, more at stake in promoting it. But your name will still be associated with the history of these games, and that's something to be proud of. Tell me the date so that I can put it on my schedule."

Anne laughed. "It is to take place October third, but I cannot ask you to come all the way to Compiègne to watch me play golf."

"You aren't asking, and I am eager to go. When I'm in my dotage, I will be able to tell my grandchildren I was there the day my friend Anne Kendrick won the Olympic golf tournament for England, and they will think I was quite the thing in my day."

Anne enjoyed a hearty laugh. "They will ask for the details, and of course, you won't recall them."

I flapped a hand. "Well, I will be in my dotage, after all. They shouldn't expect much of me."

"Frances you are making me feel so much better about the whole thing. Yes, I'd be happy to make up your foursome tomorrow. And the next day, I'm determined to begin my practice at one of the local courses."

At that point, Lily jerked awake from her catnap and sent a maid for coffee. Amelia began to fuss, so Mother got up and fairly danced around the room with her.

"I don't think I've ever seen Mother so totally infatuated before," Lily said.

"She was exactly like that with Rose." I felt a pang, missing my daughter and wishing she were here. I'd write to her tonight, sending details of her new cousin. "And while I don't recall my own experience as an infant," I continued, "or Alonzo's, I know she was enthralled with you, as well."

Lily's eyes widened. "Was she really?" She turned to Anne. "I assume Patricia was like that with all of you, too. She seems to adore babies."

"To her, infants are pure joy," Anne agreed. "Then we grow older and start thinking and speaking, and quite ruin the whole experience for her."

"Mother still dotes on Rose. Perhaps she should have stayed here with you," I said to Lily. "Then you might get some sleep."

She scowled at me.

"Truly, dear, I'm worried about you."

"Is Amelia keeping you up at night?" Anne asked.

"She is, the poor thing. I think she may be teething and she wakes herself up fussing." Lily stifled a yawn. "But it should pass soon."

"It would pass soon," I said, "if she were only to have one tooth, but that's usually not the case."

Lily looked like a startled deer.

"I understand you want to care for her yourself," I said, carefully choosing my words, "but you ought to consider finding some help. Teething can go on for quite some time. I don't think you can."

Mother returned with a much quieter Amelia and drew Anne's attention. I took the opportunity to give Lily some support. "You do not have to impress your mother-in-law. If you would like me to speak to Patricia, I would be happy to do so."

Lily took my hand and gave it a squeeze. "Thank you, Frannie, that means the world to me, but I think I will get through this."

Mother and I left shortly after that exchange for our luncheon at the Petit Bouillon Pharamond. The Kendricks' apartment was near rue St. Honoré in the first arrondissement. Our destination was close to the Louvre, so a mere city block or two away. The restaurant had been newly decorated in the Art Nouveau style for the Exposition and it did not disappoint, from the warmth of the wood paneling to the curves of the wrought iron on the staircase to the floral ceramic panels on the walls, it was polished perfection.

The murmur of hushed voices and the occasional ting of silver against china accompanied our footsteps as we followed the waiter through the dining room. The seating was rather close, but since we'd be conversing in English, I hoped we could speak without fear of being overheard.

To my surprise, Alicia was already waiting for us at a small table tucked between two windows. I don't know why, but I always pictured Alicia as someone who consistently arrived late. It seemed I would have to adjust my thinking about her yet again.

After introductions, small talk, and placing our orders, I brought up the purpose of this meeting. "Mother, I wonder what you might recall of Mimi Deaver and her son, Carlson. I know we didn't have much to do with them when I lived in New York, but perhaps that has changed in more recent years?"

Mother frowned. "I believe both of them live here in Paris now, do they not?"

"They do," I said. "In fact, Carlson has shown an interest in Alicia's daughter, Harriet. Alicia, of course, would like to know something of the man's character. If we were all in London, she would have far more resources, but Alicia is a newcomer to Paris, and Carlson has lived here for little more than two years. Not much is known about his background."

Mother placed a hand over Alicia's, drawing a look of surprise from the younger woman. "It is so difficult, is it not, knowing to whom we can trust our precious daughters? I sympathize with you, my dear. I've gone through it twice myself."

Frankly, I would never have thought she gave a fig about my late husband's character when she was negotiating our match. His social status was all that concerned her—that and his title.

"I recall that some of the so-called upper class in New York objected to *Mimi* Deaver." Mother lowered her voice a notch. "I'm sure you know her relationship with the *comte* began well before her husband passed away."

Some of them? The only reason I even knew about Mimi's affair was because of Mother's gossip.

"I've heard nothing ill of Carlson Deaver, though," she added. "I actually had my eye on him for my second daughter."

That caught my attention. "Did you? When? How did Lily feel about it?" I couldn't see her being attracted to an older man.

"It was before Mimi abandoned her husband, of course. But you know your sister. If I wanted one thing for her, she would want the exact opposite." She folded her hands and sulked. "She said he was too old for her, can you imagine?"

Indeed, I just had.

"Then your brother took her side, as if young, wealthy men of good family were thick on the ground." She made a motion as if brushing the issue aside. "It all came to naught anyway. They were no sooner introduced than Carlson's mother found some business for him to handle in Boston. Lily never had a chance to make a lasting impression on him before he was sent away."

Lily's vague recollection of Carlson led me to believe he hadn't impressed her either.

Mother sighed. "But I suppose that doesn't answer your question, does it, Mrs. Stoke-Whitney?"

I glanced at Alicia, whose tight-lipped smile spoke of extreme patience. "Please call me Alicia," she said.

Before Mother could call her anything, I broke in. "We'll get to her question, but you can't abandon the topic now. Why did Mimi interfere? What was her objection to Lily?"

Mother looked surprised by the inquiry. "I don't know that she had a specific objection. At the time, I assumed she wanted someone more established in society for her son. I hold no grudge against her. I knew Lily would have more prospects in London than in New York. Mimi was simply looking out for the best interests of her son, as Alicia is looking out for her daughter. Any mother would do the same."

As Alicia was about to speak, I cut her off once more. She could have her say momentarily, but this snub to my sister rankled. "After Carlson moved to Paris, he married an actress, right under his mother's nose and presumably with her blessing, so it appears social climbing wasn't part of her plan for Carlson, after all."

"Why are you so upset about this?" Mother looked at me in confusion. "Lily didn't care for the man anyway, and by all accounts, including yours, she is quite happy with Leo, so all's well that ends well, don't you think?"

I waved a dismissive hand. "You are right, it isn't my concern. Still, I was curious about Mimi's reasons for rejecting Lily."

"You appear to be taking it far harder than your sister did, I must say. I have no great insight into the woman's plans, so if you must know if she had an objection to Lily and what it was, you shall have to ask her yourself."

"If you do so, Frances, I hope you'll enquire about her objections to Harriet," Alicia said. "My understanding is that she is dissuading Carlson against my daughter, too. At least Harriet seems to think so."

"Well, there you have it," I said. "Her objections cannot possibly be about pedigree. Harriet's lineage goes back to the Domesday Book on her father's side. And I'll remind you, Mimi allowed Carlson to marry an actress."

"My thoughts exactly." Alicia bobbed her head firmly in agreement.

"For heaven's sake," Mother said, with a touch of pique. "Why do you both assume Mimi played a role in her son's decision?"

We turned our attention to her. "You are the one who said she came between Carlson and Lily," I said.

"And I believe that is the case, but perhaps he married this other woman before Mimi could do anything about it. Or perhaps while she was distracted by the *comte*."

I glanced at Alicia, who shrugged. "I suppose that's possible.

I wonder how well Mimi tolerated his wife while they were married."

"The marriage couldn't have lasted very long," Mother observed. "I assume his wife passed away?"

"She was murdered." Alicia and I spoke at once—and at the same moment that every other sound in the restaurant came to a stop.

Of course.

In the space of a few breaths, the other diners ceased to stare, and Mother's eyes returned to their normal size as she glanced between us. "Now I see why you are in need of information about the young man—and his mother. I shall cable some friends of mine in New York who had a closer acquaintance with the Deavers."

I turned to Alicia. "And I shall see what I can learn about Mimi's relationship with her late daughter-in-law."

Alicia placed a hand on her chest. "Thank you, ladies. I am in your debt."

After luncheon, Mother suggested we drop our cards at Mimi's home, so I gave the address to the cab driver.

"I don't expect her to receive us at this time of day," Mother said, raising her voice over the traffic noise of the busy boulevard St. Germain. "Although, now I think about it, we are in Paris, and I have no idea whether such late afternoon calls are acceptable."

"I suppose that all depends upon Mimi," I said.

"No matter, we shall ask if she is home to callers. If not, we'll leave our cards and perhaps an invitation. What do you think?"

"Not a bad idea. What are we inviting her to?"

"Why not luncheon? At your apartment. In a more intimate setting, she may be more relaxed and open."

I could find no fault with Mother's plan. We might never learn why Mimi objected to my sister, but she might be willing to talk about her late daughter-in-law. Through that conversation, we ought to be able to determine her feelings toward Isabelle.

We asked the driver to wait when we arrived at Mimi's home near the rue de l'Abbaye, a block away from the Church of St.-Germain-des-Prés. To my surprise, it was indeed a house rather than an apartment. In fact, it would be described in French as a grand hotel—a four-story, probably historical, private home. It even had its own small courtyard, garden, and fountain. If gossip was to be trusted, Mimi had completely refurnished it. I could only imagine the cost. The door opened the second I grasped the knocker, wrenching it from my fingers.

Startled, I took a step back.

The gentleman in the doorway was a distinguished fifty or so years old, at a guess, with slivers of gray in his dark hair and laugh lines around his hooded eyes. He wore an overcoat and held a hat in his hand, clearly on his way out.

"*Pardon, mesdames*," he said with convincing regret and a nod to each of us. "I hope I did not startle you," he continued in French. Backing through the door, he held it open for us to enter.

"You could not have known we were on your doorstep," I replied in the same language. "We are here to call on Madame Deaver. My mother, Madame Price is an acquaintance from New York." I held out my hand. "I am Frances Hazelton."

He bowed over my hand, then turned to Mother and did the same. "*Enchantée, mesdames*. I am Henri, le Comte de Beaulieu. I would welcome you to our home, but I am afraid Madame Deaver is away at this time."

"No matter. If you don't mind, we shall simply leave our cards right here." I indicated the silver tray on the nearby table. "We had hoped to extend a personal invitation to her, but I will send one along this evening."

"Of course," he said with a gesture to the table. Mother and I dropped our cards on the tray and stepped back toward the door. "Allow me to walk you to your cab," the *comte* said, extending an arm to each of us.

It was only a matter of a few steps but it was a gentlemanly gesture. He opened the door to the cab and assisted us inside. "*Bonne journée, mesdames,*" he called out before walking down the street, away from the house.

Mother kept her smile in place until the cab pulled away. "I didn't understand much of that. I take it Mimi wasn't at home, but who was that man?"

"That was the Comte de Beaulieu."

"He's the man Mimi left her husband for." Mother wore a look of horror. "Are they openly living together?"

"He called it their home, and it is the address I found for Mimi. It appears they live here together."

"So, he is the reason she threw her reputation away," Mother said. "I suppose I see the attraction."

I turned to her sharply. "You find him attractive?"

She lifted one shoulder in a shrug. "I don't find him unattractive, but that isn't what I meant. I assume she found the old mansion, the money, even the title far more enticing than his person."

"Is that what they said about her in New York?"

"More or less. Why? Is the rumor mill mistaken in this regard?"

"It depends on which purveyor of rumors you want to believe," I said. "Around here, and in London too, now that I think of it, it is said that Mimi pays for the upkeep of this place and for everything else they possess. He is living off her largesse and spends her money rather freely on himself."

"She is supporting him?" Mother could not have looked more shocked. "Whyever would she do that?"

"I don't know, but it gets worse. He isn't faithful to her, either. He owns a yacht and frequently sails off, with a companion, for a week or two at a time, leaving Mimi alone at home, with no idea of where he is."

Mother huffed. "And she didn't even get a title out of him. Outrageous."

"Indeed."

Chapter Five

Keep your head down. Keep your head down. And for goodness' sake, keep your head down! I twisted my torso as I drew my arms into a backswing—*hinge the wrist, now down and through.*

Swoosh! Thwack!

I liked the sound of that! When I looked down the fairway, my ball was soaring through the air—to the right.

Too far to the right.

My body slumped, and I smothered a sob as I watched it sail off the fairway, past the rough and over the rail fence, to land in the thick turf of the racetrack that I still couldn't believe wove through this golf course. I would likely never see that ball again.

"I have my eye on it," George said, giving me a buck-up pat on the shoulder. "We'll find it." He took the club from my fingers and handed it to the caddie we shared. The boy looked to be about twelve and would fit under my extended arm, but he did not seem to be struggling under the weight of both bags.

On the other hand, I was struggling, indeed—with this game.

"I don't understand what happened. I kept my head down." George and I followed Anne as she strode yards and yards farther down the fairway toward her ball, her caddie right on her heels, chatting incessantly in the hope of improving his English. Carlson was right behind her. I had been first to take my shot, since my ball had gone the least distance from our starting point on the tee box. Anne's had gone significantly farther than mine. Then Carlson, then George.

"You kept your head down beautifully, my dear," George said. "It was a lovely swing and a good shot. Look how far it went."

"In the wrong direction," I countered.

"It was mostly in the correct direction. Your ball went a little right."

I gave him a dark look.

"A lot right, then. I noticed you pulled your left elbow in when you finished. That pushed the ball to the right. Always try to finish with your arms extended."

I barely heard him over the screaming in my head. "Are you telling me I've developed a new problem?" I ended the sentence on a whisper since we'd caught up with Anne and Carlson, and Anne was about to take her shot. Like me, she wore a skirt and blouse, with sensible shoes, and a straw hat to shade her complexion. We had both started the round with fitted jackets, but doffed them, one hole before, as the day warmed.

They had been much needed on the drive up from Paris earlier this morning when the air was quite chilly. Though the motorcar had a windscreen and a roof, the sides were open to the elements. George has said the automobile is the transportation of the future, but they won't be part of my future without some significant improvements.

Carlson had chosen to take the train this morning and hadn't had to thaw out before starting the round. He and George were also in their shirtsleeves, ties, and loose trousers. Carlson had thrown off his hat, and in the sunlight, his tawny hair held the faintest suggestion of red like his sister, Lottie's. He was clean shaven, of average height, with a sturdy build, and moved with a confidence and grace his sister would have killed for.

I glanced back to Anne. None of us moved as she turned her upper torso, bringing the club back, then like a pendulum, reversed the motion with a swoosh and a solid thwack, and set the ball sailing effortlessly toward the tiny green and that tantalizing little flag.

Anne let out a small *tsk* when her ball landed on the front of the green and stopped there rather than rolling toward the hole as it had done on every other green she'd hit today.

"Well struck, Anne," I said as we all moved up toward Carlson's ball.

George concurred.

Carlson grunted.

"I could show you how to put some spin on the ball," he said to Anne. "Right after Hazelton takes his shot." He moved aside to allow George access to the ball.

George glanced at the ball. "No, it seems this one is yours, old man. Mine is farther ahead."

"George's ball has tiny squares on the surface," I said. "This one has round dimples, so it must be yours, Carlson. You can show Anne how to add a spin to her shot right now, while I hike to the outer reaches of the course to hunt for my ball."

Not wanting to slow the pace of play, I waved off George's offer of help and set off for my search alone. Without even looking, I knew Carlson would be wearing a sour expression. Perhaps he was the better golfer of his usual set, but it was clear he did not like being bested by George and truly hated that Anne's score was better than his.

I was relieved to be able to step away from whatever theatrical production Carlson would make of showing off his particular skill. It was not as though I had never experienced a man talking down to me. It happened far more frequently than I'd like. But for four hours? That was a bit too much. I had to commend Anne on her patience. She was clearly the better golfer, yet she allowed Carlson to give her his so-called advice. He'd given up on me, several holes ago.

That was one bit of luck.

I picked my way through the rough—grass as tall as unharvested wheat, for heaven's sake, taking me back to my childhood in Ohio. I swiped my club back and forth in the futile hope of uncovering my ball. When I approached the low railing that separated the golf course from the racetrack, I lifted my skirt enough to step over it and nearly trod right on top of my ball. It hadn't the decency to land in the grass. Oh, no, it rested just past the railing in the loose dirt.

With a sigh, I glanced at the green—so far away. Perhaps it was time to give up this game. It took so much practice, and frankly, brought me little enjoyment. I examined the placement of my ball. The sprinkling of soil on the surface was soft, but I knew that horses galloping over this track for years would have compacted the ground underneath to the hardness of pavement. If I attempted to dig under the ball with my club, I might find myself with a sprained or fractured wrist. But the ground was level and there was enough room for a backswing. It could be worse.

I looked back at the fairway and saw that George had already taken his shot, and the rest of my foursome were all watching me. Their scrutiny wasn't likely to improve my swing. I looked to the green. Distances were not my strong suit, but I waved away the caddie before he could trek over to me. This club should be enough to get me out of trouble and back on the fairway.

Nice, smooth, swing, I told myself. All I had to do was put the ball back on the fairway.

Turn, swoosh, thwack!

Well! That felt good—almost effortless. The ball sailed over the railing, then over the rough, down the fairway, and—oh my goodness—all the way to the green, where it finally dropped and even rolled a few inches toward the flag.

My jaw sagged open. That was incredible! Angels must be singing in Heaven. I looked down at my feet to ensure myself that I truly had hit the ball and that shot hadn't been a fabrication of my imagining. Then I raised my gaze to my foursome.

Carlson wore his usual scowl, but Anne's eyes glowed as she applauded my effort. Barreling toward me, George let out a whoop, lifting me off the ground when he arrived. "Brava, Frances!" he said. "That's the shot that will make you come back for more."

I wasn't so sure about that. Although it had felt awfully good!

Fortunately, there were only four more holes to play after that. Not that I wasn't enjoying myself. I had far more bad shots than good, but Anne offered to tutor me at a later date. George had me pick up my ball and drop it with his when my excessive number of errant shots began to slow us down. The camaraderie was wonderful.

Carlson Deaver was the one dark cloud on my sunny day. I was quite prepared to tell Alicia that Harriet ought to run in the opposite direction from the man. He was little more than a spoiled child. If he wasn't winning, he became cranky. There could be no doubt that he was a good golfer, but on this particular day, he wasn't the best. Anne had won the round, and he truly resented coming in second. And he almost hadn't. George was only two shots behind him.

In the end, however, he did congratulate Anne on her hard-fought victory, and we all headed for the clubhouse to tidy ourselves and meet for luncheon.

"I'm so grateful you brought me out here today," Anne said as we stepped into the women's lounge. "It was invaluable to get a feel for the course I'll be playing in the tournament."

"I'm relieved to hear that," I told her. "Though I'm pleased that George was able to get us on the course, I thought you might hate me for forcing you to spend the morning with such a poor sport."

Anne had removed her hat and was pinning back a few wayward strands of hair in front of a mirror. "It isn't as if I never had to deal with a man's self-importance before."

"At least you won't have to deal with it during your tournament."

"That's true." She gave me a playful grin. "Perhaps the officials knew what they were doing when they decided on separate men's and women's tournaments. The men would be so busy giving the women the benefit of their superior expertise in the finer points of the game, we might never finish the rounds." She boggled her eyes in the mirror and we both laughed.

"I was serious about coming to cheer you on," I said. "I've marked the date in my diary, but you must give me the time."

"Really?" She turned away from the mirror to face me. "That's so kind of you. I doubt my mother will come, and Lily is so busy with the baby, I can't expect her. It would be lovely to see a familiar face in the crowd."

"I wouldn't miss it for the world," I said, linking my arm with hers. "I never thought I would actually know a woman who participated in sport on an international level. If I haven't told you already, I am so proud of you. How could I not come and watch? If necessary, I would come as your caddie."

Anne's eyes were a bit damp, and she was beaming at me. "Thank you, Frances. I don't think you will have to go to such lengths, but I so appreciate the sentiment. And I stand by my offer to coach you whenever you like. I'm sure you have other things to keep you busy while you're in Paris, but once you're back in England, just say the word. Perhaps you will play in the next Olympic games."

That truly made me laugh out loud.

She turned me to the door. "Now it's time to deal with the men, by which I mean Mr. Deaver. George has been a perfect sport."

I opened the door leading back to the club restaurant. "He is, isn't he? I'm quite lucky in that regard."

We found the gentlemen at a table in the restaurant. "Ah, there you are," Carlson said, coming to his feet and holding out a chair for Anne, while George did the same for me. "Hazelton, you win this bet, and the ladies win my admiration."

I slid into the chair and grinned at Carlson. "It sounds as though you have underestimated us in some manner, Mr. Deaver. For shame. My guess is you bet George that Anne and I would be much longer."

"Foolish of me, I know," he said. "Obviously, Hazelton knows you don't generally keep him waiting, though a gentleman never minds the wait, to be sure. My wife used to keep me cooling my heels on a regular basis. Beauty takes time, she'd tell me." His eyes softened and he averted his gaze. "Seeing her was always worth the wait."

My mind stumbled in an attempt to catch up with him. What initially seemed like a criticism of his late wife, or even women in general, turned into a fond remembrance. I decided I was relieved that I didn't have to converse with Carlson frequently, and was simply glad it was he who brought up the subject of his wife.

"Although I know they come late, please accept our deepest sympathies on the loss of your wife," George said.

"Such a tragedy," I added.

"Did they ever charge anyone with the crime?" George asked.

Carlson had been bobbing his head, accepting our condolences in stride, but glanced sharply at George when he asked the question. "They never did," he said. "But oddly enough, I was notified a few days ago that the police are looking into Isabelle's murder once more. Seems they found some new evidence or something."

Anne glanced from me to George and finally to Carlson, where she rested her gaze momentarily. "Forgive me, but am I to understand that your wife was murdered?"

I'd forgotten that Anne wouldn't have known about Isabelle Deaver, but that could work in our favor.

"Indeed, she was," Carlson said. "It's been nine months now, and I still miss her desperately."

"Of course, you do," Anne said. "I'm so sorry."

The waiter stopped by with a bottle of wine the men must have requested. Conversation ceased while we all perused the menu and placed our orders. When he stepped away, Carlson picked up right where we left off, giving Anne a sad smile and accepting her sympathy.

"People were shocked when they learned we married," he said, turning to include George and me in the conversation. "My wife was an actress, you know. Our friends and my family—they didn't realize that love knows nothing of class."

Interesting that Carlson would speak of class to George and me. George was the son of an earl and I'd been married to one. Their ancestors would likely have considered Carlson, the son of a businessman, and an American, no less, to be in the same class as his actress wife. Nowadays, it's true his fortune put him at least one rung up on the social ladder, but American businessmen married actresses frequently, and he spoke as if the gap between them had been much wider.

"Well, it certainly shouldn't," Anne said, giving Carlson a curious look.

"In our case, love was truly blind."

I was willing to wager that the first thing Carlson fell in love with was his wife's beauty, so perhaps not blind. Since George seemed content to listen to the conversation while he poured the wine, I decided to act on the opening Carlson provided. "I'm sure your friends meant well and had only your best interest at heart. Perhaps their surprise was at the suddenness of the wedding, not your choice of bride." I took the glass of wine George handed to me and returned my attention to Carlson. "Your mother must have been taken by surprise."

Carlson produced a smirk. "She was both shocked and angry."

"Angry?" I asked. "Surely, she didn't object to your wife?"

He shook my words off with a shrug. "She was like any mother, I'd say. She objected at first, thinking no one was good enough for her son, but she came around in the end. She and Isabelle got along reasonably well."

So Mimi objected to Isabelle only at first. It was not the definitive answer I'd hoped for, but it was a start.

"But you say the police are investigating her death once more?" George asked.

"Yes. They sent over a short note with no real information. I'll have to pay a call on the inspector and ask about the details. It's high time, I say. It always seemed to me they gave up too soon."

"If I remember correctly," George said, "they believe she interrupted a robbery of your home."

"That is certainly possible, but I don't think it was quite as random as the police seem to believe. Isabelle did some charity work, and I've wondered if one of her poor souls followed her home, took a look at the apartment, and decided they might like to live as well as she did."

"Did you mention that to the police?" George topped off Carlson's glass of wine.

"I did. Not that anything came of it." He shook his head. "Then there were her old actor friends. I didn't like her associating with those people. She had moved up in the world, and I feared that might make her something of a target. Isabelle always wished to please me, but that was one issue we could not agree upon."

Was he saying she brought the attack on herself? I really didn't know where to go with my questions after that. Anne was gaping at the three of us as if we were complete barbarians. This was hardly polite luncheon conversation.

George looked on the verge of asking another question, but as I observed him, his expression changed to something far more pleasant. When he came to his feet, I turned to see a couple approaching our table.

Carlson stood as well and had stretched out a hand in greeting to the couple. Interesting, because I thought they were coming to greet George and me. They were Jeanne and Étienne Clement, a couple we had met during our stay in Deauville. They were a few years younger than George and I, with dark hair, dark eyes, and ready smiles. After shaking Carlson's hand, Étienne turned to George and did the same. The gesture obviously surprised Carlson.

"Do you two know each other?" he asked.

"Anne does not know the Clements," George said and performed the introductions himself while Carlson pulled up chairs for the new arrivals. "I know we said we'd get together again once we were all in Paris," George said. "But I didn't expect to see you here in Compiègne. And"—he gestured from the Clements to Carlson—"how do you know each other?"

"It is a great surprise to see all of you here," Jeanne said, taking the seat her husband held out for her. "We are neighbors to Mr. Deaver." Then turning to Carlson, she explained that George and I had met them in Deauville a few weeks ago.

It turned out the Clements had just finished their lunch. Étienne had played a round of golf that morning while Jeanne toured the nearby castle. "It is not very busy," she said, "so I can move at my own pace."

Jeanne had suffered a riding injury last autumn that left her right leg lame. Though she could walk, her pace was slow and sometimes looked painful. Prior to her accident, they had been an active couple—enjoying both tennis and golf. Jeanne had been an avid horsewoman, and Étienne played polo. When we met them, Jeanne had been attempting a new water therapy for her leg and said that swimming made her feel like her old self.

I would have loved to ask them what they knew about Carlson and the late Mrs. Deaver, but that would have to wait for another time. Our lunch arrived, and they took their leave so that the four of us could attend to our meals.

After they left, the conversation turned to the upcoming tournaments and more general topics. I couldn't find another opportunity to bring up Carlson's late wife before it was time to drive back to Paris.

The warm afternoon made the drive pleasant. In what seemed like no time at all, we were at the Kendricks' apartment, where we expected to find my mother. But upon seeing Anne to the door, we learned Mother and Patricia Kendrick had left for some shopping. Lily and the baby were taking a nap, so there was nothing for George and me to do but go home.

George had become proficient enough with the vehicle that I thought it safe to converse with him while he drove us through the crowded streets. "We didn't learn as much about Isabelle Deaver today as I had hoped, but what was your impression of Carlson?"

"He is the type of man who must always be right and, of course, better than everyone else in the room." He compressed his lips, but before I could comment, he continued, "If someone should prove himself to be better than him, Deaver will try to take that person down a peg." He glanced at me. "Do you know what I mean?"

"Watch the road, dear. There's a carriage coming this way."

George returned his attention to the task of driving. "I see it, Frances."

"As to Carlson, I didn't think he was quite that bad. He's definitely a bore, but men often talk down to women and see us as creatures that must be taught or trained, and could, of course, benefit from their superior knowledge and understanding." I turned to George to see him staring at me in horror. "The road, George!" I gestured to the windscreen.

"We are on the road, Frances, and we are not in danger of running into anything or anyone. I was momentarily distracted by your description of the so-called average man."

The wind was pulling my hair from its pins. I tucked a handful up into my hat. "I was being sarcastic. I did not mean to say that the average man behaves in such a way, at least not all the time—and I'll pause here to assure you that I consider you far above average."

"Thank you for that."

"It's only that many men do behave that way, particularly when around women they don't know. In my mind, I put Carlson in that category, but it sounds as though you see him differently."

"I believe he is an extreme version of what you describe. I saw plenty of his type back in my school days. He's full of himself, a braggart, and a buffoon."

"And I thought the two of you were getting along so well." I offered George a smile when he glanced at me, then directed his attention back to the road.

"And he cheats," George added.

"You caught him?"

"I did, and he knew it. His fairway shot on the sixteenth hole left his ball deep in the rough near Anne's."

It never ceased to amaze me that George could remember not only his own shots on every hole of every golf course, but also those of the other players.

"Deaver kicked his ball out to the fairway, thereby vastly improving his lie."

"He knew that you saw him do it?"

"He tried to involve me in his petty deception. He gave me a wink and said, 'We can't let the ladies best us now, can we?'"

George's impression of Carlson's American accent was spot on. "Did you make him put it back?" I asked.

He drew the motorcar around the back of our apartment building. "Perhaps I should have. Instead, I kicked Anne's ball out to the fairway with his. There wasn't much he could do about that."

"He won't be able to cheat like that in the tournament, will he?"

"No, I'm certain officials will be watching over the players. But it doesn't matter, because Carlson won't be playing in the tournament. He will find some way to drop out." George drove the car into its bay in the redesigned stables and turned off the engine.

"What makes you think he'll drop out?" I asked, speaking overly loud now that the engine was silent.

"Because he always has to be the best. He learned today that he doesn't play as well as Anne, and only a bit better than me. Rather than lose the tournament, he'll find a reason not to compete—something that won't be his fault. The officials will have made some mess of the paperwork—something of that nature. Mark my words."

"I shall."

We both climbed out and met behind the vehicle.

George frowned. "You are meant to wait for me to step around and hand you out."

"Am I? How are you so familiar with the etiquette of motorcars?"

He chuckled. "I always assist you in climbing down from a carriage."

"But you are usually next to me at the door and therefore don't have to circumnavigate the carriage in order to do so."

"Still, it feels as if I'm neglecting you. Humor me on this, won't you?"

"Of course." I took his arm, and we rounded the building to the gate. "So, it seems that neither of us likes Carlson Deaver or thinks very highly of him, but do you think him capable of murdering his wife?"

"That's the question, isn't it. I certainly believe anyone spending an extended amount of time in his presence could be compelled to murder him, but the other way around?" He sighed. "I'll need further research." He rang the bell for the concierge.

"We might want to find an opportunity to speak with the Clements," I suggested.

He ground his teeth. "It was so difficult to keep from questioning them right then and there."

The gate opened, revealing our young concierge, energetic and smiling. He gave George a wave. "I have a letter for you, *monsieur*."

George gave him a coin in exchange for the post. "Ah, it's from Cadieux. Shall I wait until we get inside?"

"Are you joking?"

He laughed and opened the envelope, removing a small card. "Our interview with the Clements will have to wait, I'm afraid."

"Something else has come up?"

George grinned. "Cadieux has arranged an interview with the Divine Sarah Bernhardt, herself. We are to call on her at her dressing room at the theater tomorrow morning."

Chapter Six

The traffic in the city was busy at this time of the morning. It was not quite nine and so many people were leaving home for their daily employment that we decided it best to leave the motorcar where it was and take a hackney cab, or rather, a fiacre as they were called in Paris.

"I can't believe I'm actually about to meet Sarah Bernhardt," I said, as the cab lurched into the traffic. "I'll admit, I've been incapable of any sensible thought since reading Cadieux's message."

George gave me an indulgent smile. "Have you never seen her perform?"

"No," I said, staring at him in astonishment. "Are you about to tell me that you have?"

"I don't recall having seen her."

"Surely, you would remember such an event," I said. "I was only eight the first time she came to America. We were still living in Ohio then. I used to sneak into my father's office and read his newspapers. The things they said about her before she arrived in New York were simply scandalous." I grinned at the memory of feeling that I'd gotten away with something improper simply by reading about her.

"They claimed she was the mother of four children," I continued. "All of whom had different fathers, none of whom she'd married. They said that rather than act like a fallen woman, she flagrantly paraded those children at the grand receptions and banquets given in her honor. The reputation that preceded her both shocked and tantalized my eight-year-old self."

"As it was meant to do, I'm sure," George said.

"The strange thing is that after her first performance, the papers couldn't praise her enough. She was a sort of miracle on the stage—a form of theatrical perfection. She had completely won them over, which fascinated me even more."

"What did they make of her death scenes?"

"From what I've read, nobody can die onstage the way she does."

We both chuckled. "I believe she has only one child," George said as an afterthought.

"Yes, but sensation sells newspapers. I suspect they made up most of what they reported about her."

The cab eased to a crawl as the clip-clopping of our horse slowed, the sound blending with the shouts of vendors, hawking their wares. I glanced out the window to see that the street was packed with both vehicles and pedestrians surrounding the place du Chatelet, where the Sarah Bernhardt Theater took up one corner of the square. We paid the driver and made our way to the entrance on foot.

The theater itself looked empty, though the door was unlocked. George held it for me to enter first. "I hadn't considered how we go about finding Madame Bernhardt once we got here," he muttered.

"Look around you," I said indicating the walls of the lobby. They were covered with images of Sarah Bernhardt, larger than life, depicted in some of her most famous roles, most likely by very famous artists. "She's everywhere."

"They do call her divine." George did a turn in the center of the black-and-white-tiled foyer, taking it all in. "It rather feels as if she's watching us."

"Let us see if someone at the box office can direct us."

We found the box office nestled between two staircases leading up to the balconies. The two men in the small office spent more time making excuses than it would have taken for them to actually find out if Madame Bernhardt was available.

"Madame usually does not arrive until ten," one of them told us. It was nine o'clock which was the time of our appointment. Impossible, they both insisted. George finally explained that our appointment with Madame Bernhardt was made by Inspector Cadieux of the Sûreté, and she was expecting us.

That at least caused them to pause in their protests, glance at each other, then tell us, "We will see. Wait here."

There were low upholstered benches along the wall, but we stayed by the box office, our arms folded and my toe tapping.

"Do you know I believe it would be easier to gain an audience with the president of the United States," I mused.

"Possibly," George agreed. "But he is merely a head of state. We are calling on the Divine Sarah."

I grumbled quietly. "She is expecting us. One would think those two would be loath to keep her waiting."

George touched my arm, causing my fidgety foot to settle down. "They probably see at least a dozen people every day who claim she is expecting them," he said. "All of whom are lying. It makes sense that they doubt us and want to check."

The man in the office glanced up as the other man appeared from a hallway and stood before us. "If you will follow me? She will see you now."

Hmm, no apology for the delay. I suppose George was right, her admirers were probably clamoring to get close to her. Particularly now that she had this theater and they knew exactly where to find her.

We followed the man through the theater, around the stage, and down another hallway. Unlike the lobby and the theater, which were covered in yellow velvet and gilt, this space was unadorned and a bit shabby. Finally, we came upon the dressing rooms. I heard a male voice as we approached the room nearest to the stage.

"Until tonight, my love," he said. Then before our guide could knock on the door, a large, fair-haired gentleman with a silk hat exited the room, stopping short when he came upon the three of us in the hallway. He drew the brim of his hat down to his nose, stepped around us, and headed down the hallway. That's when I noticed he was in evening clothes and wondered what sort of business he had with Madame Bernhardt.

Once he was gone, our guide ushered us into the large, well-appointed dressing room, whereupon he bowed out and closed the door.

"Someone didn't want to be seen," I said in a low voice.

George leaned closer. "I suspect Madame Bernhardt has one or two acquaintances who would rather not be caught in her dressing room."

I glanced around the room, wondering if it reflected the actress's taste. The deep red of the wall coverings, accented with gold, spoke of opulence and drama. As did the fainting couch upholstered in red velvet with a multitude of tasseled pillows. Atop the floors lay Turkish rugs, while fascinating little objects she must have collected from her many tours covered the tables and decorated the walls. The obligatory dressing table stood against one wall and above the mirror hung a stuffed bat.

I stepped away from the creature and saw George studying the painting of Sarah lounging casually in a white dressing gown, on what might be that very fainting couch. She looked like a woman daring you to tell her no.

This was all very interesting, but where was Madame Bernhardt?

As if my thought had conjured her, I heard a tinkling sound when a door opened across the room and caught a flash of ginger hair as the woman herself entered, then paused in the doorway. She was quite small, at least half a foot shorter than me. The cut of her ecru gown, high necked and very close to the body, showed that she was not as whip thin as the papers portrayed her, of course that could be because she was in her mid-fifties now. The sound I'd heard must have been her jewelry. A multitude of bracelets adorned her wrists below the cuffs of her long sleeves, and at least half a dozen ropes of beads and bright gemstones hung from her neck.

When she approached us, giving her hand to George, her presence filled the room.

"Thank goodness you are here," she said in French, her voice sonorous. "At last, someone will investigate Isabelle's murder."

George bowed over her hand and introduced himself, then turned and introduced me, which caused her brows to lift in surprise. Even they were elegant. And her eyes were absolutely mesmerizing.

"You are also involved in this investigation?" she asked.

Before I could answer, she spoke. "I like that." She drew her hand from George's, swept over to an upholstered bench in the sitting area, and beckoned us to join her. "Where do we begin?"

There was nowhere to sit but the fainting couch, so George and I moved a few pillows and settled in. "What can you tell us about the note you received?" George asked.

She tipped her head back and observed us through half-closed eyes. "The note, yes. It was delivered on Saturday—here. I was not in yet, so it was left right on my dressing table, over there. A tiny box. When I opened it, I found the earring inside. I recognized it right away as Isabelle's." The jewels on her arms jingled as she slapped a hand to her chest. "I dropped the box and jumped to my feet, wondering if this was some message from beyond. Then I gathered my courage and opened the box again." She mimed peering into an invisible box resting on her palm. "That is when I saw the note, tucked under the jewelry. My hands shook as I opened it. It read only—'I know what you did.'"

Her final words resonated through the room, the vibration seemed to come from the floor and through my body, leaving me with chills. "My goodness, then what happened?"

I'd been so transfixed I think I spoke in English. She definitely looked confused as she glanced from me to George, waiting for a translation, perhaps. Before I could do something else foolish, like applaud, I attempted to gather my senses.

George came to himself first, shaking his head as if emerging from a trance. "Only those few words?" His voice sounded dry and pitched higher than normal, but at least he remembered to speak in French. He cleared his throat. "No demand for money?"

"Nothing more. I notified the police. They have the note and the earring now. You may look at it there, if you have a need to."

"I may," he said. "Right now, I'd like to know more about Isabelle. I understand she worked with you. Were the two of you friends?"

"We had worked together on various productions for about seven years. That was before I had this theater, you understand, so she never worked for me, but we worked together. Isabelle was easy to get on with. She took direction well, always knew her lines, never wasted rehearsal time. We didn't become friends for about a year after we met. I was playing the lead in *Gismonda*, and she had a small role."

Sarah's gaze grew distant. "Isabelle thought I could help her. I liked her, so I did what I could. If I recommended her for a role, I knew I could trust her to do a good job. She wasn't the most inspired actor, it didn't come naturally to her, but she knew what she wanted and she worked hard. She might not understand her part immediately, but she understood it eventually. That makes her better than most, in my opinion."

"If she was so determined to become a successful actress," I said, "why did she take up with Carlson Deaver?"

Sarah raised a brow. "Do you really have to ask?" She leaned forward, as if preparing to explain to a two-year-old. "Before an actress can command a large salary, she must become successful, she must be in demand. That doesn't happen in the course of one or two productions. It takes time. Meanwhile, one must eat and have a place to live. That cannot always be accomplished on an actress's earnings. So we 'take up,' as you say it, with men who are willing to sponsor us—to help us pay for those necessities of life."

At least now I knew why she thought my question foolish. "What I meant was, why did she marry him? Why did she give up her dream of acting for a husband?"

"Ah, that." She swept a hand in front of her. "He asked. Isabelle thought she had to accept or lose him. As for her career, she felt certain he would have allowed her to keep working. I doubt very much that he ever told her this, you understand. But it was her expectation, nonetheless. She was very aggravated the first time she brought the subject up with him and he told her no."

George and I exchanged a look. "That seems like the sort of thing one would make clear before the marriage," he said.

Madame Bernhardt simply shrugged. "Isabelle thought it was clear. Either she was mistaken, or he changed his mind."

"It sounds as though Isabelle married Carlson in order to

keep his sponsorship." I paused to watch her reaction, hoping I wasn't offending. When she nodded, I went on. "But when faced with a choice, she decided she'd rather remain married to him than continue her career. The two of you maintained a friendship, did you see signs that she was falling in love with Carlson over time?"

Sarah stood up and strolled about the room, her head back and her gaze on the ceiling. George and I waited while she considered my question. Finally, she stopped and focused her regard on me. "It was a mercenary transaction at first—their marriage, that is. I never saw them together, so I don't know the composition of their relationship—which of them had the power. Based on the fact that a wealthy man offered a poor actress marriage, I would have thought he was madly in love with her, and therefore, Isabelle held all the power."

She spread her arms wide then dropped them at her sides, jingling her bracelets. "It may have started that way, but you are right, she gave in when he said no to acting. From that point on, Isabelle changed. As you said, we maintained our friendship. I saw her many times, always at my home or here. Never at her home. I don't think she wanted her husband to know she still associated with me. She went from a strong, independent woman of spirit, to one who lied to her husband—or let's say withheld the truth from him—because she feared losing his good opinion."

"Was it his good opinion or his money she wanted to hold on to?" I asked. "Did she fear he'd divorce her?"

"She never mentioned divorce, but it's possible. Even so, I don't think she cared about the money, at least not once her needs were met. It was his good opinion that was important. She wanted to fit in with his set, but she worried that she wasn't educated or cultured enough. I reminded her she was an actress, and she could certainly act the part of the cultured lady."

With a sigh, Sarah returned to her seat. "It was a joke. I thought she would laugh, but she took me seriously—thought it a good idea. She changed herself completely for him, then still worried that he was too good for her. She became shy and tentative, someone who wouldn't dream of making a decision on her own, even though that is exactly what she had done since she was little more than a girl."

I leaned back, almost dislodging a lute that hung on the wall behind me. The discordant notes that sounded seemed to coincide with Isabelle's life. At least my understanding of it. She was an up-and-coming actress who gave up her career to marry a wealthy man—not her wealthy lover. That was the first odd note. If she only wanted his money there was no reason to marry him. In every likelihood, he was already paying her support. And even though she told Sarah she expected to continue working, she must have had some inkling that marriage to a gentleman like Carlson meant she would have to leave the theater.

Perhaps Sarah was wrong. Isabelle may have been satisfied as an actress, but longed to be a wife and mother. Or perhaps a leader in society. To gain that sort of status, she would have needed the respectability of marriage.

It was unfortunate that we didn't have a better understanding of Isabelle. Perhaps we'd get a chance to speak with more of her friends.

"Inspector Cadieux told us Isabelle had lost contact with her family," I said. "Did she ever speak of them to you?"

"She may have mentioned family when we first met, but I recall nothing of them. We did not spend our off hours speaking of our childhood." She stood once more. Striding to her dressing table, she pulled a cigarette from an enamel box and fixed it in a long holder. "I do think she grew up poor, though." She lit the cigarette, blew out a stream of smoke, then turned to face me. "Not because of anything she told me, you understand, but that she was always generous whenever she could afford to be. She'd buy a meal for a friend, drop a coin in the poor box. A few months after she married, she began working with the Daughters of Charity. It wasn't her parish or her church." Sarah paused and frowned. "Actually, I don't know if the group is attached to a specific church at all. They help the poor in all parts of Paris."

"Her husband wonders if her killer came from that group," George said.

"From what I understand the Daughters of Charity are mostly women and nuns. As for those she tried to help, I would hate to think anyone that ungrateful." She took another draw of the cigarette. "The building she worked from was in the place des Voges, near where her body was found, so I suppose it's possible."

I wrote down the name. We might want to pay them a call. If nothing else they might provide us with a different view of Isabelle.

"There's something else I wondered," George said. "The police learned that you had an argument with Isabelle the day before she was murdered. Can you tell us about it?"

Sarah let out a huff. "We only ever argued about one thing. The same things you and I have been talking about. Isabelle would come to me and tell me how she did not fit into her husband's life. How she could never make him happy. I would ask her about her own happiness and remind her that she had been more content, more sure of herself—even happier—before she married him. She never agreed with me, and it always led to an argument."

"Did you encourage her to leave him?" I asked.

"Yes, but would she listen to me? I was sad for what her life had become, but she had to change it herself. We went our separate ways that evening, as usual. She left to go home to her husband. I went on with my performance."

"And the following evening, what time did you arrive for your performance?" George asked.

She gave him an enigmatic smile. "I arrived here an hour before the performance, which means seven o'clock. But what I think you really want to know is where I was between five and seven o'clock that evening. The police asked that same question. I was at home with a gentleman friend. My servants will vouch for me, in fact, they already have. But my friend has a right to his privacy and I shall not reveal his name"—she shrugged—"unless I am under arrest."

She observed George for a moment, as if waiting for him to shout that she was under arrest. When that didn't happen, she ground out the cigarette in a glass dish. "Now I must prepare for our rehearsal." She stepped over to the door and opened it. "Don't think I am dismissing you, at least not permanently. I don't know who killed Isabelle, but I want whoever it is caught. I want justice for my friend, and I will do whatever you need of me."

George and I met her at the door and thanked her for her time. "May I ask you one more question, Madame Bernhardt?" George asked.

At her nod, he continued. "Though you told us about the effect marriage had on your friend Isabelle, you have not mentioned anything about her husband. Can you tell us what you know of him?"

She gave her head a weary shake. "Monsieur Deaver and I have never met. As I said before, I don't think Isabelle wanted him to know she still saw her friends from the theater."

"She must have spoken of him to you," I said. "Did anything she said leave you with an opinion of him—or of his mother, Mimi Deaver?"

She narrowed her eyes in thought. "Isabelle did not care for Mimi, at least not at first. She thought Mimi was too protective of her son and involved in his life." She gestured to herself. "I am a mother who is involved in her son's life. To me this is normal. I do think she came to tolerate Mimi, though. She rarely spoke of Monsieur Deaver at all, but of course I formed an opinion. Considering the change I saw in Isabelle since her marriage, I certainly don't think he was good for her. I have no reason to believe he had anything to do with her murder, but let's say, I wouldn't be surprised to learn that he had."

Chapter Seven

Alone in the hallway outside Madame Bernhardt's door, George and I meandered in the direction of the stage. "Well," George said, "Did she live up to your expectations?"

"If I'd had any expectations, she more than satisfied them, but to be honest, I'd say I was simply curious. Now after speaking with her, I'm all the more eager to see her on the stage."

"Indeed," he said. "Speaking with her was quite an experience."

"It certainly was. She almost did it to me again—mesmerized me, I suppose you could say—just before we left. I nearly burst into applause. There is some quality about her that makes me hang on her every word."

George glanced at me with raised brows. "I have to wonder if that was her intention. She is adept at captivating people, making them believe that what they see is real and not simply an illusion."

I slowed my steps and turned to him. "She is very dramatic, but I didn't get the sense she was trying to lead us to any conclusions, did you?"

He raised a brow. "She dropped that bit about Carlson Deaver."

"After you asked about him."

"I asked what she knew of him. In reply, she barely stopped short of accusing him of Isabelle's murder, even though in her own words, she had no reason to suspect him. She was clearly pushing us to investigate the man, don't you think?"

"Something we intend to do, anyway."

"And look at the time she had us come in for this interview," he continued. "It is only ten o'clock in the morning, the theater is still empty, yet she shooed us away claiming there was work to be done."

I stopped at the entrance to the back stage area and leaned against the wall. "Now that I think about it, there is one way in which she didn't meet my expectations. She didn't push to take part in the investigation. Cadieux was rather concerned about that."

He nodded. "She may have thought answering our questions was doing her part. But I wonder why she had us call and leave so early. Did she want to ensure that no one else would be here for us to question?"

"If so, that was an error on Sarah's part. I heard at least three women pass by her dressing room door while we were in there."

"Did you? I didn't hear anything."

"Ah, you must have been more absorbed in the Divine Sarah than I thought. It sounded like they were headed in this direction"—I tipped my head toward the stage—"but I don't see anyone up there."

George stepped up and took my hand. "It can't hurt to look for them. Let's go across and see what is on the other side."

There were pools of light to guide us across the stage. I glanced up to find their source—and froze. Overhead, starting behind the heavy velvet curtain, was row after row of—what were they? I could see bits of rope and above them what looked like pulleys.

I startled when George touched my arm. "Something wrong?" he asked.

"What are those things?" I pointed upward.

He lifted his gaze to the ceiling. "Scenery, I think." He gestured toward the backdrop of a pair of Grecian columns at the side of the stage. "Like that one."

I looked from the columns back to the rows of scenery waiting in the ceiling. "There must be dozens of pieces up there."

"All part of the magic of the theater, I suppose," George said as he led me across the stage.

A pool of darkness met us as we climbed down, and beyond that a dimly lit hallway, where I found the ropes that moved all those pieces of scenery. Once George drew me away, we took the hallway to a staircase, from which I definitely heard voices. We followed the sound upstairs to a room with an open door where we found two women and an enormous collection of costumes. Racks and racks of them.

The women turned to us with questioning looks. One was on her knees on the floor, clearly the costumer. The other stood atop a footstool, being fitted for a high-waisted, puff-sleeved gown typically worn back in the days of Napoleon.

"Pardon the intrusion," I said in French. I introduced myself, then George, thinking to let him take over.

"We are conducting an investigation on behalf of the Sûreté into the death of Isabelle Deaver," he said. "Have either of you worked with her in the past?"

The actress, shook her head. I hoped she was older than she looked, which was about fifteen. "I only came to this production a month ago," she said. "I don't know the woman you speak of."

"She was Isabelle Rousseau when I knew her." The costumer spoke in a gruff voice and barely spared us a glance as she came to her feet and continued to pin the young woman into the gown. "Let me finish this, and I will talk with you."

While she added the last few pins, George found a couple of wooden chairs and pulled them forward. Finally, the costumer patted the actress on the shoulder. "That should do. Go take that off and leave it on the table for me. Then tell Berthe and Shantal to come out here. I don't intend to wait all day for them."

With a glance at us, the young woman did as she was bid. The costumer stuffed a few pins into the cushion attached to her left wrist before she looked at us, her lips compressed tightly. "Isabelle died months ago," she said after examining us. "Why has the Sûreté waited so long to ask us about her? And why send you?"

She was an older woman, somewhere in her sixties, I imagined, and she didn't look well. Pale and thin, her gray hair was twisted and pinned, but wiry curls escaped her attempts to tame them and bounced as she spoke. She wore a black wool shawl crisscrossed over a gray shirtwaist and skirt. Since she didn't look angry or aggressive, I assumed the growl in her voice was just something that happened over time.

George frowned. "Some new evidence has surfaced. We were asked to step in and conduct our own investigation. The file we have from the Sûreté indicates officers interviewed all of you shortly after Isabelle Deaver's death. Did they somehow miss you, *madame*?"

"They missed a great many of us. They spoke to only a few lead actors, the stage manager, and of course Madame Bernhardt."

"That's unfortunate," I said. "It happened so long ago as you say, and memories can fade. But if you would be so kind, we do have some questions, and hope you will answer as best you can."

She sighed. "I will try, but you will have to ask those questions while I work. These costumes are for tonight, and that doesn't give me much time to alter them." She leaned back toward a curtained opening and shouted, "Did you hear that, mesdames? I don't have time to wait for you. Bring yourselves out here if you want to be fitted."

Now I knew where the gravelly voice came from.

Another woman in an empire style gown stepped through the curtain into the room. The costumer waved her over to the crate. This one was not quite so young as the first actress, probably about twenty. "This is Mademoiselle Shantal," the costumer said. "And I am Madame Gervais. Go ahead and ask your questions."

Madame Gervais proceeded to fit the costume, while George asked about Isabelle. Both her answers and Shantal's coincided with Sarah's. Shantal agreed she had heard Sarah and Isabelle arguing the day before, but it was nothing out of the ordinary. "They were friends," she said with a shrug. "Friends argue. You should attach no importance to it."

By the time Shantal's costume fit her to a T, George had asked about everything I could think of. Neither of them had ever met Carlson, though they knew Isabelle had been his mistress before becoming his wife, something they shrugged off as easily as the argument. As far as they knew, Isabelle had left on good terms with everyone in the company. She even maintained a friendship with Sarah. They could think of no one who would want to murder her.

"Did either of you happen to attend her funeral?" I asked. It might be helpful to know who had.

Shantal shook her head, and Madame Gervais scowled. "I heard nothing of a funeral. If the family held a service, it must have been small." She gave Shantal a final look of approval. "Now where is Berthe? Doesn't she need alterations?"

Shantal glanced at George and me before she replied. "I think she left."

The costumer followed the direction of Shantal's gaze. "Ah, yes. I don't think she would want to talk with you."

"Whyever not?" I asked. "Was she a friend of Madame Deaver?"

The costumer let out a chortle. "She was, and is, a very good friend of Monsieur Deaver."

Shantal let out a tut. "You are planting thoughts in their heads." She turned to George and me. "Berthe would never hurt anyone. She spoke to the police when they came here months ago. She probably didn't want to go over it again, so she left."

"Thank you," I said to Shantal. "But I need to back up a bit in this conversation." Madame Gervais still wore an evil grin. "You called Berthe a 'good friend' of Monsieur Deaver. What did you mean by that?"

The costumer let out a cackle. "She is his mistress."

"Now?" George asked.

She bobbed her head. "And then. They have been together for at least two years."

Shantal cocked her head, giving us an impatient glare. "These things happen all the time. It's not as if Berthe and Isabelle fought over the man. They ignored each other's existence. They had no problem with one another, and Berthe had no reason to harm Isabelle."

George and I shared a look. We'd definitely want to speak with Berthe.

Other than a few workmen setting up some scaffolding on the stage, we found no one else to speak with at the theater. Rather than wait for hours for the players to arrive, we left and headed to the Sûreté, hoping to find Cadieux in his office. George flagged down an available cab, and we were on our way.

"Well, I think my assignment can be considered complete

now," I said, grasping the door handle as the driver made a tight turn.

My words seemed to come as a surprise to George, who simply stared at me.

"Alicia wanted me to investigate Carlson Deaver," I explained, "to find out if he has any objectional traits. I have learned he is a philanderer. No mother would want to marry her daughter to such a man."

"Your mother did," George said, looking at me as if wondering how I could have forgotten that little detail.

"That's not fair. Nor is it precisely true. Mother had no idea what Reggie was like. She assumed all members of the nobility were above such things." I rolled my eyes. "That was a rude awakening."

"For you, certainly. I don't know that it did your mother any harm."

"No, I suppose not, but she felt bad when I told her the truth about Reggie. My point is that Mother didn't know about him beforehand. Alicia will. She asked me to vet Carlson before there is any thought of marriage, and I have done so."

George wagged a finger. "That's not what you told me. You said she wanted to know if the man was involved in his wife's murder. A different matter altogether, and one we have no answer for yet. She may not care about Carlson's mistress." He tipped his head and narrowed one eye. "This is Alicia Stoke-Whitney we're talking about, after all."

"And it's Harriet, her daughter, that Alicia is concerned about. Not even Alicia would allow her daughter to become engaged to a man who kept, and may intend to keep, a mistress and a wife at the same time."

George smiled, clearly enjoying the debate. "I still don't believe you have completed your assignment. Mrs. Stoke-Whitney may believe Carlson will give up his mistress. She may insist upon it. But not until she knows if he is a murderer or not."

"You could be right," I said, thinking he very likely was. "Well, it's not as though I objected to the investigation."

"I should hope not. I thought you were interested in getting to the truth for Cadieux's sake. I thought you wanted to help me." George allowed his lower lip to tremble.

"Oh, stop, George. You know that pout never works on me."

"You are heartless, *madame*."

I patted his leg. "I'm far too intrigued to bow out of the investigation now. Let's go over what we've learned, shall we?"

"And what exactly is that?"

"Unfortunately, not much about the night of the murder, but we learned something about Isabelle. She was an actress who was motivated to rise in her profession. She met Carlson and became his mistress while she continued to work at her craft. She and Carlson later married, so should we assume he fell in love with her?"

George held up a hand. "No assumptions, if you please. Carlson might have married Isabelle for any number of reasons, not the least of which may have been to annoy his mother. Surely, you noticed his smirk when he told us his mother was shocked by his marriage?"

"That's a good point, but so far, I've seen only two expressions from Carlson—a smirk or a scowl. Otherwise, he's displayed no animosity toward his mother. And now that you mention Mimi, I do wish we'd thought to ask Madame Gervais and Shantal if Isabelle had ever spoken of their relationship. If Mimi was so particular that she passed over my sister, how did she feel about her son marrying an actress?"

"Madame Bernhardt didn't have much to say about Carlson's mother."

"I suppose that might be because she was steering us toward Carlson, as you suspect. Still, if Isabelle confided in anyone at the theater, I would think it would be Sarah."

"She did say we could return if we had more questions."

"We may need to do so. Now, where was I? It must have been shortly before his marriage to Isabelle that Carlson took up with Berthe, don't you think? Madame Gervais said they had been together for at least two years. Heavens, he might have met them both at the same time. We don't know when Isabelle learned Berthe was her husband's mistress, but it does sound as though she knew. That may have contributed to her self-doubt and feeling that she wasn't good enough." What an irksome man. "Carlson didn't have to say anything to her. She could easily have convinced herself."

"Or her mother-in-law did," George suggested.

"That's another possibility. I'm interested in learning more about Mimi and what she knows about their marriage and Isabelle's murder. As well as her opinion of both. I ought to be able to do that this afternoon."

"Indeed? What happens then?"

"Mother and I are having Mimi to lunch at our apartment. Along with Lily, Anne Kendrick, and Jeanne Clement."

George took my hand and kissed the bare skin above my glove. The shivers his action induced almost had me calling for the driver to take us home.

"I'm so proud of you," he said. "That is an excellent plan."

After that delightful kiss, I had no intention of telling him it had been Mother's idea.

"Should I be there," he asked.

"You should definitely not be there. Women are generally more relaxed and unguarded when there are no men in the room."

"I'm sure I shall find something else to do. Mimi does seem like a good next step, as does Jeanne Clement. Perhaps I will pay a call on her husband." He grinned. "Men are also less guarded when there are no women in the room."

"Funny how that works, isn't it?" We had finished our planning just in time to be set down outside the Sûreté, the large building on Île de la Cité that housed the criminal division of the French police. George paid the driver, and we headed inside.

Ten minutes later, we were in Cadieux's office, on the third floor. The space said a lot about the man. Smallish, with room enough for his desk and two visitor's chairs, which could be moved to a narrow table at the back of the room. The wall slanted on one side beside a window that looked out over the Seine. A shelf behind the desk held a calendar, a clock, and three coffee cups. A stove in the corner would likely heat the room with efficiency, but at the moment it heated only a ceramic coffee pot.

George and I were in our usual seats on the visitor's side of his desk, trying to ignore the lovely view of the Seine outside the window. Cadieux sat opposite us. We gave him a summary of our interviews at the theater. "Was it you or Madame Bernhardt who requested the time for our meeting?" George asked.

"She did, of course. That was the time she found most convenient."

"I suspect it was also the time she knew few others would be at the theater. I don't think she wanted us speaking to anyone else. I'll have to review the interviews your officers did of the other actors and see if anyone said something contrary to what Madame Bernhardt told us."

"I sense that you are inclined to be suspicious of her." Cadieux rested his hands on the desktop and studied George.

"You want a thorough investigation, do you not?" George asked.

"That goes without saying, but I'd like to remind you that Madame Bernhardt came to us with the new evidence. She has been very cooperative."

George gave the inspector a nod. "As an innocent person would do—or one attempting to appear innocent."

"We will, of course, keep open minds," I said, determined to end their staring contest. "Fortunately, we were lucky enough to meet up with three other women who were at the theater for costume fittings. One of them was new and hadn't been there when Isabelle was murdered, but the other actress and the costumer gave us some food for thought."

Cadieux lifted an inquiring brow, and I tapped George on the arm, urging him to continue the story.

"Do you recall if your officers interviewed an actress by the name of Berthe?" he asked. "I'm afraid we neglected to ask for her surname."

"That name does not sound familiar," Cadieux said. "But it was a long time ago and you have all the interviews we conducted. Can you not look through them?"

"I will, but tell me this, did any of the actresses you interviewed admit to being Carlson Deaver's mistress?"

"Now, that I would remember," Cadieux said, his eyes wide. "And the answer is no, but it sounds as though someone has admitted as much to you. I take it the woman is named Berthe? How did you learn of her?"

"The costume designer likes to indulge in a bit of salacious gossip," I said. "Berthe, herself, slipped out rather than speak with us, and if she never told the police about her relationship with Carlson, I can understand why."

"Yes, that's very interesting. I assume you intend to speak with her?"

"I will look her up this afternoon," George replied.

Chapter Eight

"How does the table look, Mother?"

Madame Auclair and I were in the dining room on either side of the table, trying to determine if the floral arrangement in the center was too large. I could see over it, but few women are as tall as I, so I called Mother in as soon as I heard her steps in the foyer.

"Too tall," she pronounced, then reached out and plucked the uppermost carnations from the center of the arrangement.

"Mother! That took half an hour to arrange."

"But it works, *madame*," the housekeeper said to me in French, gesturing to the table.

Hmm. So it did. Without the carnations, the roses weren't crowded and the whole arrangement looked more casual. This was a luncheon after all. Not a state dinner. I wanted everyone to feel comfortable.

"What did she say?" Mother asked.

I repressed a smile as I lied. "That it was very rude of you to break off those flowers."

Mother looked stunned. "But I was only trying to—" She

cut herself off when she caught sight of Madame Auclair struggling to repress a laugh. She shook a finger at me. "I will learn French one day, and you will no longer be able to play this little game."

She gave the table a final perusal. It was laid with our landlord's lovely china and crystal atop a white linen cloth. "The table is lovely," Mother said with a note of finality. She handed the plucked blooms to the housekeeper, then she and I crossed the foyer to the salon.

"So," Mother said, taking a seat in the middle of the sofa, "what are we trying to accomplish at this luncheon with Mimi Deaver? I can't believe I am actually entertaining that notorious woman. I dearly hope no one in New York hears of this."

Was she serious? "If I recall correctly, it was your idea to invite her, but since we are at my home, you can honestly deny entertaining her."

Mother raised her index finger. "Good point."

I rearranged some knickknacks on the sofa table behind her and returned a bottle of brandy to the cabinet below. "You really needn't worry. It's not as if New York society is clamoring to hear about whom I'm entertaining in my salon."

Mother turned around, and I paused my fidgeting long enough to look her in the eyes. "Are they really still interested in Mimi's activities? She left New York well over a year ago. Her husband has been dead for almost a year. Why do they care about how she lives her life?"

"You know how catty society women can be," she said, adjusting her position to face front.

"I also know how convenient their memories are." I rounded the sofa and took a seat across from Mother. "Why do they still gossip about Mimi?"

"Well, it might be because we—*they*"—she paused, then heaved a sigh—"*we* resent her for the freedom in which she lives her life. And the fact that she pays no consequences." Mother leaned forward and tapped her finger on the coffee table, emphasizing her words. "They—*we* tell our daughters, as our mothers told us, that there would be heavy consequences for flouting society's rules. Surely, I don't have to tell you that living with one man when one is married to another is a significant flouting of the rules."

"Yes, Mother. While I don't believe it's written down anywhere, I think we all understand that society would indeed frown on such behavior."

Mother raised her hands helplessly. "Yet she gets away with it. She pays no price whatsoever."

"I don't know about that. She's been cast out of New York society."

"And why should she care, I ask you, when Paris welcomes her with open arms? Especially since Paris is far more entertaining."

"*Welcome* might be too strong a word," I said. "They accept her because she has money and because of the *comte*'s influence."

Mother scowled. "You seem to be missing my point. I will concede that the people of this city do not throw rose petals at her feet. But they do accept her. Our family is accepted in New York society because your father has money and you have a title. Acceptance is acceptance, no one cares why. But in exchange for that acceptance, we are expected to comport ourselves according to a certain set of rules."

"Of course."

"Mimi does not, so her acceptance in Paris is almost a reward for bad behavior. Prior to your father and I sorting out our problems, I must admit I envied her."

I was coming to regret pushing Mother for an honest answer. The image of her leaving Frankie to be some strange man's pampered love interest was one I truly did not want to contemplate. "Please tell me you don't mean that literally. You didn't actually wish to have what she has?"

"Not at all. What I'm saying is that if Mimi can break the rules and end up smelling like a rose, what is to stop other women from leaving their husbands and taking up with exciting foreign men? What is to stop our daughters from doing the same?"

It was becoming clearer now: Mimi made them nervous. "It seems as though the matrons of New York wanted Mimi to be a cautionary tale. They needed her actions to produce a horrible outcome with which to frighten themselves and their daughters into following the rules. Is that a fair analysis?"

Mother frowned and looked about to quibble over my choice of words, but instead, raised her hands in surrender. "Fine. Seeing her as a fallen woman would have been helpful, yes."

"I find it hard to believe that any woman in a good marriage is going to hear about Mimi's acceptance in Paris and leave her husband because of it. I certainly wouldn't think of it."

"Yes, but not all women are in good marriages."

"Aha!" I straightened my spine and raised a finger.

"What?" Mother looked sincerely perplexed.

"Perhaps those rules you want your daughters to follow are actually unfair. Perhaps society pushes women into arrangements that are not to their benefit. We lose our names, our independence, our money. If marriage were more favorable to women, maybe we wouldn't have to frighten our daughters into the married state."

"Well! You sound like one of those radicals, Frances. I don't know what's gotten into you, and I think we should end this conversation right now." She crossed her arms over her chest, a clear sign that there was no point in arguing.

To be honest, I wasn't sure what had gotten into me, either. Perhaps because I'd had both a happy marriage and a bad one. And I didn't want my daughter to find herself stuck in the latter.

"In fact," Mother continued, "I don't believe you ever answered my original question. What do you hope to accomplish with this luncheon? I noticed you didn't invite Mrs. Stoke-Whitney or her daughter."

I smiled at Mother and allowed the previous subject to drop. "I'm hoping to learn something of Mimi's relationship with her daughter-in-law and of her son's relationship with his wife. Inviting the woman her son is currently interested in—and her mother—might keep Mimi from speaking freely. Not that I'm certain she'll speak freely anyway, but it's worth a try."

"It should be easy to engage her in conversation on the topic of her son," Mother said. "The deceased daughter-in-law might be more difficult."

"I've also invited Carlson and Isabelle's neighbor, Jeanne Clement. As it turns out, we met her and her husband when we were in Deauville and struck up a friendship. When we golfed with Carlson yesterday, we learned they were neighbors."

Mother bobbed her head in approval. "That's convenient. Our neighbors often know more about our lives than we think."

"I hope so." The doorbell rang, and I checked the clock in the corner. One o'clock. Someone was right on time. I came to my feet and waited while Madame Auclair opened the door to Jeanne Clement. Jeanne leaned on her cane while she removed her wrap and handed it to the housekeeper.

"I'm so glad you could make it," I said. I led her into the salon, matching my steps to her slower ones. As I introduced the young woman to my mother, the housekeeper opened the door to Mimi Deaver. I returned to the foyer just as she took

Mimi's fur-trimmed coat to reveal an afternoon gown in black, reminding me that she was still mourning her late husband, at least technically.

Mimi was an attractive woman in her middle fifties, about the same age as Sarah Bernhardt, though there was little else about the two women that was similar. Mimi had golden blond hair that she wore in curls over her forehead. They ended just above brows that sloped downward in nearly diagonal lines from inner to outer edge. Her skin was surprisingly smooth, and her figure, womanly. She looked like what one would expect of a middle-aged society matron.

"Thank you for coming to my little gathering, Mrs. Deaver," I said, leading her into the salon.

"It's Mimi," she said. "I appreciate the invitation. I was surprised when I saw that you had called." Though her words were cordial, there was no warmth in her tone, and her expression was indifferent. I was immediately reminded of the stiff formality of a reception I'd attended long ago at the Fifth Avenue home of one of the old monied elite.

"We New Yorkers must stick together, mustn't we?" I said.

She raised her brows. "That hasn't been my experience, but I like the sentiment."

"I believe you and my mother are already acquainted." I waved a hand toward Mother.

The two older women exchanged disingenuous smiles. "Mimi," Mother said with a nod of acknowledgement.

"Daisy." Mimi glanced at Mother's afternoon gown and sniffed. "Is that the fashion in Egypt these days?"

Ugh! If Old New York haughtiness could be captured in a sentence, that would be it.

"Still in mourning, I see," Mother said. "My condolences on the loss of your husband. I heard you returned to New York for his funeral. I'm surprised *monsieur le comte* could spare you."

Mother's words were chips of ice, leaving me speechless. I glanced at Mimi, hoping to deflect Mother's comment, only to see her eyes narrow and her lips tighten. This might be a battle to the death.

"At least someone desires my company," she said. "I understand your husband dropped you off at the train station and continued on his way."

Mother's nostrils flared. "My husband and I have been traveling together for the last six months."

"I suppose that explains his rapid departure." Mimi faked a sympathetic pout.

Mother was not faring well in this exchange of poisonous quips. She looked ready to stamp her foot. "He'd been away from his office for half a year. He could not spare any more time and headed home only to mind his business."

"Indeed?" Mimi said. "You might try doing that yourself."

Taking advantage of a pause in their hostilities, I drew Mimi's attention to Jeanne. "And this is Madame Clement."

Jeanne shrank back, giving Mimi a nervous smile. "J-J-Jeanne," she said.

With the present company introduced, everyone took a seat, with Mimi next to Jeanne, and Mother on the opposite side of the coffee table, where she and Mimi could glare daggers at each other. I honestly didn't know what had gotten into Mother. She'd been so calm and relaxed since she arrived. Perhaps it was a reaction to seeing another New Yorker.

Before we could begin any conversation, the doorbell rang once more and the housekeeper admitted Anne Kendrick and Lily. Amelia alerted me to her presence before I reached the entry by releasing a howl that caused Madame Auclair to cringe.

"And you brought the baby," I said, taking custody of her while Lily shrugged out of her coat.

"I don't know how I could have done anything else," she said, taking Amelia back into her arms. She indicated a bag the size of a small trunk she'd placed on the floor. "Would you be so kind as have that taken to a bedchamber?" she asked the housekeeper, then turned to me. "Amelia will have to take a nap at some point, or be fed, or need to be changed, so if I may borrow a room for that purpose, I'd appreciate it."

Lily was speaking so quickly, I barely had time to agree to her plan, before she went on: "Anyway, Patricia is at an Exposition meeting, and Anne was coming here. There was no one to leave Amelia with, so I brought her."

Lily continued to chatter as I led her and Anne to the other guests in the salon. "I suppose I could have stayed at home," she said, "but I'm tired of being left out."

I waited for her to draw breath so that I could introduce the new arrivals, but as I opened my mouth, Mimi came to her feet, both hands over her heart. "What a darling baby," she said. The joy that lit her eyes seemed to be the first genuine expression she'd shown since arriving. Stepping close she extended a finger to Amelia, who wrapped her own tiny fingers around it and pulled it to her mouth.

"You may have met Lily during her season in New York," I said to Mimi.

Glancing at Lily, Mimi frowned. "I don't believe we have met. I'm sure I would remember you."

Mother harumphed.

Lily managed to disengage Amelia's fingers before Mimi's hand became covered in drool. Nevertheless, Mimi persisted in her attentions to the baby. "May I hold her?"

"Of course." Though she looked surprised by the request, Lily joyfully turned Amelia over to Mimi, then, exhaling volubly, took a seat on the overstuffed armchair beside the sofa, looking more relaxed than I'd seen her for days.

Amelia, on the other hand, seemed less than pleased at being so easily surrendered to a stranger. Fearing a burst of outrage from the baby, I finished the introductions as quickly as possible while Mimi cooed and fussed over the child. The attention appeared to be exactly what Amelia needed—she was Lily's daughter, after all. Within seconds, she was making little gurgles of delight.

"Well, isn't that amazing," Anne said. "My mother told Lily that Amelia would fuss at being handled by a stranger."

"Did she indeed?" Mother looked adoringly at her little granddaughter. "Amelia was perfectly content the first time I picked her up, and of course, I would have been a stranger to her at that point."

Mimi stopped cooing to Amelia long enough to respond. "She seems quite happy now, as well."

As did Mother and Mimi. It seemed the wailing baby had brought on a truce of sorts. Surrendering to this arrangement, at least for now, I took a seat next to Lily, who turned to me. "I shall take her away momentarily. As happy as she seems right now, it is time for her nap, and she will be fussing very soon."

"I shall ask Bridget to sit with her so you can enjoy lunch with us," I said, referring to my maid.

Lily sighed, and I believe she blinked away a tear. "That would be perfect."

Mimi reluctantly gave up the baby to Lily, who followed me to my room. I happened to know Bridget was there, attending to some sewing. Once Lily found Amelia's trunk and got her settled, the baby fell to sleep almost instantly. Bridget agreed to watch her, and Lily and I tiptoed out of the room.

"Amazing, isn't it, how Amelia felt so comfortable with Mimi," I said, closing the door quietly behind us.

"You may be right," Lily muttered. "I ought to at least consider hiring a nurse."

"You needn't sound so glum about it. A nurse will free up your time, but it's not as if you will never see your daughter again."

"It's not that. I had hoped to live up to my mother-in-law's standards, and I feel as though I'm failing terribly. I was so relieved to hand her off to Mrs. Deaver for a few minutes. What kind of mother feels that way?"

Before I could assure her that she was completely normal, she continued. "How can one little baby be so exhausting? Simply dressing her is enough to require a rest. And it's impossible to schedule anything. I almost had to miss a dinner party last night. It was held by one of the company's suppliers, and Leo had asked me specifically to attend on his behalf. If Anne hadn't returned from her practice in time and graciously agreed to watch Amelia, I would have had Leo cross with me."

"You mean you didn't think to bring her with you?" I teased.

Tears clouded her eyes again. "Believe it or not, I do know where to draw the line. Frannie, am I just bad at this?"

"Patricia's standards for motherhood are such that we would all fail. Do not let her set the rules of your household," I said. "You must raise your child as you see fit. Don't do as I say either, by the way. I only want you to know there are other options."

She gave my arm a squeeze. "You are a good sister."

I linked my arm with hers. "Let us go have some lunch."

A little over an hour later we were all back in the salon with dessert and coffee. Lily had gone to check on Amelia.

"Mother brought a new camera back from her travels," I told the ladies. "It appears to be very simple to use, so I hope to take a few photos of Lily and the baby."

"What a wonderful idea," Anne said. "May I see it?"

"Of course." Anne and I crossed the room in a few steps to where I'd left the well-traveled little Brownie camera on a desk next to a wall of bookshelves. Frankie had purchased one the instant they became available and brought it with him from New York for my wedding, but he had never used it. Then he and Mother took it with them to Egypt, and even with the wonders of the pyramids before them, they never used it. It was of rather flimsy construction, so I was surprised it was still in one piece when Mother had fished it out of her luggage. With luck, it would be in working order.

While I showed Anne how the camera operated, Mother and Mimi sipped their coffee and chatted on the sofa behind us quite congenially—amazing when little more than an hour ago it had been poisoned barbs at ten paces. Perhaps that's how ladies in New York society sized each other up—each matron must make some show of dominance and then simply move on. I don't know how Mother managed to bring up the subject, but somehow, they were talking about Harriet Stoke-Whitney.

"I've not had the pleasure of meeting her," Mimi said. "I'm sure she's a lovely girl, but I hope she isn't taking Carlson's attentions to heart. He still grieves the loss of his wife. I doubt he has plans to remarry any time soon."

"I completely understand," Mother said. "After the earl died, Frances was bereft. It was nearly two years before she married Hazelton."

Well, half of that was true. Bereft was hardly the word for what I felt after Reggie's death, and I hadn't failed to notice that Mother managed to slip his title into the conversation. Mimi's eyebrows only lifted a fraction of an inch.

"How long ago was it that you lost your daughter-in-law?" Mother asked.

"It was January, so it hasn't even been a year yet. If we were in New York, Carlson would still not be going out in society.

His father passed away last autumn and even that mourning period isn't officially over."

Bless Mother for not mentioning Mimi's attendance at all the society events regardless of her recent widow status. I saw her lips tighten, but she managed to restrain herself.

"Now Carlson tells me that the police have reopened the investigation of Isabelle's murder." Mimi's words were short and crisp, and she let out a little sound of disgust. "After all this time, all that serves to do is stir up the pain again."

"I'm so sorry," Mother's tone was soft and, frankly, convincing. "I understand that memory is painful to both you and your son, but if they are investigating once more, the police must have some new evidence that could lead to the killer. While it won't bring your daughter-in-law back, someone might be brought to justice. Surely that would help."

I couldn't resist the urge to take a look at Mimi, my head was only tipped a bit, but my eyes were turned so far to the corners it was beginning to make my head ache. It was worth the effort when I saw the fear in Mimi's eyes. It was only for the briefest of moments before she buried it behind a mask of doubt. It was enough to send a chill through me.

"I have lost all confidence that the police will ever bring her killer to justice," Mimi said. "And I don't think Carlson appreciates the false hope, either. It's time they stop chasing after every little clue and close her case so that we can move on."

The words sounded harsh and her voice even more so, but I could see Mother wasn't any more convinced than I that Mimi was speaking out of anger. It was clear that she feared this new line of investigation. But was she afraid for Carlson or herself?

"Frances?"

I swiveled my gaze back to find Anne wearing a frown and staring at me. Of course she was. I'd been more than obvious in my eavesdropping. Before I could make an excuse, she held up a hand. "I'm not going to ask," she said in a low voice. "Apparently there is something going on here that I'm not privy to, and that is fine with me. I'd like to save all my drama for the tournament."

"Thank you," I said. "Now, perhaps we should take some photographs. Would you like to give it a try?"

"Yes, I would." As she passed by me, she leaned close. "Should I be sure to take one of Mrs. Deaver?"

"At least one, but it might be better to wait until she has the baby so as not to look too obvious."

Lily came down the hall with Amelia a few seconds later. "Look who's awake again," Lily singsonged as she entered the room, bouncing the baby on her hip. She stifled a yawn as she moved toward one of the armchairs to take a seat.

Mimi came to her feet. "I'd be happy to take her, if you'd like to have your coffee."

Lily jumped at the offer and handed Amelia over right away, which meant it was time for a photo of the baby. Anne got to work immediately. I only hoped the light in here was good enough.

Jeanne had been quietly enjoying her coffee and dessert on the other side of the table. She seemed so serene I took a seat next to her, hoping some of her calm would rub off on me. "I ought to have warned you," I said in French, "that there would be non–French speakers here today. I hope we haven't made you feel uncomfortable with everyone speaking English?"

"Not at all," she said. "I enjoy the practice." She leaned forward to see around me. "I knew Isabelle," she said to Mimi, who quickly covered her surprise with a smile.

"My husband and I live in the same building as your son and were friends to them both. Isabelle was a kind person and a thoughtful neighbor who didn't deserve such a terrible end." Jeanne swiped at a tear. "I'm sorry for your loss, and your son's," she continued. "And I'm sorry if the investigation causes you pain, but I'm pleased to see the police follow every clue they find. Someone must pay for what they did."

With her gaze on Jeanne, Mimi dropped all artifice and simply looked weary. "You are right, of course. The police must do their job, but I do wish it weren't so painful. You must forgive a mother for trying to protect her son. He suffers every time he is made to relive that memory."

Mimi actually seemed to appreciate Jeanne's support of Isabelle. I didn't know quite what to make of Mimi. Was she a femme fatale? A catty socialite? An overbearing mother? At the moment, she seemed like any other woman. Her life was complicated, but what life wasn't?

I still had no idea whether she'd murdered her daughter-in-law—or if she thought her son had done so.

It wasn't long after that exchange that the gathering came to an end. Hardly a surprise, as it hadn't exactly been stimulating, intellectual, or even fun. Fortunately, Anne had taken a great many photos.

Mimi was the first to move. She handed Amelia back to Lily, and thanked me for a lovely afternoon and actually seemed to mean it. Anne and Lily were next. Mother bid me sit while she walked them to the door, so I took a seat next to my remaining guest, Jeanne.

"I hope you don't mind that I spoke up to Madame Deaver," she said. "I fear our somber conversation rather broke up the gathering."

"Not at all," I assured her. "Lily would have had to leave soon regardless, and I'm glad you spoke up for Isabelle. I understand that Mimi might prefer to deal with her grief privately, but I'm sure she wants the police to continue their efforts to find Isabelle's killer."

"I would hope so," she said.

"I'm surprised you and Mimi weren't acquainted," I said,

"considering you and Étienne were friends with her son and his wife."

Jeanne shrugged. "We were friends, but we didn't see each other daily, and I don't believe Mimi visited often. Our apartment was across the courtyard from theirs, so if I happened to look out the window, I might see Mimi pay a call on her son and daughter once in a while. Though we never met, I recognized her from Isabelle's description."

"You never met? Not even at Isabelle's funeral?"

"The funeral was a private affair. Étienne asked Carlson about it a few days after we'd heard of Isabelle's death. First, Carlson said he assumed I'd be unable to attend." She pursed her lips and color suffused her cheeks. "I could not move as easily back then, but I would have managed. Étienne told Carlson as much, so Carlson was forced to admit that he wanted everyone to remember Isabelle as she had been." Jeanne drew in a breath and blew it out. "Apparently, the injuries to her face were significant."

I could see Carlson's point, but it had been cruel to assume Jeanne wouldn't wish to say her final goodbyes to her friend.

Since I'd met her, Jeanne hadn't seemed much hindered by the injury to her leg. She had used a cane today, and when I'd seen her in the past, she had Étienne to lean on. Still, stairs had to be difficult to manage, and her words about seeing Mimi come and go had me imagining her stuck in her apartment, two floors up, alone while her husband was at work, and watching out the window with longing. I wondered if my image was anywhere near the truth. "Did Isabelle and her mother-in-law get along?" I asked.

"They did, as far as I knew. Isabelle had told me the two of them were at loggerheads in the beginning. She told me that Mimi was horrified when she heard about the wedding. Isabelle was sure Mimi disapproved of her." Jeanne paused to consider, then shrugged. "But they were already married, and there was nothing Mimi could do. They seemed to get past their differences rather quickly. In fact, it was usually Isabelle that Mimi came to call on. Mr. Deaver was rarely at home when she came by."

Sadly, my image of Jeanne was starting to sound like a reality. "Indeed?" I said. "I'm glad to hear it."

"In fact," Jeanne continued, "I believe she and Mimi were meant to go to the opera together the night Isabelle was murdered."

Chapter Nine

Jeanne left within a few minutes of the rest of my guests. Once I'd closed the door behind her, I requested tea from Madame Auclair and dashed back to the desk in the salon where George had stored the police file.

"What has you so flustered?" Mother had returned to the sofa, watching as I leafed through the pages of the file.

"Something I just heard about Mimi and Isabelle." I glanced at her as I recalled the initial exchange between her and Mimi. "Whatever came over you when Mimi arrived today?"

"Me?" Mother looked the picture of innocence. "She fired the initial salvo. I had to respond in kind. Sadly, my skills are rather rusty from disuse. I'd never survive a gathering of the upper four hundred with such a paltry defense." She clucked her tongue.

"Please tell me you don't plan to practice on us," I said, returning my attention to the file.

"You needn't fear. My heart simply isn't into crafting deadly repartee these days. What was it you heard about Mimi?"

I brought the file back to the sofa, having found the write-up of Mimi's interview. "Mimi and Isabelle had plans to go to the opera the night Isabelle was killed."

Mother was unmoved by the statement. "We have plans to go to the opera tonight. Does that mean one of us intends to murder the other? I assume that's what you're thinking."

"Perhaps, I ought to set the stage for you," I said. "First of all, we've known from the beginning that it was Mimi who discovered the burglary and that Isabelle was missing. We then heard from Carlson that Mimi disapproved of Isabelle when they were first married, but eventually the two women ended up tolerating one another."

Mother nodded. "Go on."

"This afternoon, Jeanne confirmed that the two women were at odds in the beginning of their acquaintance but overcame their differences to the point where Mimi would come to the apartment to visit with Isabelle."

"Visiting her daughter-in-law," Mother said, feigning shock and horror. "Clearly the sign of a dangerous woman."

I gave her a cold stare. "I thought you weren't going to use me to sharpen your wit."

She flapped a hand. "I think you are making too much out of a mother's concern." She sighed. "And perhaps I'm tired." She came to her feet as Madame Auclair arrived with the tea tray. "I'm going to my room for a rest before dinner."

"That sounds like a good idea." I already regretted sharing so much of the murder case with her. I tended to forget this was not normal drawing room conversation. Perhaps Mother was right, and I was making too much of Mimi's actions.

I poured myself a cup of tea and read Mimi's statement. She had arrived at the apartment at approximately seven o'clock the night Isabelle was murdered. That would make sense if they were to attend the opera. Indeed, the report indicated Mimi was dressed in an evening gown and an opera cape.

It would be fair to assume Mimi knew Carlson would be out

or she would have included him in the evening's entertainment as well. She would also have known that Isabelle would be at home to make herself ready at least an hour before Mimi called to collect her.

I let my gaze drift off. "To be successful, she would have to have known that the servants were given the evening off. But then she might have suggested it herself."

"Who suggested what," George said, entering the salon. "And who are you talking to?" He stopped long enough to drop a kiss on my head, then dropped himself next to me on the sofa. "Ah, a spot of tea is just what I need."

"Then you must join me," I said. "That will keep me from talking with myself."

George took custody of the teapot and poured himself a cup before glancing around the room. "Where is your mother?"

"She's resting. We are all going to the opera tonight, in case you forgot."

"I'm not certain I ever knew." He savored a long sip of tea and sighed. "But if so, I did indeed forget. What time is that?"

"Eight o'clock. I'm sure I mentioned it when I bought the tickets, but much has happened since then."

"And now you're going through the police file again."

"Shall I tell you why?" I asked.

He shook his head. "Let me finish my tea first. Tell me, how did your luncheon go?"

"It certainly wasn't a typical social gathering," I said. "I wouldn't be surprised if everyone in attendance burned all future invitations from me."

"That bad?"

"It was, but Amelia brightened things up a bit."

George paused as he raised his cup to his lips. "The baby was here? Isn't she a little young for society events?"

"Apparently not. In fact, once she arrived, everyone seemed to relax. And I learned a little more about Mimi."

"Well, I haven't finished my cup, but you have me curious. Tell me more."

I told him that Jeanne had concurred with Carlson's opinion that Mimi and Isabelle had a rough beginning but eventually reconciled themselves to one another. Then I explained my theory of how Mimi could have been the killer. "If Carlson arrived at his club by five o'clock, he must have left the apartment shortly after four. That gives Mimi over two hours to kill Isabelle, dispose of her body at that café, and return to claim she had just arrived to find the apartment door open and Isabelle missing."

"The plan to attend the opera together would explain why she was the first one on the scene," George said, looking less than convinced by my theory. "Cadieux said she notified the police when she saw the state of the apartment. She may have mentioned something about that in her statement."

I moved next to him, and handed him Mimi's statement. "It's right here. She said she arrived at the Deaver apartment to find the door open and the place in a shambles."

"Hmm, the door itself was undamaged," George said.

"Wouldn't that indicate that Isabelle let her assailant into the house?" I asked. "Thus, it was someone she knew."

"Or someone adept at picking locks, or someone with a key." He waggled his brows. "Carlson surely had a key."

"He also has an alibi."

George rifled through the pages of the report. "Aha, I thought I saw this." He handed the papers to me. "Mimi also has an alibi."

I read the statement. According to her staff, Mimi was in her bedchamber from four o'clock until half past six with her maid. "Her alibi is her maid, George. That is highly suspect. If I were to murder someone, Bridget would swear I was at her side during the pertinent time without batting an eye."

"You might want to keep that bit of information to yourself," George said with a chuckle. "And what you've just said, in fact, everything you're saying, could pertain to Carlson Deaver, too."

I gestured for him to go on.

"Carlson's alibi consists of three friends and the staff at his club, all of whom he could have bribed. He, too, knew Isabelle had plans that evening, and he knew she'd likely be home alone for the hour or so before Mimi arrived." He narrowed his eyes. "What was Isabelle doing prior to six o'clock that day?"

"She was working at the charity Carlson had mentioned." I had read the report enough times to memorize Isabelle's day. "She left there at four o'clock, right about the same time Carlson states he left home for his card game."

"So he says," George said with a smirk.

"So he says," I repeated. "Either of them could be lying, and either of them could have done it. What do we do?"

"Keep digging."

"Which reminds me, did you manage to speak with Berthe this afternoon?"

"She is proving to be rather elusive. The address she gave to the police was actually the address of the theater. She wasn't there, so that did me no good. However, when I was unable to find Berthe, I paid a call on Étienne Clement and had a nice chat with him."

"Learn anything?"

"Nothing about the murder. They live on the opposite side of the apartment building from Deaver, so it's not as if they would have heard someone breaking in that night or dragging Isabelle out of the apartment. What did Jeanne have to say?"

"She cares about Isabelle. After her accident, Jeanne was bored and lonely, and Isabelle provided friendship and distraction. She is obviously much recovered, but I think she spent quite a bit of time observing what goes on in the building."

George nodded. "Étienne told me Isabelle was a great friend

to his wife. I gained the impression that she enjoyed the company of Isabelle far more than Étienne enjoyed that of her husband."

"Poor Carlson. No one seems to like him. Lily thought him a bore. Anne thought him a braggart. Even his own mother seems to think he would be helpless without her."

George shrugged. "Let's face it, he's a helpless, boring braggart. No wonder no one wants him around."

"Except his mother," I reminded him. "I can't quite make her out. I'm glad I managed to take some photographs of her this afternoon."

George's eyes widened in surprise. "How did you manage that? And why?"

"I supposed a photograph might come in handy if we ever find a witness and need to identify her."

"You do have strong suspicions about her."

"She was at the apartment that night." I held up a finger. "She is overly involved in her son's life—was so, even back in New York. And that's another thing." I popped up two more fingers. "When he moved to France, she followed a few months behind and essentially moved here herself, without her husband."

"I thought that was due to the *comte*?"

"The *comte* may have been nothing more than a convenience. But even if she did move here to be close to him, her relationship with her son continued in its odd little way."

"Odd how? Perhaps she's a devoted mother."

"May I remind you that with no prior acquaintance with me, she dropped her daughter off at my home in London while on her way to Paris? Carlson, on the other hand, receives her full attention. If he shows an interest in a woman, Mimi does her best to keep them apart. She did so with Lily, and she's doing it now with Harriet. Then when Carlson married Isabelle, she made no attempt to hide her disapproval."

George raised a finger. "But then Carlson said, and Jeanne confirmed, the relationship between Isabelle and Mimi changed."

"Yes, I don't know if it happened suddenly or over time, but she and Isabelle seemed to be getting on. Even Madame Bernhardt mentioned it. What I have heard of Mimi over the years doesn't bring to mind a warm, caring person. Her change of heart toward Isabelle strikes me as suspicious. And that brings me back to the fact that she was there the night Isabelle was murdered."

George waved a hand. "All right, your theory has some merits. I can't believe you just stepped up and aimed a camera at her."

"Anne helped me by taking numerous photos of the baby. Mimi happened to be holding her. We took a few of Jeanne, too."

"Jeanne, too?" He grinned. "My, you never cross a suspect off your list."

"She and Étienne live in the same building, and Carlson doesn't hide the fact that he has a great deal of money. And now that I think of it, I didn't see a statement from either of the Clements in the file."

"Étienne told me the police never spoke with them." George stroked his beard, lost somewhere in his thoughts. "Have you a plan for developing your film?" he asked.

"I had planned to find a photographer," I said. "But Mother told me that the entire camera is meant to be returned to the Kodak Company. They develop the film and return the photographs along with the camera loaded with a new roll of film. That could take weeks."

"Just because that is what the company wants you to do, doesn't mean there isn't another way," George said. "In fact, I believe Cadieux could arrange to have the photos developed. They take photos of crime scenes. They must have a specialist to process them, and I'd imagine they do it very quickly."

I could always count on George to know his way around a

rule. "Excellent idea," I said. "There are still two hours before dinner. Shall we go and ask him now?"

"We could, but why the rush?"

"I want to leave before Mother wakes. I spoke to her about my suspicions of Mimi and she became rather disturbed. She'd been so helpful, I forgot momentarily that she wasn't used to dealing with murder."

He looked incredulous. "Your mother was helpful?"

"Very much so. She's taken to this sleuthing business quite well. Most of what I learned today about Mimi was due to Mother's questioning. And she is the one who brought the camera."

"Did she?" I could tell from his tone that Mother had risen a notch or two in George's esteem. He came to his feet. "In that case, are you ready?"

"I'll need to fetch a hat and gloves. Are we taking the motorcar?"

"For such a short ride, a cab would be easier."

"Find one, and I'll meet you at the gate."

It took only a moment to slip down the hallway to our room. Bridget, who was inspecting my gown for the opera, quickly found a hat while I pulled on a pair of gloves and picked up the camera. I arrived at the gate at almost the same moment George and the cab pulled up. He helped me in, and we were on our way.

George had been right, the cab had us at the Sûreté in fifteen minutes or so. We would have slipped down the hallway to the stairs that led up to Cadieux's office if not for a bruhaha taking place in the lobby. Several uniformed officers were gathered around another man waving his arms and shouting in French—with a terrible accent.

We were too far away to recognize anyone, but since all attention was on the man causing the commotion, we wove our way into the crowd gathered around him without much notice until we had a front-row view.

The man shouting was Carlson Deaver. Standing behind a reception desk, his arms crossed and seemingly impervious to Carlson's shouts was Inspector Cadieux. How interesting.

Carlson was in high dudgeon and clearly not done airing his grievance. "You have all the evidence you need," he said. "And yet you don't arrest her."

"Monsieur Deaver, what you see as evidence is not as straightforward as you think," the inspector replied. "We must act within the law, yes? You must allow us to do our jobs."

Carlson sneered. "If you were doing your jobs, that woman would be behind bars. She murdered my wife!"

A murmur of indignation rippled through the group of officers. Cadieux, looking up, noticed George and me standing nearby. Acknowledging us with a nod, he addressed Carlson with a kindness and patience that he must have dug deep to find. "Why don't we go back to my office, Monsieur Deaver, so we can discuss this quietly." Cadieux gestured to the hallway.

Carlson batted his hand away, then leaned forward until he was a mere inch from Cadieux's face. "I don't need to discuss this or stay quiet. You have the note. You have my wife's jewelry. If you don't arrest that murderer, and soon, I will go over your head."

Cadieux remained non-plussed. "Of course, *monsieur*. You are well within your rights to do that. Though we don't see eye to eye on this matter, we have the same goal, you and I—to arrest the guilty party and find justice for your wife. We are doing all we can to reach that end."

"See that you do." Carlson popped his hat back on his head and turned on his heel. He strode blindly past George and me without any sign of recognition, and pushed through the pair of large wooden doors to the street.

Cadieux glanced at us, then tipped his head toward the stairway. We made our way up to the third floor and waited outside his office until the inspector arrived. He waved us inside and followed behind.

While we settled in, Cadieux took up two of the cups from the shelf behind him and placed them next to his own on his desk. He poured some of the delightful elixir from the coffee pot on the stove into the cups and handed them to us. Picking up his own, he led us to the table at the back of the office where a small box lay atop a sheet of paper.

"Since you are here," he said, "you may wish to view the items that were sent to Madame Bernhardt."

George picked up the box which held an earring—a cluster of tiny rubies and diamonds forming a flower on a curved stem of gold. I glanced at the paper he'd uncovered. It held just a few words—*I know what you did*. They were hand-printed in ink, in a slapdash manner on blue tinted paper that looked very familiar. It was thick and of good quality, with an image of something frothy in the upper left corner.

"I think I've seen this paper before," I said. "It could be sold everywhere, but I saw it at a stationer in Deauville, on rue Olliffe." I held the note out to the Inspector. "This frothy bit in the corner is meant to be a wave."

"A wave," George mused. "Indicative of the seacoast. Perhaps this is a product of Deauville, or at least the Normandy coast."

Cadieux took custody of the note. "Thank you, Madame Hazelton. I'll have an officer find out where this paper can be purchased. Possibly, it will be a lead."

I let out a sigh. "Or it will be available at every stationer in Paris. Otherwise, this is exactly as you described, but somehow, I'd hoped you had left something out. Madame Bernhardt has identified the jewelry as belonging to Isabelle Deaver. I assume Mr. Deaver has confirmed that, but this note—it could mean anything."

"I wish you could explain that to Monsieur Deaver," Cadieux

said. "The man is determined to believe the note means Sarah Bernhardt murdered his wife, and nothing I said could change his mind."

"Yes, I saw that," I said. "I think he must be allowed to be overwrought upon learning of this new evidence. One cannot be expected to be reasonable and rational about the murder of one's spouse. Carlson must be beside himself."

"Perhaps," George said. "Or maybe he finds Madame Bernhardt a convenient scapegoat."

Cadieux cut his gaze to George. "You have suspicions of Monsieur Deaver?"

"He's on my list of possible suspects. He wouldn't be the first husband to murder his wife."

"Then what is this letter about?" I asked.

"That's what we must find out," George said. "And I did say possible suspects, did I not? If Deaver murdered his wife, then the letter may be a ruse—a way to divert suspicion from himself."

"What of his alibi?" Cadieux asked. "It was confirmed not only by his friends but the staff at the club."

George frowned. "I had wondered if they had been persuaded to lie, but at some point, they must have learned that his wife was murdered that night."

"Yes, it's hard to believe one of them wouldn't have suspected Carlson and come to the police with the truth." I pulled out a chair and seated myself at the table, feeling rather deflated.

"He may not have done the deed himself, but—" Cadieux paused and raised a finger.

"He could have paid someone to do it," said George, finishing the thought.

My stomach did a flip as I followed their line of thinking. "Are you saying he might have paid someone to get rid of his wife and make it look like a robbery?"

"We're saying it's one possibility." George turned back to Cadieux, who shrugged and took a seat next to me.

"It would be very hard to prove," the inspector said. "Deaver gave us a list of the stolen goods, and we've been on the watch for the items at all the usual locations. We have seen nothing of them."

"Until now," George said.

"If you believe Carlson Deaver might have organized this murder, wouldn't he have all those stolen items in his possession?" I asked.

"I would think so," George said. "Whoever actually did the deed wouldn't want them. Too easy to identify for a quick disposal. They'd have looked for cash, or if they were in Deaver's employ, they'd have demanded it."

"It would be helpful to search the house, but I don't know how that could be accomplished." I turned to Cadieux. "Could the police do it?"

George answered first. "They'd have to have some evidence that points to Deaver in order to obtain a warrant to search his home."

"Perhaps you will be able to provide that evidence," Cadieux said.

"If it exists, we'll do our best to find it for you," George replied. "But Deaver is not the only relative to raise our suspicions."

"You mean Mimi Deaver?"

"I had her over for lunch today," I said. "She was not pleased that you have opened Isabelle's case once more. She claimed it upset her son, but from what I saw downstairs, I rather think he approves of the investigation." I gestured to the Brownie camera I'd left on his desk. "I took a few photos of Mimi and wonder if someone on your staff would be able to develop them rather quickly."

Cadieux's eyes widened. "Yes, I believe we can help you with that. You must have strong suspicions about her."

"Along with Carlson," I said.

"Not to mention the friends across the courtyard," George added. "It doesn't appear the police questioned Étienne and Jeanne Clement. They were friends of the Deavers."

"There are a few photos of Jeanne on that film, too."

"Everyone in the building would have been asked if they saw or heard anything that night," Cadieux said, "but we would only have statements from those who said yes, and those who claimed an acquaintance with the couple."

"They definitely fit the latter category," I said.

George gave me a sly look. "Perhaps they denied it."

We left Cadieux's office a little later than expected and had to make great haste to return home. Mother had woken from her nap and was more than a little annoyed at our tardiness. But the wonderful staff, both our landlord's and our own, came to our rescue. Bridget and Blakely, my maid and George's valet, had us dressed for the opera in record time. Madame Auclair only had to hold dinner for twenty minutes. And at only a few minutes past eight o'clock, we were in the Grand Foyer of the Palais Garnier, climbing the steps with the rest of the latecomers, of which there were few.

"Heavens," I said. "There's something to be said for a late arrival."

"No crowds," George said with a grin.

Mother scowled. "Another few minutes and we'd be waiting in the foyer until the second act."

"But what a spectacular place to spend an hour." As Mother pushed us along, I tried to drink in the beauty of the curved double staircase, the stone columns, the marble floors, and the amazing sculptures everywhere I looked.

"Nobody can say the French don't know how to do opulence," George said, bringing up the rear.

I had to agree. "But they do it with such elegance."

Mother had reached the top of the stairs and turned to glare at us. "You may admire the building later, but if you don't move smartly, they will be dimming the lights by the time we reach our box. Then we will have no chance to look about us and see who else is here, whom they are with, and what they are wearing. Isn't that why one attends the opera, after all?"

George offered an arm to each of us as we reached our floor and made our way to the box Mother had obtained for the night. "I was under the impression one attended for the performance," he said.

Mother made a rude noise. "Not the performance on the stage, at any rate. Here we are." She pointed out the door, and George ushered us inside the box, papered in red silk and fitted with eight red velvet chairs. We were the only occupants.

I glanced at Mother in surprise. "Did you purchase all of the seats?"

"No, some friends your father and I met on our travels took this box for the season, but they won't arrive in Paris for another month. When they heard I would be here, they suggested I use it. I'd have invited the Kendricks, but I feared they'd leave Lily at home with Amelia."

"Knowing Lily, she'd have come with the baby," I said.

No sooner had we taken our seats than the lights dimmed. Mother moaned in disappointment, but frankly, I was relieved to be able to lose myself in whatever performance was about to begin.

It turned out to be Wagner, not my favorite, but I knew Mother had a fondness for his operas. While she sat entranced, I scooted closer to George so we could whisper about the case. Unfortunately, I moved toward him just as he leaned into me and my forehead made contact with his nose. To his credit, George reacted to the obviously painful strike with no more than a quiet groan, but Mother shushed us anyway.

I touched George's nose gingerly. It didn't seem to be broken. "Sorry, darling," I whispered. "I didn't realize you were moving, too. I thought we could take this time to consider our next step in the investigation."

"Do the two of you intend to chatter throughout the performance?" Mother had leaned toward me and somehow managed to shriek and whisper at the same time.

George leaned forward on my other side. "We could go out and admire the foyer."

"An excellent idea," Mother said.

"But if we go out to the foyer, we won't be able to return until the interval," I said.

George grinned.

Mother scowled. "I must have missed seeing the guard at the door to this box. Go. Now. You should be fine as long as you don't leave the theater. Be back when the lights come up."

Not needing to be told twice, George was on his feet, reaching for my hand. Mother had turned back to the stage. I hated to leave her alone, but it was her idea. I took George's hand, and we slipped out to the curved hallway.

Oddly enough, once we left the box, we didn't discuss the case at all. With our fingers intertwined, we simply strolled in a circle, from the hallway, to one beautiful salon after another, and finally, to the Grand Foyer and its gold and crystal glory.

"You are right," I said. "There is not one square foot of this building that isn't gilded, sculpted, or somehow embellished. It's the very definition of opulence."

George gazed around the foyer. "So you think it's too much?"

I laughed. "For one's home, far too much, but this is intended to be a showplace."

"Still a little too much gold for my taste."

"Nonsense." I gave him a bump with my shoulder. "It's the perfect amount."

With the muffled strains of Wagner in the background, we moved to the forward foyer and stepped on to a balcony that overlooked the entry and grand staircase. We had passed few other theatergoers on our procession, but here, the only people we saw were a floor below us. George drew me behind a column and into his arms, and for a few moments, we were the only two people in the world.

Until we heard voices. "My love, my heart," a smooth male voice spoke in French. "You must promise to meet me tonight."

His love's voice was softer, compelling, but I couldn't make out what she said. I realized I must have been straining to listen when George stopped kissing me and whispered in my ear. "If that couple below is more interesting to you than I am, consider me highly insulted."

I looked into his eyes, ready to whisper an apology, but the next words the smooth voice spoke snatched the attention of us both.

"You needn't worry about Mimi. She will do as I say."

I met George's gaze. "Carlson?" he whispered.

"Carlson's French is horrible," I replied. "It can't be him."

George moved us to the outer corner of the balcony, then stretched over the rail, taking me with him, and giving us the perfect view of a lovely young woman of perhaps twenty and Comte Henri de Beaulieu, a man well past his fiftieth year.

Though the sight didn't come as a surprise, I sighed from disappointment. *Oh, Henri, you are such a cliché.*

George and I returned to the box in time for the interval. Mother was raving about the performance and likely hadn't missed us one jot. All the while she spoke, she scanned the audience through her opera glasses. At one point, the glasses paused, then Mother wiggled her fingers at someone in another box. It was clear she'd already lost interest in us.

"Alicia is supposed to be here tonight," I said to George. "I'm going to look for her in the Grand Foyer. I assume whoever Mother just waved to will be joining her here in a moment. Do you mind waiting?"

He shook his head. "Go ahead. I'll find you shortly."

I made my way around the curved hallway and through one of the salons, either the sun or the moon. I smiled at a group of people who looked vaguely familiar and exited to the grand foyer, which was rather like walking into the Hall of Mirrors at Versailles. The low murmur of voices belied the fact that a large percentage of tonight's audience was in this vast space. Everyone must be speaking *sotto voce*. I doubt I'd ever have found Alicia if she hadn't tapped me on the shoulder.

"How did you see me in this crowd?" I said, when I saw who it was.

She let out a snort. "You are a head taller than the majority of the people in here. I looked up, and there you were." Alicia lifted her arm indicating the long foyer. "Shall we promenade while you tell me everything you've learned about Carlson Deaver?"

I linked my arm with hers so that we could speak quietly while we followed the flow of the crowd. "One of the first things I must tell you is that he has a mistress. She's an actress."

"Pish," she said. "I'd be more surprised if you'd told me he didn't have one. Should he propose marriage to Harriet, I will of course insist that he cut all ties with the woman. Please tell me that's not all you've learned."

I scowled, hating that I'd have to tell George he was right, Alicia didn't see a mistress as a problem. "It's all that I can state as a fact, and I'd like to point out that he didn't give up this mistress while married to Isabelle."

"That's because Isabelle's mother wasn't involved in the negotiations."

"What good would that have done?" I asked. "Do you really believe that while Carlson might be comfortable cheating on his wife, he'd hesitate to upset his mother-in-law?"

Alicia pursed her lips and drew her eyebrows together. "Any man who marries my daughter will learn that I am not to be crossed."

"While I'm sure your scowl would send shivers up Carlson's spine, I doubt it would separate him from his mistress."

"I'm not worried about the mistress," she said, "but I am concerned about his mother."

"Mimi? What's she done now? Still disapproving of Harriet?"

"Nothing that simple. It seems she only disapproves of Harriet and Carlson." She glanced around and leaned slightly closer. "I was at a reception last night where I met a Frenchwoman who expressed disappointment that my daughter wasn't with me. She has a son and was eager for them to meet, because she'd heard such glowing praise of Harriet—from Mimi Deaver!"

"You're joking?"

"I'm not." Alicia's eyes bulged as she pronounced the words. "Mimi Deaver is trying to push my daughter into the arms of another man. What do you make of that?"

"It reminds me of her creating a distraction to keep Carlson and my sister apart."

"So maybe it's nothing personal to Harriet." Alicia's shoulders rose and fell on a sigh. "I wonder if I should simply let Carlson Deaver go by the wayside. This is becoming entirely too much work, even for the likes of him. By the way, do you have a better sense of who may have murdered his wife?"

"He is not above suspicion yet. And neither is his mother, so your instincts to drop any attachment to him may be on point." A glance at Alicia's face told me she wasn't pleased with this information. "There are other fish in the sea," I reminded her.

"Of course, but we can't return to England to find them. We're still meant to be in mourning, and because of my late husband, the Stoke-Whitney reputation has lost some of its luster."

She gave me a sour expression, and I patted her hand in sympathy. "What of the French gentleman whose mother you just met?"

"Frenchmen are delightful." Alicia's dreamy smile appeared to indicate that she knew this firsthand. "But they are so—French. I thought Harriet might be more comfortable with an American, and it appears I was correct: She and Carlson get on well. If we let go of Mr. Deaver, where are we to find another American? I have no wish to take my daughter across the Atlantic, and I have no acquaintance there." Her copper curls bounced as she shook her head firmly. "No, until we know more, I think we shall keep him as a possibility."

"We do have more stones to turn before we are even close to determining who murdered Isabelle, so yes, he may be innocent."

"None of them are innocent, Frances, but I know what you mean." She glanced around the room. "Ah, here comes your husband. I'll leave you to him. Hopefully, you'll have more to report in the coming days."

She gave George a finger wave as he took her place by my side. "Is someone visiting with Mother?" I asked.

"Yes, an American woman and her husband. Didn't catch the name. Mrs. Stoke-Whitney looked less than pleased with your report of the investigation."

"She was. It seems she isn't ready to give up on Carlson yet."

"And speak of the devil," George murmured, looking out over some nearby heads.

"Is he here?" I did not have George's view.

"His mother." George gave me a wink. "And the naughty *comte*. And they are coming this way."

In fact, they were upon us before he'd even finished his sentence. Fortunately, I'd pasted on the social smile one wore for these occasions. "Good evening, Mimi. *Monsieur le comte.*"

We proceeded with bows, air-kisses, and introductions. "How are you enjoying the performance?" George asked them.

The *comte* pressed a hand to his heart. "Wagner is one of my favorites. This opera, in particular."

"My mother shares your preference for Wagner."

"A very discerning woman, I take it," Henri said. "I hope she enjoys the rest of the performance. I, alas, will not, as we must be off."

"Yes, we have a busy day tomorrow," Mimi said. "But you have seen this opera many times, Henri. Surely, you don't mind leaving?"

Henri kissed Mimi's gloved hand. "I am yours to command, my dear." He fairly cooed the words, then turned to us. "We will have some friends at our box at Longchamp tomorrow. Have you been to the races yet?"

"No, we haven't had that pleasure," George said.

"We will be there most of the afternoon. I hope you will join us." His mustache twitched as he smiled. "And bring your most discerning mother, if she is willing."

"Thank you," I said. "We'd be delighted."

Mimi's mouth tightened a bit at our acceptance, but only for a moment. "Excellent," she said. "We'll be happy to see you there."

"Until tomorrow," the *comte* said.

George and I shared a glance. "Until tomorrow."

Chapter Ten

Mother was delighted at the prospect of attending the races at Longchamp as a guest of the Comte de Beaulieu. So much so that she chose to do what everyone else in Paris society had done regarding the relationship between the *comte* and Mrs. Deaver—look the other way.

Or in Mother's case, she attempted to do so. "After all," she said, "they are both adults."

"Indeed, they are," I said.

We were aboard one of the steam boats that conveyed Parisians and tourists alike up and down the Seine. Since Hippodrome de Longchamp was on the westernmost end of the Bois de Boulogne, alongside the river, this was the most efficient manner of transport. Mother balked when she first realized that we were not using a private watercraft, but she soon came around to the festive air aboard the steamer, and seemed to enjoy the breeze on her face and the sun warming her back as we stood along the rail, watching the Eiffel Tower grow smaller behind us.

I know I did.

"It is truly no one's business but their own," she added.

"I must agree with you on that point as well," I said.

"Still . . ." She let the word drift off on a sigh.

"Mother," I said, doing my best to quash an impatient tone. "I shan't tell you what to think, but I shall tell you to make up your mind. You cannot partake of the man's hospitality while secretly condemning him and Mimi for their behavior."

She threw me a dark look. "Don't be silly! How are they to know if I am silently condemning them? Besides, his behavior is not that unusual. But Mimi? She ought to be past the age for such scandalous carrying-on."

"I think she considers herself past the age of reproach for her behavior. And they are nearly the same age. Why judge her and not him?"

Mother clucked her tongue. "I'm only saying that if she has no intention of marrying him, she should step away and allow some young woman to try her luck. He would be such a prize."

The *comte* was in his mid-fifties. His late wife had already given him an heir. And unless rumor was very much mistaken, he had no money to speak of, but instead lived off the generosity of Mimi and the credit of his family name. If that was Mother's idea of a prize, she must be thinking only of his title. "Must I remind you that you have no daughters left to marry off? His eligibility can mean nothing to you."

"I suppose you are right. This is Paris after all, and since I have accepted the invitation, I have no business judging him."

"Or Mimi," I added. "Unless of course, she's a murderer."

Mother's eyes widened. "Have you learned something new?"

I turned away from watching the river to face her, leaning an elbow on the rail. Like me, Mother was dressed in race day finery with a nod to the cooler temperatures of the season; a close-fitting dress of fine wool, with a highly decorated picture hat. "Not new, exactly," I said. "But she and Isabelle were meant to go to the opera together that night. In fact, it was Mimi who discovered the house had been burgled and that Isabelle was missing when she came to collect her."

"How horrible for her."

"Even more horrible if it was Mimi who did the damage and murdered her daughter-in-law."

Mother peered at me through a plume that floated over the brim of her hat. "Do you have any reason to believe that actually happened?"

"No reason to believe it, plenty to suspect it. Her protectiveness of her son. Her reported disdain for Isabelle, and though I have heard they were getting along better toward the end, that could well have been an act on Mimi's part to gain Isabelle's trust. Finally, if we assume the burglary and murder were done by someone Isabelle and Carlson knew, Mimi was one of very few people who had the opportunity."

"She was there right after it happened," Mother agreed.

"So she says. It's also possible she was there *when* it happened. She may have hired a couple of thugs to kidnap and murder Isabelle. Or she might have done it herself, then returned to her son's home and thrown a few things about to make it look as if someone broke in."

Mother looked doubtful. "You are making a great many assumptions."

"Indeed. And there's every chance that I'm wrong. But I do feel that Mimi bears watching."

"Is there something I can do?"

"Yes, there is." My eagerness seemed to startle her at first, but she stepped closer, so I continued. "I cannot keep asking her about Isabelle, particularly if Carlson is there today. However, I would like to learn how she feels about the potential of Carlson marrying again."

"Are you thinking of Miss Stoke-Whitney?"

"I'm thinking of marriage in general." I spread my hands toward Mother. "You have a son. She has a son. If you express how you feel at the thought of Lon's marrying, you may encourage her to do the same."

"I see." Mother nodded. "Yes, I should be able to engage her in a discussion of marrying off our sons."

"I was certain that you could," I said. "And should the topic of his mistress come up, I'd be curious to know how she'd feel at the prospect of Carlson marrying her."

Mother gave me a look of utter disbelief.

"He's done it once already," I said.

"That may well be, but how am I to introduce such a topic?"

I allowed my disappointment to show in my expression. "Well, if you can't do it—"

"I didn't say that." Mother's glare was sharp enough to cut me off.

"If anyone can, it would be you."

"We shall see." Mother cast a glance down the rail and back at me. "It appears we are about to go to work." She directed my attention to the front of the steamer, from where George was striding toward us. As usual, the sight of him put a smile on my face.

"Ours is the next stop," he said. "The racetrack is just ahead."

"Are all these people getting off with us?" Mother glanced around in dismay. "I have never attended a race, but considering the invitation came from the *comte*, I assumed it was a rather elite function."

"I do believe many on board are simply taking a ride on a rare sunny day," George said, with a bit of mischief in his tone. He leaned closer to Mother. "You needn't worry about rubbing shoulders with the common people. They won't have access to the *comte*'s box."

"You shouldn't tease her, George," I said, placing a restraining hand on his arm.

"Don't be silly, Frances," Mother said. "He was simply being helpful." She gave George's arm a pat. "That puts my mind at ease."

"You see?" George gave me a wink. "I can be helpful."

"It would seem so. I've never been here, either, so perhaps you can lead the way?"

George escorted us both across the gangplank to solid land. Only a few fellow passengers disembarked with us. Then we had to cross the carriageway to the entrance of a magnificent venue. We entered between the grandstands, which were about half full. It seemed that most of the attendees preferred to stroll the spacious grounds between the stands and the track, or enjoy a drink at one of the many café tables scattered about.

That must be the social section. If one wished to watch the races, one sat in the stands or the boxes, but if one wished to see and be seen, the promenade was the place to be. I was not surprised to see it was far busier than the stands. I looked around, taking it all in. Every manner of Parisian made use of this area. I had to rush Mother along before she saw the woman seated on a man's lap right out in the open.

"Where is Henri's box?" I asked.

"This way, I think." George was looking up toward the back of the grandstands where the seating was sheltered by a roof. I took Mother's arm and followed George up. Though there were throngs of people here, it was all quite orderly and within a few minutes, we had not only found Henri's box, but the man himself was offering us cool drinks.

Henri was clearly in his element hosting a social gathering. He had the mayor chortling over some *bon mot* and a debutante giggling behind her fan, when we joined him. He drew my mother aside to ask about the opera and practice his English.

As I watched the two of them, I wondered how long it would take for her to fall under the spell of his charm.

George and I took the opportunity to see who else was in attendance. The box was rather like one at a theater—an enclosed area with four rows of seats and an open area behind them for walking, standing, or entertaining. Henri had a full buffet available for us with fruit, croissants, and various breakfast items. Mimi and Carlson were currently filling their plates. Two other couples I didn't know were already seated, anticipating the races to come.

I faced the track, and George stepped up beside me. "Do you have a plan?" I asked him.

"You know I rarely do things by plan," he said, giving my elbow a nudge with his arm. "I'd like to observe how Carlson and Mimi act toward one another. See if she is as overbearing as people claim, and if so, does it bother him?"

I only took in part of what he said because Mother had stepped up to my other side and tapped on my arm. George and I both turned to her. She tipped her head toward the promenade. "Do you see the two women walking together down there? They are passing by the couple at the table just below us."

I spotted them. "Two well-dressed women?" I asked.

"That's them," she confirmed. "The one with the red hair in the black and white hat is Carlson's mistress."

The astonishment on George's face was almost comical. "How do you know that?" he asked her.

Mother looked coy. "The *comte* is quite indiscreet." She patted my arm. "I'm off to speak with Mimi."

I gave her my thanks, then turned to George, who was focused on the woman in the distance. "So that's the elusive Berthe," he said. "I wouldn't have expected her to be so finely dressed. Actresses don't earn a great deal, do they?"

"I don't believe they do, but remember, she's an actress and a mistress."

"Interesting," he said, glancing back to the buffet. "She's down there, and Carlson is up here."

"With his mother," I added. "I'm going down to try to speak with her."

"Shall I come with you?"

"It would be better if you keep Carlson distracted. I don't want him to see me chatting with his mistress."

George agreed and headed back to the buffet and Carlson. I worked my way down to the promenade area. It took a moment to find Berthe again once I was on the path. She and her companion seemed to be strolling up and down the length of the track, and they were about to come my way. As they passed me, I fell in with them.

The companion scowled at me. "You're not wanted here. There are only meant to be two of us."

"Then I'm terribly sorry to intrude, but I must speak with your friend." I turned to Berthe who kept her gaze straight ahead. "We haven't met, Berthe, but I suspect you remember me from the theater yesterday."

She glanced at me as if I'd lost my senses. "No," she said. "And I'm working, so please go away." Without breaking stride, she tossed her head, which was topped by a wide-brimmed black straw hat, the crown of which was wrapped with white tulle that trailed behind her.

That's when it hit me. Both women were dressed in the height of fashion, in very figure forming garments at that, traipsing before the crowd. That could only mean one thing.

"You are mannequins," I said.

"Your friend is a genius, Berthe," the companion muttered rudely before glaring at me. "Now, if you don't mind, we would like to get back to work."

If she thought ill manners would stop me, she was in for a surprise. "What house are you working for? If you give me fifteen minutes of your time, I promise to purchase your complete ensemble."

Berthe stopped in her tracks to stare at me, leaving her friend a step ahead and pulling on her arm, but Berthe was immovable. Watching her, I was struck by her resemblance to Sarah Bernhardt. The red hair, the small frame, even the way she held her head tipped back, her eyes partially closed. "Who are you?" she asked.

"Frances Hazelton—"

"Yes, yes, but what do you want with me?"

"If you had allowed me to finish, I'd have told you. I'm attempting to investigate the murder of Isabelle Deaver and—"

"That again?" She shook off her friend's hand and placed one of hers on her hips. With her other hand she jabbed her finger into my face. "So that was you asking questions of the costumer? You were with the handsome man?"

I suppose I ought not to find it annoying that it was George who stood out rather than me, but cutting me off every time I spoke and pointing her finger at my nose was trying my patience. "Yes, it was me. Then, as now, I merely wish to ask a few questions."

She stared at me a moment, considering her choices, I assumed. At least she let me finish my sentence, and retracted her finger. Things were looking up.

"You'll buy my ensemble?" she said at last. "All of it—including the hat, shoes, gloves, and bag?" She held up a dainty silver mesh bag with a bejeweled frame.

"Well, I don't really need another pair of—" This time I cut myself off when she turned and made as if to walk away. "Yes, all of it," I amended.

Berthe's companion looked at me as if I'd lost my senses until Berthe jabbed her in the arm. "You go on ahead, Sophie. I'll catch up with you soon. After my little *tête-à-tête* with Madame Hazelton."

Sophie didn't look happy about the arrangement, but she took a step away, then quickly turned back to face me. "My outfit is much prettier than Berthe's, don't you think, *madame*? Why do you want hers?"

"She doesn't want it," Berthe said. "But she'll buy it anyway, because she wants to talk with me. Now, go."

"I've never known your conversation to be worth that much." Sophie tossed the words over her shoulder and flounced off.

Berthe took my arm. "We may as well keep walking while we talk. We'll attract less attention that way."

I noticed her gaze travel to the box I'd just left. She must know Carlson was there. Since I had no desire for him to see us together, either, I fell into step beside her. "How long did you know Isabelle?" I asked.

"Since I took up with the Sarah Bernhardt theater about two years ago. We both came from the Comédie Française, but we really didn't work together until we became involved with Madame Bernhardt."

"Were you working the night she was killed?"

Her eyes widened. "You go right to the point, do you not? The police asked me that, and the answer is yes. I'm sure they checked with the theater to verify my claim. You should check with them." She gave me an artificial smile.

Mine was every bit as sincere. "Your interview must be missing from the police file. Perhaps you could indulge me. Do you recall what time you arrived at the theater?"

"I would have arrived shortly after six o'clock. That gives me time to get into my costume, my makeup, and my character before the performance."

"Can anyone confirm that?"

I had braced myself for an explosion, but she remained calm. "I share a dressing room with several of the other actresses. We all arrived about the same time."

"I see. And before six o'clock?"

Though she presented a placid expression to the crowd, she slanted her gaze at me from the corner of her eye. "Prior to arriving at the theater, I was on my way there. I left my house at half past five, right after a light dinner. My sister, whom you just saw, lives with me and dined with me that evening. We also prepared the meal together. I'd say we began about four o'clock. Does that account for enough of my time?"

"It does," I said, trying to hide my amusement. "Have you known Mr. Deaver as long as Isabelle?"

"Longer. I was his mistress before his marriage, during his marriage, and after his marriage." She paused and frowned. "That is to say, after Isabelle was murdered."

"Are the police aware of that, too? Should I check with them?"

She pouted. "I may have forgotten to mention it at the time.

Hmm, more likely that she forgot to speak with the police at all. "Did it bother you that he married Isabelle?"

"And not me?" Her tone was mocking. "That is what you mean, isn't it? Was I insulted that he thought me good enough to be a mistress but not a wife?"

Blast, I had been rather transparent with that question. "I suppose that is what I mean, yes."

She smirked. "Let me tell you something about Carlson. He is an arrogant man—somewhat overbearing but still weak. He would never have married anyone with spirit. Isabelle was exactly what he wanted in a wife. Someone who would answer to him and follow his orders. Someone who thought so little of herself and so much of him that she would try to anticipate what he might want and feared she would never get it right."

She made a face of disgust. "Isabelle laid herself down, and Carlson walked all over her. Within a week of the wedding, he'd lost all respect for her."

"Yet, you said she was exactly what he wanted."

She held up a finger. "What he wanted—yes. What he needed—not at all. I am what he needed. I don't put up with his nonsense. If he tries to lord it over me, he finds himself on the other side of a locked door, and it takes a very fine piece of jewelry for me to unlock it. Isabelle was too eager to please him, and she found him very difficult to please." She lifted her shoulder in a shrug. "I put myself first. *He* has to please *me*."

"Was Carlson bored with his wife, then?"

"He was bored with her by the end of their wedding day. From that time on, he despised her and took pleasure in making her jump through his hoops like a circus animal." She cut her gaze to me. "I don't mean actual hoops, of course."

"Of course." Heavens, Carlson was worse than I thought him. Berthe made it sound like Isabelle led a miserable life.

We'd come to the end of the promenade. Berthe caught the edge of her demi-train and swept it wide as she made a full reverse turn, smiling as she caught every eye in the vicinity. Dropping the train, she headed back toward the stands. I continued beside her. "Did Carlson object to her acting?"

"She said he did."

That came as a surprise. "Isabelle told you that?"

"Theater gossip," she said. "It came from somewhere. I assume it was Isabelle. Carlson and I never spoke about it, but it wouldn't surprise me if he didn't want his wife to have a career, or any life outside of being his wife." She held up a finger. "Or it could be his mother who stopped her. She may have decided Isabelle must give up acting. To hear Carlson tell it, his mother was more high-handed than he."

As if Carlson wasn't bad enough. "Do you think he had anything to do with her murder?"

She looked genuinely surprised. "Carlson? No. Isabelle was his pet. Without her, who would build him up? Not me. No matter how badly he treated her, she apologized. He could never do any wrong in her eyes. He would not want to lose that."

From the description Berthe gave, it's a wonder Isabelle stayed with him as long as she did—as well as a wonder that Berthe stayed with him. He might be rich, but the man was detestable. Still, while I couldn't quite give up on Carlson as a suspect, after such a categorical denial from Berthe, I ought to move on in my questions. "Did Isabelle have a good relationship with Madame Bernhardt?"

She glanced at me in astonishment. "You don't think Sarah killed her, do you? You can't be serious?"

Her voice had risen on her last words, and I shushed her. "I doubt it very much, but it's not out of the realm of possibility." She gazed at me, disbelieving. "Madame Bernhardt won't tell the police what she was doing that night," I said. "I would have a better idea of her possible culpability if you tell me how they felt about one another."

She flapped a hand. "Sarah had no reason to kill Isabelle. They were friends, even after Isabelle left the theater. Isabelle wielded no power and couldn't cause the *grande dame* any harm. If Sarah doesn't want to tell the police where she was or who she was with, it's likely because she was with someone of importance and she is saving his reputation." She shook her head. "Sarah is almost never alone."

That was pretty much the way I had assessed the situation, so I dropped that line of questioning. "What about Mimi Deaver?"

"Carlson's mother? Is there anyone you don't suspect?"

"At this point, only those with a solid alibi. Do you know how Mimi and Isabelle got along?"

Berthe stared out to the distance, thinking. "Again, it's only gossip, but it sounds like Isabelle was appalled by her mother-in-law. Madame Deaver hated that her son had married an actress and did not pretend otherwise. They say she told Isabelle to her face that she was after her son's money. Carlson also let on that his mother wasn't happy about his wife, but it was clear that he found it amusing."

"So, no love lost between them," I said.

"It didn't sound that way." She glanced at me and shrugged once more. "After a while, the gossip about Isabelle and Madame Deaver stopped. I really can't recall when it stopped, but it did. I don't know if Mrs. Deaver ceased hounding her or if Isabelle stopped talking about it. It's very strange, now that I think of it."

"You don't suppose they suddenly became friends, do you?"

"I'd find that hard to believe. Mrs. Deaver does not want to give up her son to any woman." She pursed her lips, then said, "Do you want to know what I think?"

Was she serious? "Why else would I be asking you these questions?"

"Well, I think the police got it right, that Isabelle was killed by the people who broke into her house. But they must have you looking into it for some reason you don't wish to reveal, so if the burglars didn't kill her, I wouldn't be surprised to find her mother-in-law had something to do with it."

We were within sight of Henri's box when she came to a stop. "Now you have heard everything I know about the matter, and I must get back to work. By the way." She raised her arm and did a pirouette. "This is all Callot Soeurs." She spread her hands, indicating her clothing. "You know where their *maison* is located?"

"I do."

She smiled. "I'll tell them to expect you one day next week."

"I shall, indeed pay them a call. And thank you for your help."

She gave me an assessing gaze. "I'd be very curious to hear the outcome of your investigation."

With a nod, we parted. She continued down the promenade, and I made my way up past the stands to rejoin my party. George looked relieved to see me and broke off his conversation with Carlson with the excuse of bringing me a refreshment from the table at the back of the box. As I wandered over to him, I noted that Mimi was completely absorbed with Henri. I couldn't help thinking about the young woman from last night.

"How did it go?" George asked as he handed me a glass of lemonade.

""I hope you like her ensemble," I said, then took a sip from my glass. "I'll be purchasing it this week."

"Blue suits you better, in my opinion. Was her information worth the cost?"

"I believe we covered everything. Berthe was quite thorough." I gave him a quick summary of our conversation. "What about up here? Did Carlson notice the two of us talking?"

"I doubt it. He was too busy airing his grievances about his mother and her gentleman friend."

"Really? Do tell."

"He very indelicately revealed that his mother is essentially supporting Henri. Carlson has tried to put an end to her throwing her fortune away, as he put it, but as it happens, it is her fortune. She doesn't depend on Carlson for support."

"That's not so unusual in American families. The husband usually leaves the wife a comfortable income. Did Carlson say anything about chaffing under his mother's control? Complain about her interference? Something of that nature?"

"Not at all. He'd just like her to stop spending her money on her lover."

Before I could respond, I noticed Mother cross toward our side of the box. "Speaking of lovers, here comes Mother."

George gaped. "I fail to see the connection."

"It's merely a line of inquiry I asked her to take," I said, as Mother joined us. "Did you have a chance to speak with Mimi?" I asked her.

"Of course," she said. "We discussed the travails of having sons of marriageable age."

"Did you ask about Berthe?"

George's eyes grew wide. "Her son's mistress? You wanted your mother to inquire about that?"

Mother held her hands out in a calming gesture. "I didn't have to. She brought it up herself."

That shocked both George and me into silence.

Mother was clearly pleased. "Mimi said she's quite given up on Carlson. That he's as likely to marry his mistress as a girl of good family."

"She's not wrong," I said.

"When I replied that such a possibility must upset her," Mother continued, "she told me quite sincerely, that if he chose to marry the woman, it would be fine with her."

"That's interesting—"

I was cut off by shouting at the front of the box, which had the three of us goggling to see what had happened.

Carlson stood at the entrance, shaking his fist and shouting at someone walking past.

"How dare you show your face in public? How dare you mingle with genteel society?"

Oh, dear, I feared I knew who he was shouting at, but by now, by-standers were putting themselves between Carlson and his target. One of Henri's friends had come up behind Carlson and pulled him back, forcing him into a seat. It didn't stop his shouts, but fortunately for him, it did make him look harmless to the men who came to the rescue of the Divine Sarah Bernhardt. Otherwise, he might have been pummeled to death where he stood. Her only reaction was to spare him a glance filled with pity.

Carlson shook with rage. As Madame Bernhardt walked past our box, she couldn't help but hear him shout, "Murderer!"

Chapter Eleven

"Well, this is remarkable!"

George, Mother, and I were in the dining room of our apartment enjoying coffee and a light breakfast of soft-boiled eggs and buttery croissants, when Mother made this pronouncement, likely based on something she was reading in the newspaper. We only received one copy of the morning edition, and George and I were rather chafing to get our hands on it. I suppose her reading the articles out to us was the next best thing.

"What is remarkable, Mother?"

"There is some sort of protest at the police headquarters over on Île de la Cité."

"Huh, what have they done to annoy the public now?" George asked.

Mother dropped the corner of the newspaper and peered around it. "It sounds as though they are persecuting Madame Sarah Bernhardt. Accusing her of murder. Weren't the two of you meant to prevent that?"

My stomach soured. This did not sound like a good development. I dropped my croissant on the plate and reached for the paper, but Mother had surrendered it to George already—not that he gave her much choice.

"For goodness' sake!" she said, leaning away from him, a fragment of the paper she'd been holding still between her fingers. "I see we shall have to request two copies in the future."

"Forgive me, Daisy," George said, though he looked not a bit repentant. "As you mentioned we were meant to keep this from happening, so it's quite distressing to hear that it has."

"I wonder if Carlson Deaver is at the bottom of this," I said. George was scanning the paper in search of the article, so I turned to Mother. "Did you notice him yesterday, shouting accusations at her? I wouldn't be surprised if he went right to Inspector Cadieux and demanded her arrest."

"I don't think that would be quite enough to induce Cadieux to do so," George said. "The article doesn't confirm that she's been arrested. It could be the protestors are taking some preventive action."

"Do you mean to say they are protesting something that hasn't happened yet?" I asked. "How can that be?"

"They're French, Frances," Mother said. "They invented the art of protest."

Finished with the article, George folded the paper and handed it back to her. I raised my open hands. "Well?"

"They aren't protesting her arrest, just what they see as police intimidation. They are protecting their beloved Sarah. I'm sure it will all blow over, but you and I had better continue our investigation before the police are left with no choice but to arrest her."

That had to be a hint for me to get ready for the day. George was already dressed, but I was still in a wrapper with my hair down. It was still early, only seven o'clock. "What do you have in mind?"

"We've yet to visit the charity Isabelle volunteered for," he said.

Which happened to be near the place where her body had been found. Good thinking on George's part. "I'll need half an hour at least. Do you think the police photographer will have my photographs ready today? We can pick them up on the way."

George stood up from the table. "I'll fetch them now and come back for you." He finished the last of his coffee and set the cup in its saucer with a *chink*.

"If you are going to the Sûreté," Mother said, "be careful of the protestors."

"Thank you for the reminder, Daisy. I shall." Stepping up behind me, George placed a hand on my shoulder. "Thirty minutes," he said. Then he dropped a kiss on my head, bid Mother a good day, and departed.

"Do you have plans for the day, Mother?"

She glanced at me in surprise. "Don't tell me you are asking me to join you?"

"I don't believe you'd care for our destination, but I wouldn't rule it out another time. You were very helpful at the luncheon."

"Indeed?" She preened a bit. "As it happens, I have some correspondence to take care of today. I'm also expecting a reply or two to the cables I sent a few days ago."

"Cables to New York?" I asked. "Are you expecting information about the Deavers?"

She smiled. "I certainly hope so."

I came to my feet. "Then I'll look forward to hearing about them, but for now, I must make myself ready. You heard George, I have only thirty minutes."

She took hold of my hand before I could leave. "I believe the two of you know what you are about with all this investigation and spying, but I do hope you are taking every precaution. Do not make me worry about you."

"We are being very careful, Mother, but I'm quite sure you

will always worry about me." I kissed the top of her head and headed up to my room.

George was a few minutes late, so he had no idea that I had practically sped through my toilette and pulled on the first gown that came to Bridget's hand in order to arrive at the gate on time. He pulled up in front of the gate and I climbed in beside him, moving the camera and the large envelop of photographs before seating myself.

I nearly dropped them when George accelerated before I'd settled. "A little warning would be nice, dear," I said in a voice loud enough to be heard over the motor. Fortunately, I'd thought to use a scarf to keep my hat attached to my head, so it was safe for now.

George cast a glance my way. "Apologies, but you know I'm new to this, Frances."

"And much better at it than I. Please forget I said anything." I looked out through the windscreen as he negotiated the traffic. "You seem to know where to go."

"I found a notation in the police file with the name and address of the place. Daughters of Charity they're called. They seem to be a well-rounded foundation, offering assistance in finding work, clothing, lodgings, and food."

"Sounds like a worthy organization." The wind had taken hold of my scarf, and it required both my hands to keep the ends from obscuring my view.

"It seems Isabelle found it so," George said, ignoring my battle. "She volunteered several times a week."

"And her body was found there."

"Not there exactly. She was outside a café a little farther down the square."

My face reflexively pulled itself into a grimace. "Where is the charity, exactly?"

"It's in the place des Vosges. Number four."

"Did the police interview anyone there?"

"I have their names in my coat pocket. Someone from the charity and another person from the café."

"They only spoke to two people? That can't be right."

George shrugged and turned the motorcar onto the gravel-covered square while I peered through the windscreen, looking for number four. "Over there," I said, pointing straight ahead. "Between the grocer and the bookshop." I let my gaze travel along the square. It was tidy, but it definitely wasn't as grand as I had expected.

"Weren't these royal residences at one time?" I asked George.

"The royals had many residences to choose from, but I believe the aristocracy lived here in the seventeenth century. Paris has been through both revolution and war since then, so I'm sure the place has changed."

I'd never seen the square before, but still felt sure he was right. The four-story buildings that outlined the park, fronted with brick, slate, and stone, were attractive but shabby, as if they'd seen better days. At least the parklike grounds at the center were inviting, shaded as they were by leafy plane trees.

George nodded in that direction. "I suspect what the royals really liked was that large square—good for tournaments and parades."

"Wasn't a king killed at one of those tournaments?" I could imagine two knights on horseback, lances out, running toward each other.

"Yes, I remember reading about that in my school days. Henry II, I believe." George parked in front of the grocer and shut off the motorcar. "Right now, I'm more interested in who killed Isabelle Deaver. Shall we go inside?"

This time I waited while he walked around the front of the vehicle to my side, opened my door, and handed me out. "Where to first?" I asked.

"The Daughters of Charity, I think."

The ground floor of each of the buildings was recessed, which allowed for a covered passage, or arcade, along the four lengths of the square, where several merchants displayed their wares. George led the way to the open door of the charity.

The interior looked as if it might have once been a dry goods store, and prior to that, a residence. We walked through a small entrance that faced a staircase and turned left into what must have been a drawing room in a past life. Instead of sofas and chairs, there was a man seated behind a desk speaking to an older, bewhiskered man who leaned against it. At a long table in the corner, a woman dressed in white shirtwaist and black skirt interviewed a younger, painfully thin woman.

"*Bonjour*," the seated man said, drawing my attention back to the desk. "How may we be of service?"

We crossed the bare wood floor and approached the desk. Speaking French, George introduced us and explained our business.

Both their faces grew solemn when he mentioned Isabelle. "Such a tragedy," the whiskered man said. He introduced himself as Marc Leblanc, the general manager. He was gray-haired and stout. His seated companion, Victor Garaud, was somewhere in his twenties with dark hair and eyes.

"I often worked alongside Madame Deaver," Monsieur Garaud said, "and I like to believe the two of us became friends in her short time with us. You may ask me anything you like. I am relieved to learn that the police have not given up on her case."

Monsieur Leblanc pulled up a chair, placing it across from Monsieur Garaud, and indicated I should sit. "We all held Madame Deaver in high regard. She was a kind and caring soul."

"What exactly did she do for your organization?" I asked, taking the seat.

"Often, she sat at this very desk, taking care of anyone who came through the door, whether they sought our help or offered theirs by way of financial assistance," the manager said.

"And did many people come through your door?" George asked.

"There is generally a steady stream. Far more often are those seeking help than those willing to provide it."

"I understand Madame Deaver was working here on January 26th—the day she was murdered," I said. "Do either of you recall what time she left?"

"I know she never worked into the evening," Leblanc said. "She always wanted to be home at night for her husband. The building is never open past seven anyway. Since we don't house anyone here, everyone is gone after the evening meal." He poked a thumb at a doorway behind him, so I assumed a kitchen lay behind that wall.

"As I recall she left early that day," Monsieur Garaud said. "Around four o'clock. I believe she had some event to attend that evening."

Leblanc concurred. "She was a volunteer and did not have set hours as we do. Although the kitchen remains open later, this office closes at six o'clock. Madame Deaver would normally leave here at five o'clock."

The burglary story was beginning to sound more likely. If someone had been watching her and knew her movements, they'd have expected her to be in the office until five o'clock that day.

"Did Madame Deaver ever have to turn people away?" George asked. "People with needs you were unable to meet?"

"We do, occasionally, turn people away—there are some we simply cannot help. But it was never Isabelle's job to do so," Monsieur Garaud said. "She would take their information and direct them to the person best able to assist them."

"You are wondering if she was the victim of someone who was angry with our organization, are you not?" Leblanc gazed at us with an assessing eye. "While she was a public face for the Daughters of Charity, it ought to have been clear to anyone seeking help that she did not make the decisions."

George tipped his head to the side. "That may be so, but someone who is angry or frustrated may not make that distinction."

"It might also have been someone who was simply greedy," I added. "Madame Deaver was very wealthy. All someone had to do was to follow her home and conclude that everything they needed could be found inside her apartment."

Monsieur Leblanc stroked his gray whiskers, his eyes troubled. "Yes," he said at last. "That could be so."

"Can you think of anyone who may have a grievance or some resentment against your organization?" I asked.

The older man's gaze slipped between George and me while we waited patiently for his answer. "As you suggested, it's possible someone, or the family of someone we were unable to help, might bear us a grudge, but those people tend to be unstable. At least, that would be one reason we would be unsuccessful at helping them obtain employment. I doubt they'd be able to carry out such an endeavor as you imagine—watching her, following her home, finding a way to enter her home—the people I have in mind could not manage it."

"Do you by chance keep a list of such people?" George asked.

"In a manner of speaking, yes, but I wouldn't have enough information to locate them for you."

"If you could provide a list," George pressed, "we will check with the police and see what they can do with it. Perhaps these people are on a similar list of theirs."

"Of course." Leblanc instructed us to wait while he went out a side door. The woman at the table in the corner was alone now. George shifted his gaze from Garaud to her. Turning back, he gave me a wink, then wandered off to speak with her. I leaned closer to the desk and smiled at Monsieur Garaud. I guessed his age to be about twenty-five, but his lack of facial hair made him look younger.

"How long have you been employed here?" I asked.

"Nearly six years, now," he replied.

"Goodness, only six years," I eyed his pristine suit, the neat white cuffs at his wrists, and his manicured hands. His shoes were highly polished and one foot was shaking where it rested on the opposite knee. "You have worked you way up through the ranks quickly to become second in command." I had no idea what position Garaud held, but if his smile was any indication, he seemed to like the title I chose.

"Daughters of Charity administers to the needy all over France, *madame*," he said. "This is only one small office, but I like to think I do my part."

"I'm sure your wife must be very proud."

"I have not been fortunate enough to find a wife yet."

"Really? I can't imagine what the young ladies of Paris are thinking."

He compressed his lips. "My work doesn't give me the opportunity to meet many unattached young ladies. Those who volunteer here are married women."

"Are all the women volunteers?"

"Yes. Some are involved in raising funds. Others, like Madame Deaver and Madame Fabien over there," he nodded at the female volunteer, "work in the offices, interviewing those who need our help."

It seemed the only paid positions were for men. As annoying as that was, I didn't think it factored in Isabelle's murder. "Tell me, were you working here the day Madame Deaver was killed?"

"Yes, of course. We were working together. That's how I know she left early. I stayed until the office closed."

I nodded, but said nothing, hoping he'd elaborate.

"I usually take my evening meal at the *brasserie* around the corner. That is to say, I stopped there for a meal that night." His fingers twisted a scrap of paper.

"Is the food good there?" I asked.

"The food?"

"Yes. It must be good if you dine there every evening. Do you know if Madame Deaver ever stopped there for a meal? Heavens, that isn't where . . ." I let the sentence drift off.

"Where Isabelle was found?" he asked, almost choking on the words. "No, that was the café on the other side of the square."

"I see. So, after you dined, presumably you went home to your bachelor apartment? Or do you live with your family?"

He frowned. "My family is not in Paris. I share an apartment with a friend." He glanced to my left, where George had stepped up.

"Do you have those photographs, Frances," George asked. "I'd like to show them to Madame Fabien and see if she recognizes anyone." He gave Garaud a quick glance. "Perhaps we could show them to Monsieur Garaud first."

"Excellent idea." I opened the envelope on my lap, sifting through the photos of Mother, Lily, and the baby until I found one of Mimi. I handed it to the young man. "Does she look at all familiar to you?"

By this time, Madame Fabien had come over to us and Monsieur Leblanc had returned. Garaud shook his head and passed the photo on to Leblanc, who in turn handed it to *madame*. None of the three had recognized her. I tried again with a photograph of Jeanne Clement and obtained the same result.

Leblanc handed the photograph back to me and gave George

the promised list. "Our cooks have arrived," he said. "You may show those photographs to them if you like, but they will be preparing for the midday meal soon, so it would be best to speak with them now."

George and I took the hint and thanked them for their time. Monsieur Leblanc volunteered to walk us back to the kitchen. Once there, he waved to the two men in white coats at the stove and asked them to join us. We showed them the two photographs. One of them took a long look at Mimi and sighed. "I can't be certain if I saw her here, but she looks familiar."

"Are you a chef at another establishment?" George asked.

The man gave us a rueful laugh. "Not somewhere she would dine," he said, then held up a finger. "It was here, or rather, back there." He pointed outside to the square. "I saw her getting into or out of a cab. I don't know if she was coming or going, but I was taking a break after preparing the evening meal and didn't pay much attention. I only noticed her because she was so elegantly dressed. She didn't seem to belong here."

"If you were finished preparing the evening meal, that would have been about six o'clock." Monsieur Leblanc turned to George. "If this person is associated with Madame Deaver, why would she be here when Madame Deaver wasn't? As I said, she never worked at night."

"Good question," George said. "I don't suppose you recall what night this happened?"

Sadly, we were not that lucky. We thanked the men and left the building.

Once outside, George took my arm and we moved away from the buildings to stroll across the square. "What do you make of that?"

"That the chef recognized Mimi? We'll have to ask her about it, though her being here could be as innocent as checking up on her daughter-in-law to make sure she was truly working for a charity." I stopped for a moment and passed a hand over my eyes. "I can't believe I said that. There is nothing innocent about her spying on Isabelle."

George let out a mirthless laugh. "No, but it is better than Mimi murdering her."

I could not argue with that.

"Now for Monsieur Garaud," he said. "What made you suspicious of him?"

"You noticed that, did you? He slipped and called Isabelle by her given name—more than once. Plus he's an unmarried man who worked closely with a beautiful young woman. He may have fancied himself in love."

"And you suppose she didn't reciprocate his feelings?"

I pondered that a moment as our shoes crunched across the gravel. "I'm not sure it matters. If they did indulge themselves in an affair, he could have threatened her with a confrontation with Carlson unless she continued it. If she had no feelings for him, he may have paid a visit to her home that evening. She tries to send him away. He kills her." I sighed. "We might have some difficulty verifying his alibi, considering it was eight months ago. He dined at his usual place, then went home, where he lives with a friend."

"Let's keep him in mind," George said. "But I still have to wonder what Mimi was doing here."

"So do I."

We'd reached the café across the square, and I let George ask questions of the staff. Only two of them had been working in January when Isabelle's body had turned up outside their establishment. Only one had worked that day. He visibly blanched when we brought up the subject. He had been the one to find her and verified the day—January 27th, the morning after the Deavers' apartment had been broken into and Isabelle had gone missing. "I'll remember that date forever," he said and went on to describe the state he'd found her in.

That's when I blanched. Cadieux had told us Isabelle had been beaten before she was strangled, but I hadn't been prepared for his description. Poor Isabelle. Hard to believe Mimi could have recognized her, though as Cadieux had said, her height, age, and hair color matched Isabelle's. Perhaps her clothing was also familiar to Mimi.

Unfortunately, the waiter told us nothing that wasn't in the police report. None of the staff recognized either Mimi or Jeanne, so we decided it was time to take our meager findings to Cadieux.

George drove us to the Sûreté, but we had to leave the motorcar around the corner, near the courthouse, due to the crowd of protestors chanting outside the entrance.

"Heavens, they are quite persistent. I had expected them to break for lunch, at least."

George shrugged and pushed his way through the crowd. I followed close behind him until we made it through the door into the building, where an officer stopped us and asked our business.

"We are here to see Inspector Cadieux," George said.

"He left not more than fifteen minutes ago." The officer cocked his head. "Monsieur Hazelton?"

At George's nod, he continued. "You have excellent timing, *monsieur*. Inspector Cadieux asked me to find you and deliver a message. He was called out to the Sarah Bernhardt Theater less than an hour ago. It seems there was a murder."

I let out a gasp. "At the theater?"

"That is where the body was found. He asks that you meet him there as soon as possible."

George's hand tightened on mine. "Please tell me the victim wasn't Madame Bernhardt?" he said.

The officer put a hand to his heart. "*Mon Dieu!* No. Though this is surely a tragedy, it is not *that* tragedy. *Le chef* mentioned a name, but I don't recall. It was another actress, I believe."

George and I exchanged a look then turned back to the officer. "Berthe?" I guessed.

"That's it," he said. "Berthe Pepin. She was found in Madame Bernhardt's dressing room."

Chapter Twelve

Rather than attempt to drive the motorcar through the crowd of protestors once more, we left it at the courthouse and hailed a cab to travel less than a mile to the theater. We were met in the lobby by an officer posted in front of one of the floor-to-ceiling images of Sarah. He was determined to send us on our way until George told him Cadieux had asked for us himself.

Though this seemed to annoy the older man, he relented. "I have to wait for the coroner, but if you know your way backstage, you may go ahead."

George assured him we knew the way, and we walked past him into the dark theater. "Ugh, a little light would be helpful," I said, following him down the aisle.

He pointed to the stage where a dim light glowed. "We only have to determine how to get behind the stage. I'm certain we are up to the task."

Once we got closer, all we had to do is follow the sound of voices and within minutes, we found ourselves in Madame Bernhardt's dressing room—one of them, that is. "This isn't the room we met her in," I said, glancing around the much smaller space furnished with a wardrobe and a dressing table and mirror. This was not the tidy table from her other dressing room, but one covered with jars and brushes. The mirror was surrounded by notes stuck into all its fasteners. This must be the room she used to make herself ready, while the other was for visitors.

"The voices are coming through this wall." I indicated the door, which must lead to one of the other rooms in her suite, and headed that way. George took hold of my arm to stop me.

"Not so fast," he said quietly. "We may not get another chance to look around here. If she is hiding something, it certainly won't be in the room where she receives the police."

"She'd have a difficult time hiding anything in here." I waved a hand at the scant furnishings. "Besides, what are you looking for?"

"I don't know," he said, rifling through the small scraps of paper. "Correspondence, perhaps?"

A letter could easily be hidden. Still, it seemed foolish to hide anything in the theater. Particularly if others could simply walk in here as we did. Sarah didn't strike me as foolish, but nothing ventured, nothing gained. George had moved on to the wardrobe. I followed his example and glanced around the room. The first thing my gaze landed on was Inspector Cadieux, standing in the doorway, a scowl on his face and a hand on his hip. I nearly jumped out of my skin.

"I thought I heard someone moving around," he said. "What are you two doing in here? You are needed two doors down."

"Of course," George said. Closing the wardrobe, he took my arm and drew me toward the inspector. "You see, Frances, I told you they must be farther down the hall."

I waved a hand. "Silly me. We were simply following the voices and this was the first room we came upon."

"Um-hm." Cadieux looked doubtful. "The body is down the hall. Follow me."

"How was she killed, Inspector? Was it similar to Isabelle's murder?" If Sarah was in the room with Berthe, I might not get another chance to ask.

Cadieux paused at the doorway. "She was strangled with a silk scarf, probably her own as Madame Bernhardt doesn't recognize it. There appears to be a bruise on her cheek, but she was not beaten like Madame Deaver."

"Do you know if she was murdered in the dressing room, or if her body was placed there afterward?" George asked.

The inspector shook his head. "If she were moved right after death, it would be difficult to determine, but we'll see what the coroner can tell us. One thing we know is that she shares a dressing room with other actresses, and Madame Bernhardt left the theater immediately after the performance."

"So if she were meeting someone and she wanted privacy," George said, "she would know that Madame Bernhardt's dressing room would be empty."

"That is a possibility," Cadieux agreed. "Shall we go?" He led us to a room next door to the one Sarah had used when George and I interviewed her. Since we were waiting for the coroner, presumably Berthe's body was still in that room. How many dressing rooms did the woman have? This one reminded me of a boudoir, with fluffy rugs, a few chairs, and several small tables cluttered with bric-a-brac the actress likely deposited as she walked by them.

Sarah was reclined against the arm of a fainting couch of red velvet and gilded wood, her face blotchy from crying, her dark eyes luminous with tears. She was dressed in a white wrapper trimmed in feathers that appeared to swallow her up and make her look both helpless and fragile—the complete opposite of the Georges Clarin painting I'd seen of her on our first visit.

As we exchanged solemn greetings, I wondered if Sarah was more in control of the situation than I'd given her credit for. The woman was an accomplished actress, and she was certainly wearing the right costume for playing the grieving friend. And why on earth was she wearing a wrapper anyway? Wouldn't she have been fully dressed when she came to the theater? Or did she have a bedchamber somewhere in this suite of dressing rooms?

If Cadieux had arrived only ten minutes ahead of us, had he asked her any of these questions yet? Considering his reverence for the woman, would he dare to question her?

"Would you be so kind as to stay with Madame Bernhardt?" Cadieux asked me. "Then Hazelton and I can examine the other room before the coroner arrives."

I agreed readily, and the two men left through a side door that led to yet another connecting room. I assumed it was the crime scene. When I turned back, I realized I was alone with the Divine Sarah. And I had to admit, I was a bit dazzled by her, but I couldn't just stand here gawking.

"Is there anything I can do for you, Madame Bernhardt?"

She raised the back of her hand to her forehead and brushed back a clump of curls. The wide sleeve edged in feathers slipped to reveal an armful of bracelets. "Please call me Sarah," she said. "There's a bell over there by the table. Ring for my maid, won't you? She can bring us some coffee."

I pushed the button on the wall, partially hidden by a framed photograph of—who else? When I turned back, the actress was up and pacing in front of the couch. Her steps were quick, her turns jerky, and her bracelets jingled and clinked as she flung her arms about. Coffee might not be the right beverage for the moment.

"How I despise this inactivity!" she said. "I wait and wait and wait while the police plod their way through an investigation that seems to take forever. Meanwhile, another beloved friend has been taken from me. And I am told to sit and do nothing."

Her voice carried as if she were trying to reach the farthest balcony. I was certain Cadieux and George could hear her. When she turned, her face was that of a woman tortured. "I don't know how to let other people handle matters. I don't know how to do nothing."

She paused when the maid arrived with a tray holding a carafe of coffee, cups, sugar, and cream. Apparently, she knew Sarah well. Without a word, she laid everything on the low table in front of the couch. When she left, Sarah wrapped her arms around herself and flopped down on the velvet couch, her gaze on me. "If I were investigating, this horrible killer would already be in prison, that is if I didn't kill him with my own hands." She lifted the carafe and poured herself a cup.

I seated myself across from her and took the carafe when she offered it. "Are you saying you have a suspicion of who might have killed your friends?"

She widened her eyes and spread her arms, sloshing a bit of coffee on the floor. "I have not been allowed to investigate. How would I know? Tell me what to do, Madame Hazelton. There must be something."

"To begin with, please call me Frances," I said, pouring a cup for myself. "Then why don't you tell me about Berthe? It would help to know what she was like."

Sarah focused her gaze on the far wall, her lips quirking up on one side. "Berthe. She was sharp like a razor, that one, and I don't mean merely smart. She could be kind and generous at times. She would be the first to offer help to anyone in difficulty, but no one could play her for a fool. She had good instincts about whom she could trust."

Those instincts must have failed her last night. "She struck me as a no-nonsense type of person. How long have you known her?"

"Several years. Longer than Isabelle. Berthe and I go back to the Odéon theater, before my last American tour. She was brought on because she resembled me and could, in the event of illness, stand in for me." She gave me an intense look. "Not that I am ever so ill I would miss a performance."

"Now that you mention it, the two of you could be sisters," I said.

Sarah's smile was tight. "Perhaps mother and daughter makes more sense. And you are right, she was straightforward. If you asked for her opinion, she would give it honestly, not really caring about what you might want to hear."

That certainly sounded like the woman I spoke with yesterday. Sarah took a sip of coffee while I wondered what to ask next. "Did Berthe have family?"

"Not in Paris. Well, her sister is here. They arrived together about ten years ago. They had a plan to become actors. Her sister didn't have the fortitude to persevere in the theater, but she did well enough modeling for the fashion houses. Berthe found a gentleman to help her financially. That ended three years ago. She had been working enough since then that she did not need to make such an arrangement again, but then she met Monsieur Deaver."

I noticed Sarah wrinkle her nose as if she smelled something unpleasant. "I thought you weren't acquainted with Carlson Deaver?"

"Should that stop me from forming an opinion?" she asked. "Besides, the man is calling for my arrest almost daily."

I suppose that would leave a bad impression of him.

"Otherwise, I only know him through Isabelle. Though Berthe and Deaver had an arrangement, she never spoke of him. What I do know is that he was involved with two of my friends, and I think he used both of them very badly."

Not to mention they both ended up dead. "Did Isabelle know Berthe and Carlson had an arrangement before she married him?"

Sarah shrugged. "I believe so. She may have assumed he'd give Berthe up once they married. He was American, after all, and they often do. But eventually, she learned she was not the only woman in her husband's life. I don't think she minded all that much."

"Don't you?" I drummed my fingers on the arm of my chair. I hadn't been the only woman in my first husband's life, and I definitely did mind it. I minded it very much.

"Isabelle was the one he married," Sarah continued. "That gave her far greater status than Berthe had as his mistress. And considering they were both poor girls from the country, they were both enjoying success." She paused for a beat, gazing sadly into the distance. "At least Berthe was. As I mentioned the other day, Isabelle seemed to feel she wasn't up to the task of being Madame Deaver."

"Did Isabelle ever mention another man? Perhaps in a romantic sense or perhaps someone who was bothering her?"

She leaned forward with interest. "Do you mean since her marriage? Was Isabelle having an *affair de coeur*?"

"That's what I am asking you."

"I have no knowledge of an affair, but something must have prompted your question." She watched me through narrowed eyes. "Is there some man you suspect?"

For goodness' sake, she was better at this than I was. "Yes, there is a man at the charity where Isabelle volunteered who might have had an attraction to her, but I have no evidence that he acted on it. It's possible they were simply friends."

She looked less than convinced. "Chances are her husband would not have believed she and this man were simply friends."

I hadn't even considered that possibility. Monsieur Garaud only struck me as a suspect, someone who might have followed her home that night. But he might also have been a catalyst, setting Carlson off on a murderous rage. But Carlson did have an alibi for that night. I would have to have Inspector Cadieux look into Monsieur Garaud's life a little more thoroughly.

"Back to Berthe," I said. "Do you know of anyone who might want to hurt her?"

Sarah shook her head, looking perplexed. "Berthe always seemed to get along with everyone. But she did keep her personal life to herself. As I said, she never spoke to me about Monsieur Deaver or anyone else she was seeing."

That perked me up. "Is it possible that she was seeing someone else—other than Deaver? I assume he would call for her at her home. It looks like she may have intended to meet someone here last night."

Sarah scoffed. "She might have come here to meet someone, but it would be a poor lover who couldn't do better than a theater dressing room." She crossed her arms over her chest. "No, Berthe would have demanded more."

I glanced around at the opulence of this room and thought it quite luxurious enough for a tryst with a lover, but I did see her point. Berthe would want to know the man in question would be able to provide for her, and if he had no rooms of his own, he was unlikely to get very far with her. Still, the man may have desired nothing more than a private conversation. "Did men ever call for her backstage after a performance? I assume she was part of the performance last night? And how did she get inside your dressing room?"

"Men often call on the actresses after a show, but Berthe was very cautious about whom she met. As to how she got into my dressing room, I do not lock it. All she had to do was walk in."

Or be dragged in, I thought. "If someone waited for her after the performance, one of the other actresses who share the dressing room might have seen him."

She brightened. "That's possible. We should check with them."

"But if she had planned to meet someone in your dressing room, it seems to me she would have kept that to herself and slipped out of the shared dressing room without anyone seeing her."

"That doesn't sound like Berthe."

Voices from the adjoining room caught our attention.

"Do you think that is the coroner?" Sarah asked coming to

her feet. "I want to see my friend once more before they take her away."

"I rather think Inspector Cadieux wants you to stay here," I cautioned.

"These are my rooms." She squared her shoulders, and her voice vibrated with emotion. "This is my theater. He can hardly stop me from going anywhere I choose."

I followed her as she pulled open the door and strode into the other dressing room. I gave Cadieux a shrug when his head snapped around, but rather than the scowl I had been expecting, he extended his hand to Sarah and led her over to a velvet upholstered chair. Two men, one a uniformed police officer, the other likely the coroner, were on the floor effectively hiding Berthe's body from our view, something for which I was grateful.

"Where has George gone?" I was speaking to Cadieux's back as he bowed over Sarah's hand.

"To speak with the cleaning women," he replied over his shoulder, barely taking his eyes from Sarah, who had suddenly begun weeping again. "Madame Bernhardt, do you know why Mademoiselle Pepin was in the building last night?"

"She was part of the performance," I replied, taking the chair next to Sarah, who promptly clasped my hand.

"Do you know if she stayed behind to meet someone?"

"Frances asked me the same thing," Sarah said. "We think you should check with the actresses who shared her dressing room."

Cadieux scowled at me. I knew I'd see that scowl sooner or later. What did he think I would do with my time alone with Sarah—have her sign photographs for me?

"Perhaps the cleaning staff will be able to shed more light on what happened here last night," I said.

"Madame Bernhardt, have you had any further communication with the person who sent you the blackmail note?" He asked.

She blotted her eyes with a handkerchief. "No, I've heard nothing more."

"We found a very similar note near Mademoiselle Pepin's body."

"Did it say anything beyond, 'I know what you did'?" I asked. "Was it the same paper?"

"It was the same paper, and only held those few words," he said, still watching the actress closely. "Madame, forgive me, but I must ask where you were between eleven o'clock last night and four o'clock this morning?"

"I was with my son," she said, surprising me. She'd still not revealed her alibi for the time of Isabelle's death. "That is why I left here so quickly last night," she continued. "I had a letter from Maurice telling me he'd call on me at home after the performance. He arrived at half past ten."

She drew a handkerchief from her sleeve and dabbed at her eyes. "We have been at odds lately, so I rejoiced at seeing him again. We stayed up talking well into the morning. I left him at my home this morning, sound asleep. You might still find him there."

Relief showed in Cadieux's eyes and in the relaxing of his jaw. The Divine Sarah had an alibi. Yes, it was her son, but it was still an alibi. He wouldn't have to arrest her.

"Odd that Berthe also received that accusatory note," I said. "Perhaps it isn't related to Isabelle at all."

"Or perhaps the killer is only guessing," Cadieux said. "Sending such notes to people with whom Madame Deaver was acquainted."

"If so, do you think whoever murdered Berthe was exacting revenge for the death of Isabelle?" This was becoming very confusing. "Did the killer believe Berthe killed Isabelle so he killed her? And considering Berthe's fate, is Madame Bernhardt in danger now since she received one of those notes, too?"

The coroner cleared his throat and gestured to the body on

the floor. Cadieux once again offered his hand to Sarah. "Ladies, please, let us return to the other room, shall we?"

I was happy to comply. I had no desire to watch them take Berthe away.

George returned when we headed into the visitors' wing of the dressing room suite. His report was not promising. The theater isn't cleaned until the morning after the performance. They had arrived this morning before Sarah, but none of them had seen anything out of the ordinary, and they hadn't yet cleaned any of the dressing rooms.

"Frances and I can go to the actress's apartment and see what might be found there," he said.

Cadieux declined the offer. "I have already sent an officer there to break the news to her sister. I may go myself once I have taken Madame Bernhardt's statement." He turned to Sarah. "We have no reason to suspect you of this heinous crime, *madame*, but if you would come to the Sûreté and make an official statement, I would be greatly obliged. In fact, many of your supporters and admirers are already there." A wry smile played about his lips. "They fear we plan to arrest you and would be relieved by any words from your own lips."

Sarah placed her hand over her heart. "That touches me so," she said in her sonorous voice. "Of course, I will come and tell them I am safe from harm."

Cadieux returned to the coroner's side, and since it seemed we were no longer needed, George and I took our leave of the actress.

"But you must go with us," she said. "It will take only a moment for me to dress."

"There really is no need—" Cadieux began.

"I have need of you," she said, taking a step closer to me. "You wish to speak with Berthe's sister, do you not?"

George and I exchanged a look before I replied. "Yes, of course."

"Then you will join us."

We agreed to drive with Sarah and Cadieux to the Sûreté. Since more officers had arrived, George and I left the crowded room to wait for them in the lobby.

"She has such a dramatic manner," George mused as we walked through the empty theater. "One would be hard-pressed to know if she were truly upset about Berthe or only acting."

"I believe she is truly upset about Berthe, but I know what you mean," I said. "I think acting is something of a refuge for her. A way to deal with her emotions when they become too much to bear, which I suspect is frequently. She becomes a character dealing with tragedy rather than herself."

George opened the door to the lobby and followed me out. "If that is so, then how do we know who is the woman and who is the character?"

"I begin to think that they are one and the same."

Chapter Thirteen

We returned to the Sûreté in Madame Bernhardt's spacious carriage along with Inspector Cadieux. It gave us the opportunity to tell him what we learned at the Daughters of Charity and of Monsieur Garaud.

"Madame Hazelton believes he and Isabelle were involved in an affair." Sarah, who was seated next to me in the carriage, supplied this little tidbit eagerly.

"I haven't proof enough to suspect anything of the sort." Flustered, I sputtered a bit, but I had no idea if the inspector heard me or not as he sat gazing in awe at the actress. Frankly, I couldn't tell if he had heard her, either. I wagged my hand in the air to gain his attention. "Monsieur Garaud did seem very interested in Isabelle and closer than a mere colleague. George and I questioned him as best we could, considering we are not the police, but I would suggest someone more official pay him a visit."

Cadieux awoke from whatever he'd been dreaming, agreed with me, and jotted down a note to himself.

"On the other hand," I said, "I would like the opportunity

to speak with Berthe's sister. I believe we already have a slight acquaintance."

This prompted George to give me a look of surprise.

"It was she who was walking with Berthe at the races yesterday. She works as a mannequin, and she and Berthe shared an apartment."

"My officer is there right now," Cadieux said. "He will question her."

"I think she'll speak more openly to me—another woman."

Sarah cast a glance at me, then turned back to Cadieux. "Frances is right. In fact, she and I should both go and console Berthe's sister. The poor dear must be devastated."

Cadieux looked horrified at the suggestion. "Madame, it is our intent to keep you completely separate from this case."

"Of course, you have only my best interests at heart." Sarah placed a long, slender hand on his arm. "But would it not be clear that I had nothing to do with the crime if I were actively involved in the investigation—working to find the killer?"

I had thought all the color had already drained from Cadieux's face, but as he turned a shade paler, it seemed I was wrong.

"That is very noble of you, *madame*," George said. "But the police are determined to keep you safe. Following potential killers is definitely not safe."

She heaved a sigh. "Yes, I suppose not." With a deft movement, she took Cadieux's hand in hers. "But you must let Frances speak with Berthe's sister. It would be so much more comforting to the woman than speaking to one of your officers, don't you agree?"

Cadieux nodded mutely and stared at the fingers Sarah had just released. She turned to me with a wink. Things went swimmingly when she was on my side.

George leaned closer to me. "It seems that sometimes it is better to ask for permission."

"That completely depends on who is doing the asking," I whispered back.

We left Cadieux and Sarah at the Sûreté and took the motorcar to Berthe's apartment, which was in the opposite direction from the protestors, on the third floor of a well-tended building with a smart address. Not a home I would think an actress could afford on her own. I assumed Carlson Deaver paid the rent.

Cadieux had given us the address. George was right, it was refreshing to be working out in the open, with the permission of the police, rather than sneaking around.

The door was answered by the woman I had almost met at the races—Sophie Pepin, Berthe's sister. Her red, watery eyes and blotchy face told me the police had already been here. Though she was dressed, her hair was down, floating like a dark shroud over her shoulders.

"You," she said. The single word was uttered with no expression or emotion, but at least I could presume she remembered me.

"I'm so sorry about your sister," I said. The claims I'd made to Cadieux—she will be more open with another woman, and I'll get more from her than an officer—drifted away on the breeze. She was a woman in pain due to no fault of her own, and I had nothing but sympathy for her. "May we come in and speak with you?"

I truly don't know why she agreed. Maybe, like Berthe, it was George's good looks that decided her, but whatever her reason, she pushed the door wider and retreated to the salon. We followed.

"How do you know Berthe," she asked, eyeing me with a touch of suspicion. Yes, it must be George that made her willing to talk with us. She had taken a seat in an oversized chair, leaving the sofa for us. "Berthe told me you were investigating someone's death, but I can hardly credit that."

"She told you the truth," I said, taking a seat. "I wanted to speak with Berthe because she was a friend of Isabelle Deaver's."

"Isabelle?" She drew a shaky breath. "Tell me, does everyone you speak to end up murdered?"

That stung, particularly since I'd never even met Isabelle. However, arguing over such a detail was not likely to make her more willing to talk with me. "Fortunately, they do not," I said. "My husband and I are working with the police to find out what happened to Isabelle, and now your sister, too. It seems their deaths might be related. I am sorry to confess I had once thought your sister might have been responsible for Isabelle's murder. Obviously, that doesn't seem at all likely now."

Sophie blew out a puff of air. "The reverse would have been more believable. Isabelle had nothing Berthe wanted. More than anything, my sister wanted to be an actress. One of the great ones, like Sarah Bernhardt. She could not have cared less about Monsieur Deaver and whom he married. He was nothing more than a way to pay the bills."

"She and Deaver had been together for over two years," George said. "No matter what her feelings actually were, he must have believed she cared for him or why would he stay with her? A man like him wants more than a mere physical relationship."

"She was an actress, wasn't she? He believed her." Sophie paused to blot her eyes. When she glanced up, she was frowning. "That's not right. She did not act with him. She made it clear what she was offering to him and what she expected in return." She shrugged. "If he wanted more than a physical relationship, I suppose that's why he married."

"Were Isabelle and Berthe friends?" George asked. "Or did Isabelle resent your sister?"

Sophie tutted with impatience. "Isabelle got what she wanted. Berthe got what she wanted. They were more acquaintances than friends, but I don't see any reason for resentment from either of them."

Time to change the subject. "Did you sister mention any plans to meet with someone after the performance last night?"

"The officer asked me that, too. Berthe told me nothing. She and I were together most of the day. We went to the designers late in the morning to dress. You saw that Berthe and I were at Longchamp all afternoon. After the races, we returned the clothing. I came back here, and Berthe went to the theater." Sophie's eyes welled up with tears. "And someone killed her there. The policeman could tell me nothing more. Do they know who did this?"

"I'm afraid they don't," I said.

"Since she never left the theater," George said, "her assailant had to be someone in the cast or who worked there, or someone who was allowed backstage."

"Could it have been Monsieur Deaver?" I asked her.

Sophie looked genuinely shocked. "Carlson adored Berthe," she said. "Besides, he wasn't at the theater, he was here."

"Here?" George and I spoke at the same time.

"Yes, here. It can come as no surprise to you that this is his house. He came by here around seven o'clock to see Berthe. He didn't know she had a performance last night." She shrugged. "To make it up to him, I cooked him dinner. We ate, we had some wine, and he left about nine o'clock."

"Could he have gone from here to the theater?" George asked.

"He said he was going home," she said. "He looked tired." She came abruptly to her feet. "In fact, he left her a note." Sophie stepped down a hallway and into another room, returning in a few seconds with a slip of paper she handed to me.

"Until tomorrow, my love," I read.

"It sounds like he expected to see her again," George said.

It did. I handed the note back to Sophie. "Was there another man in Berthe's life?" I asked.

Sophie shook her head. "For Berthe, Carlson was manageable. A second man would have driven her mad."

I could understand that. "Did the officer ask you about the note they found in her possession?"

Fat tears slipped from her eyes. She blotted them quickly and sniffed. "Do you mean the note that claimed to know what she did? He asked me about it, but I don't know what it could mean. Berthe and I have lived together most of our lives. I know her as well as I know myself. She has never done anything that would make someone want to hurt her."

I was coming to that same conclusion. This seemed a senseless killing. I said the only words I could think of. "I'm so sorry that someone chose to do so."

"So am I," she said. "I hope you find them and make them pay."

George and I made our way back to our apartment in the motorcar. "Do you honestly think that there was no hostility at all between Berthe and Isabelle?" he asked over the chugging noise.

"Over Carlson Deaver?" I sounded as incredulous as George had.

"He was Isabelle's husband. I understand a married man having a mistress is hardly a rarity, but I can't believe she didn't at least mind that he was with another woman."

"Whether she did or not is of little consequence, George. What good would that do her? Isabelle minding would not stop her husband from cheating. She would simply have to live with it. What other recourse did she have?"

George shrugged. "Divorce, I suppose."

I gave that some thought. "Yes, divorce has been available in France for at least a decade, maybe longer, so she had to know that was an option, particularly since they had no children."

He gave me a quick glance. "Is that why you remained married to Reggie?"

"He would have been awarded custody of Rose, and I could

not bear to lose her, but divorce comes with scandal. Regardless of the whispers about Reggie and his many loves, we were still welcomed in society. The scandal of divorce would have ended that." I gave George a sidelong glance. "Can you imagine my mother's reaction? I would not have received a warm welcome home, either."

George grimaced. "I suppose not. And if you had returned to America, we might not be together."

"That would have been the real tragedy," I said. "But when one is stuck in a situation such as mine and such as Isabelle's, one tries to make the best of what one does have. I had status, a large house to run, good friends, and most importantly, my daughter. The women Reggie dallied with had no interest in taking any of that away from me. Isabelle might have minded a great deal about Berthe, but not enough to ask for a divorce."

"On the other hand," George said, "they weren't married for long before she was killed."

"That's true," I said. "She may have held out hope that Carlson would give up his mistress." I shook my head in an attempt to clear it. "However, after a year of marriage, I would think the time for hoping had come to an end. She might well have come right out and asked Carlson to give up Berthe. They may have argued about it. Perhaps it became heated. Perhaps he killed her."

"In the heat of an argument?" George blew out a breath while he considered the possibility. "Unfortunately for your theory, Carlson does have the card game as an alibi for the night Isabelle was murdered."

I sighed. "She didn't leave the Daughters of Charity until four. Carlson would have been gone before she arrived at home."

George frowned and shook his head.

"And I so liked that possibility," I said. "Carlson commits murder in a moment of passion, then sets the stage for a break-in to cover it up. It explains so much."

"But it doesn't explain the threatening letters or who killed Berthe," George said, looking equally glum.

"Regardless of what Sophie said, it is possible that Carlson murdered Berthe."

"Cadieux sent an officer to Carlson's house when we left to call on Sophie. We'll see if he has an alibi," George said. "Though I'm at a loss for his motive for either of the murders."

"There is still the possibility of Victor Garaud, the man at the charity, being involved," I said. "Perhaps Cadieux will learn something from interviewing him. After all, he would have been one of the last people to see Isabelle alive."

Chapter Fourteen

I was not allowed the luxury of forgetting about my obligation to Alicia Stoke-Whitney. News of Berthe Pepin's murder made the afternoon papers, and Alicia showed up at our door the very next morning. Though I still didn't have the definitive answer she wanted, I had the housekeeper take her to the salon, where I met her a few minutes later.

She came to her feet as I entered the room. "It seems as if things are going from bad to worse."

I took the hand she held out and led her back to the sofa, seating myself on the opposite end. "I have to agree with you. I take it you've heard there's been another murder."

"And in Carlson Deaver's milieu, too." She gave me a rueful smile. "I can't decide if the man is a murderer, or simply unlucky in love."

To a most extreme degree.

She cut her gaze to me. "What do you think?"

I thought it was amazing that without even trying, Alicia had managed to give voice to what had been nagging at me for the past few days. It was difficult to imagine what Carlson would have to gain by the death of his wife and mistress. George checked the police file to learn that the gentlemen in Carlson's company the night of his wife's murder said they had met up at five in the afternoon and had played at cards right through to an early breakfast the following morning. In light of this, I began to wonder if the murderer was someone with a grudge against Carlson, rather than the victims, making them the ones who were unlucky in love.

While I pondered silently, Alicia mused aloud. "I begin to question whether he is worth the risk, regardless of his fortune," she said with a sigh. "But he does have a sizable fortune, so I thought I'd come to you to hear what you have learned."

I grimaced, knowing I was about to disappoint her. "I wish I had an answer for you, but the details are still very opaque."

"So you don't know who killed either of the women?"

"I'm afraid not."

"But it's been days. What have you been doing all this time?" she asked. "I thought you would have completed your investigation by now."

"These things take time, Alicia," I said, rather resenting her attitude. "Our questions keep leading us to new avenues of investigation."

She pouted, then brightened suddenly. "But do you still suspect Carlson?"

Did I? Both Berthe and Sarah had at least intimated that Carlson mistreated Isabelle, but Berthe said her experience with him was different and that he treated her well. A fit of temper causing Carlson to murder them both seemed unlikely. Besides, Isabelle was alive when he began his all-night card game.

Sophie Pepin believed Carlson adored Berthe and hadn't gone to the theater last night. And I had yet to determine what he might have to gain from her death. "I suspect him less," I said, meeting her gaze. "But I cannot completely exonerate him. I'm sorry."

I quite expected her to rail at me, demanding I find evidence to prove him either guilty or innocent, but at that point, my mother entered the salon. After greeting me, she turned to Alicia. "How lovely to see you again, my dear."

"And you, Daisy." Alicia stood up, and the two diminutive women executed perfunctory air-kisses near each other's cheeks. It was odd seeing Mother behave so congenially to someone whose reputation would normally bring out her most stinging insults. Even more odd was to see Alicia behave sociably to any woman.

"I'm afraid I must run," Alicia said, still holding Mother's hand. "But you and I must meet for tea sometime soon."

I walked her to the door where she simply said, "I look forward to receiving some word from you in the near future."

I turned wearily from the door to see Madame Auclair with a tray of coffee. Mother must have requested it. We both entered the salon as Mother settled herself on the sofa. "I suppose Alicia was referring to news of her daughter's gentleman friend," she said. Clearly, she had heard Alicia's parting comment.

"More like news of his late wife's killer." I took a seat opposite Mother and poured us each a cup of coffee. "Frankly, without finding the culprit, there will always be a shadow of suspicion around Carlson Deaver, enough so that Alicia would likely dissuade Harriet from seeing him."

Mother gave me an odd look. "I would hope so. Such suspicion ought to put off any woman."

"It should, indeed," I said. "I assume that is why Carlson is so eager for the police to arrest Sarah Bernhardt. He simply wants them to arrest someone—anyone—other than himself, of course."

"I'm afraid I don't have any information about Mrs. Deaver's assailant, but . . ."—Mother left the last word hanging and patted the drawstring bag that lay beside her—"I have heard from my friends in New York with a little more background about the Deavers." She removed several folded pages from her bag. Mother was the only person I knew who regularly corresponded by telegraph and cable. "I hesitated to bring these out while Alicia was here. I wasn't sure if you wanted her to know how much digging I'd done."

To be honest, I couldn't say who knew what about anything at this point. Cadieux had recruited George into this investigation. Alicia had recruited me, and I had recruited Mother. And we all shared different bits of information. What an unlikely band of sleuth hounds we were.

I took the pages Mother offered just as George entered the room. He hesitated for less than a second upon seeing her, then, with a brave smile, he continued forward and greeted her. Clearly, he still didn't believe she'd mellowed.

"Mother has brought us some intelligence, dear," I said, holding up the telegraph forms.

"I don't know how much help it will be, but I knew my friends would have more recent particulars of the Deavers than I. Though I'd expected it to be nothing but gossip, there are some firsthand accounts, as well."

George sat down in the chair next to mine and poured himself a cup of coffee. "Even gossip is a start," he said. "At this point, I'll take what I can get."

"Take this, then," I said and handed him one of the forms. The one I kept was two pages closely written and must have cost a fortune to send. "Heavens, it seems this person had quite a bit to say on the matter."

"Not everything in there is about the Deavers." Mother leaned toward me and directed my gaze to the bottom of the first page. "I believe it begins about here—yes, that's right. At Prudence Henbeckler's dinner party."

Prudence was a member of the old guard in New York. Mother must have done some strategic social climbing to be corresponding and swapping gossip with such a grand lady. I perused the first few sentences which referred to decorations and food, let my gaze drift to the second page, caught the phrase, 'train your servants,' then backed up a paragraph or two.

"Heavens!"

Mother, knowing what I'd just read, nodded in agreement.

George, who had no idea, stared at me with raised brows.

"I can't believe this." I blinked a few times and reread the passage.

"Do you intend to share?" George prompted.

I allowed my gaze to leave the shocking words on the paper and met George's. "He slapped a servant."

"And not even his own servant, mind you," Mother added. "It was Prudence's parlor maid, a woman who could name her own price at the best houses in New York."

"Her price as a parlor maid," I clarified for George, whose expression told me he had attached a different meaning to Mother's words. "And at the best *homes*."

Mother gave me a narrow look. "That's what I said." She tutted and faced George. "The point is, he slapped her."

"And it sounded as though he might have done worse had he been given the chance," I said.

"That is serious," George said. "Somebody stepped in to stop anything further from happening, I take it."

"Exactly. Let me read it to you," I said, scanning the page for the particular passage. "Here it is. It says, after dinner, Mr. Deaver didn't wish to partake of the port and requested a cup of coffee from the footman."

"But the coffee wasn't ready yet," Mother said.

I glanced up from the letter. "Do you wish to tell this story, or shall I?"

"Go ahead." She made a little shooing motion with her hand. "But do get on with it."

"The coffee wasn't meant to be served for another hour," I continued, "so it had to be brewed. After ten minutes or so,

Mr. Deaver thought he'd waited long enough and went in search of it, catching the parlor maid as she brought it up to the butler's pantry."

I glanced up at George. "Where she would then hand it off to the housekeeper who would then notify the footman." I made a rolling gesture with my hand. "You know how that goes."

"Yes, of course. A parlor maid serving in the drawing room is quite impossible," George said, imitating a royal drawl. "Go on."

"Deaver demanded the coffee, which startled the young woman, who would never expect to see a guest in the butler's pantry. She hesitated a moment too long, and it seems that enraged him. He batted the cup from her hand, then slapped her across the face."

"The devil he did!" George did indeed look shocked.

"At that moment, the housekeeper stepped into the pantry and saw what he'd done. She courageously placed herself in front of the maid, apologized to the man, who had caused all the trouble, and only avoided a slap herself because Prudence, who had been coming down the hallway and heard a commotion, walked into the little room."

"That's a rare bit of luck," Mother said. "Generally, the mistress of the house never sees the mistreatment of those who work for her."

"Or she mistreats them herself," George added.

"When Prudence asked what had happened, he gave her an angry sniff and said she ought to train her servants better." Stunned by the man's audacity, I lowered the letter and stared at George. "Can you imagine such a scene?"

Mother grumbled in disgust. "Prudence managed to get Mr. Deaver back to the drawing room, but she didn't find out until the end of the evening exactly what had happened. She swore she would never have that man in her house again."

"Madame Bernhardt mentioned that Isabelle often felt that

she wasn't good enough and that she was always in the wrong," I mused. "I wonder if she ever said anything about Carlson striking her."

Mother reached out and placed her hand over mine. "No, no, Frances," she said. "This isn't about Carlson. It was his father whom Prudence refused to entertain again."

"The late Mr. Deaver?" I knew I was gaping at her, but I simply couldn't help it. "I always assumed he was a benign sort. Nor did I know he went out much in society."

Mother pursed her lips. "Perhaps he shouldn't have."

"I have something more along the lines of what Madame Bernhardt told you," George said, shaking out the folds from his page. "This is the gossipy stuff. It appears a young lady favored Carlson with one dance at a ball."

He looked up and met my eye. "This story is definitely about Carlson. The following day she turned down his offer of a ride in the park, because she had already promised her afternoon to someone else."

"A completely reasonable response," Mother said.

"One would think so," George said. "But Carlson did not take her rejection at all well. He made her feel so bad about her refusal that she later told her mother she must have led him to believe she admired him."

I sighed. "Why must young ladies always blame themselves?"

George tapped the page with a finger. "In this case, the young lady came to her senses when gossip surfaced, claiming that she had indeed led him on with very specific words of love she knew she had never uttered."

I sat back in my chair and blew out a breath. "So we have one story revealing the late Mr. Deaver to be a brute, and another that Carlson tried to intimidate a young lady. When that didn't work, he attacked her reputation," I said. "But they are only two examples."

Mother held up one more cable. "Three." She passed the

pages to me with a frown. "This one is from Ethel Cuddymore, a very reliable source. It involves Mimi."

I took the pages cautiously and skimmed through the salutation and the first paragraphs, finally settling on some very interesting words farther down the page. I cast a glance at George before I began to read.

"*Goodness, Daisy,*" I read, "*you can hardly blame Mimi for leaving her husband. The man was a beast. No, perhaps that's too strong. He comported himself well enough in the business world, when he was around other gentlemen, which leads me to believe he simply had no respect for the fairer sex. If one dared express an opinion, it would be met by him with a look of pure loathing. It was as if the footstool or his pipe had the temerity to speak up.*"

George and I exchanged worried frowns, then I continued: "*Frankly, I don't know how she stayed as long as she did. Have you never glimpsed the bruises she attempted to disguise?*"

I raised my hand to my cheek, both of which were burning with anger. "*Who else would dare strike her? I don't know how he treated their son and daughter, but I assume Mimi stayed only to protect them. The moment Carlson left for the continent, she and Lottie moved to a less fashionable part of town and socialized very little. While I don't approve of divorce, I certainly understand her need to separate from such a man.*"

I skipped over the part where Mrs. Cuddymore exhorted Mother to keep that information between the two of them. Fortunately, Mother had ignored that request.

"So, the late Mr. Deaver abused his wife," George mused.

"And possibly his children," Mother added. "No wonder they all left him."

"I didn't know that Mimi had already left her husband before coming to Paris," I said. "When did that happen?"

"It was several months earlier. As Ethel said, she left him immediately upon Carlson's departure from the family home.

There was no divorce, but they no longer lived together. Mimi didn't move to Paris until July of last year, well after her son's marriage."

"That was right when she dropped her daughter, Lottie, off with me in London."

"She may have wanted to get Lottie out of harm's way, too," George suggested.

"If I remember correctly, Lottie got on well enough with her father, but I never asked her directly what he was like." I folded the telegraph paper and returned it to Mother. "I don't want to lose focus on Carlson. What do you two make of these revelations? His father may have been horrible, but that doesn't make Carlson so."

"True," Mother said, "but it doesn't necessarily make him a victim, either."

"From what I've seen of Carlson, he hasn't much character, nor a great deal of respect for women," George said. "While this isn't conclusive proof that the man is violent like his father, the stories we've just read about the Deavers tell us what sort of example he grew up with. Carlson also seems to find someone else to blame for all his own shortcomings."

He leaned forward and shot me a look. "Do you recall my prediction about the golf tournament?"

"That Carlson would find a reason to back out?"

"And lay the blame elsewhere. When we were all at the racetrack, I mentioned the upcoming competition. Carlson told me that the French committee overseeing the tournament had lost his paperwork. Of course he could simply complete the application again, but he claims this means the judges are favoring the French players. According to him, the winners are predetermined, and he won't be participating."

Mother gave us each a glance, looking perplexed. "And this means what, exactly?"

"The truth of the matter is that Carlson doesn't play golf as well as he thought, and doesn't want to be shown up by the skilled players," I said. "To avoid such an embarrassment, he made up a reason to be offended by the hosts so that he may back out of the tournament altogether."

"I believe that is a defining trait in Carlson's character. His lack of anything is always someone else's fault," George said.

"Which might have upset Isabelle or led her to ask for a divorce," I countered, "but provides no reason for him to murder her."

"It might, if he believed she was to blame for any and all problems he may have been experiencing," Mother suggested. "Moreover, he might have hated the blow to his reputation if his wife divorced him."

"It's not out of the realm of possibility," I said. "But neither is the theory that someone broke into the house and later killed her. Besides, Carlson could not have felt that way about Berthe. What reason would he have had for murdering her?"

George's brow furrowed. "I've been wondering if we are dealing with two murderers."

"But is Carlson one of them?" I asked.

George smiled. "An excellent question. We have no real proof of that and no reason to suspect he murdered Berthe."

"He has a good alibi for the night of Isabelle's murder," I said. "As for Berthe, it sounds as though she was universally liked. In fact, the only person who may have had a grudge against her is already dead."

The three of us returned to our coffee, completely stumped. "On the other hand," I said, "Carlson is not particularly well liked. I still think we might consider the possibility that both women were murdered not by him, but because of him. Perhaps the notes—*I know what you did*—relate to him, something he did."

"But then why would one have been sent to Sarah Bernhardt?" Mother asked.

"You're right. She didn't have any type of interaction with Carlson, even though two of her fellow actresses did."

"But wait." George held up a finger. "Isabelle didn't receive a note. Two of her friends did. Does that tell us anything?"

"That my theory is a lot of rot," I said glumly. "What do the two victims have in common?"

"The theater and Carlson," Mother said.

"The theater leads us back to Madame Bernhardt, and I really can't see any reason for her to murder two women she cared about."

George sighed. "If the theater leads us to Sarah Bernhardt, where does Carlson Deaver lead us?"

"Marriage? One illicit relationship? Do you suppose it's possible Berthe was jealous of Isabelle?" I gave the idea some thought. "I know her sister said that was not the case, but Berthe had been working in the theater quite a long time now. Perhaps she was growing tired of it. Perhaps she thought with Isabelle out of the way, Carlson might marry her."

With no evidence to back them, my theories felt flat even to me. "However, I'm not convinced Berthe even wanted marriage with him. In fact, I'm not convinced of anything I'm saying."

George reached out and clasped my hand. "What about Mimi?" he asked.

"I can guarantee you Berthe didn't want to marry Mimi."

Mother *tsk*ed, and George rolled his eyes.

No sense of humor, either of them. "Then what did you mean?"

George turned to Mother. "When you posed the possibility of Carlson marrying Berthe to Mimi, you indicated that she seemed indifferent to the idea."

"Indeed," Mother said. "I was rather surprised."

"Yes, her reaction is surprising." George raised his brows.

"She had disapproved of Isabelle. Would she have let Carlson marry another mistress? Perhaps that was the first time she considered the possibility. Berthe was murdered that very night."

I had always thought Mimi was a good suspect.

"Now that I've heard these tales about her husband," Mother said, "I wonder if he would have given Mimi anything to live on when they separated—or in his will once he died. Perhaps she followed Carlson here to Paris because she relies on him for support. She would not want another woman to interfere with that arrangement."

"No, no," I said with a wave of my hand. "Carlson told George he objected to the way Mimi lavishly supports the *comte*. It sounded as though it was her money."

"Then money may have nothing to do with her behavior toward her son," George said, "but it's possible that she has been protecting him from his father all his life. She may now feel that she has to protect him from the women in his life."

I tried to put myself in the actress's shoes. "If Berthe found Mimi Deaver outside her dressing room door, asking to speak with her, she might be curious enough to take her to a private place like Sarah's dressing room. But knowing Isabelle had been murdered, do you think she'd meet Mimi alone?"

Mother's eyes widened. "I've never met this Berthe, but if the mother of the man who has been her lover showed up at her door, she might easily have been shocked enough to have forgotten all about Isabelle."

"Mimi might have wanted to hear directly from Berthe if she was angling to marry Carlson."

"Would Mimi have believed the woman if she had denied it?" George mused.

Mother paled. "Would Mimi go so far as to kill her?"

"The night Isabelle was murdered, she was supposed to be going to the opera with Mimi," I said. "Our earlier speculation about Carlson murdering Isabelle, disposing of her body, and making the house look as though someone had broken in, could apply to Mimi, too. And one of the chefs at the charity where Isabelle volunteered recognized Mimi."

George frowned. "Near the place Isabelle's body was found."

"We could be completely off course," I said, "but I think it's time we take a closer look at Mimi."

Chapter Fifteen

Our ruminations about the victims and killers were put to an end when Lily stopped by with the baby. Since George had yet to meet Amelia, we spent the first fifteen minutes of her visit introducing them. It didn't take long for both man and child to tire of repeated rounds of peek-a-boo. Amelia grew fussy, and George handed her back to Lily and returned to his newspaper. Back in her mother's arms, the baby began to cry in earnest.

Lily's face collapsed into a grimace of despair as she drew Amelia to her shoulder and paced the room with her. "She does this all the time lately. I fear I shall have to call in a doctor."

"The way she's chewing on her fingers, she may be teething," Mother suggested, coming to her feet and hovering behind Lily.

"Indeed," I said, "she seems to have her whole fist in her mouth, which is generally a sign."

"Stop walking away, and let me look at her." Mother held on to Lily's arm, and standing behind her, put her face level with Amelia's. That served to make her cry louder. While opening her mouth was precisely what Mother had wanted, it clearly drove Lily to distraction.

"I do believe I see a tooth in there," Mother said.

"Let me see if the housekeeper can find something cold for her to gnaw on," I said, coming to my feet.

Lily sputtered in indignation. "Gnaw on? She's not a wild animal, Frances."

I stepped up behind Lily and stood next to Mother. Both of us bent to peer at Amelia's face. "But you sound so much like one," I cooed to the little girl, who screwed up her face and let out another bellow.

"I'm so sorry, dear," I said in a soothing tone. "You are the sweetest, prettiest wild animal I've ever seen." I circled around to face Lily. "She definitely has a tooth coming in."

"Giving her something cold to soothe her gums is a good idea." Mother reached for the baby. "Let me have her. I'll take her to the kitchen and see what the housekeeper can find. Lily, you sit down and rest."

Lily handed the child over, then collapsed on the sofa as Mother and Amelia left the room. George had been quiet during the recent exchange. When I sat down next to him, I noticed him looking at my sister with some concern.

"You look rather done in, Lily," he said. "Shall I send for some tea?"

Before she could reply, she was overcome by an enormous yawn.

"Lily has not been sleeping," I told him. "The baby has been crying all these nights, and Lily has been caring for her by herself."

"Ah, then a brandy might set you to rights."

I placed a hand on his arm to keep him from jumping up to pour a glass for her. "She's not suffering from insomnia, dear, the baby is keeping her awake. Lily needs a nurserymaid."

"I would be useless at that, I'm afraid," he said.

"I just need a little rest." Lily curled up on one end of the sofa and closed her eyes.

"You need a good night's sleep," I said. She made no response. "I believe she's sleeping." I stood up to leave the room and gestured for George to follow me. "We'll let her nap."

"She did look exhausted," he said. "Shall I carry her to a room?"

"Let's leave her be. It's one o'clock and time for luncheon anyway. Here's Madame Auclair now." We'd just stepped into the dining room to see the housekeeper setting a lovely quiche on the table. "That looks delicious," I told her. "Did my mother find anything for the baby to chew on?"

"She has a shard of ice wrapped in a *serviette* and seems to be happy with it for the moment," she said, turning away from the table with a sympathetic frown. "The baby was making it clear she was uncomfortable, no?"

"Teething is unpleasant for everyone," I said, "the baby, the parents, and anyone within earshot." Madame Auclair left us to serve ourselves with salad and quiche. Before we could take a bite, the housekeeper returned to inform us that Inspector Cadieux had arrived. "I told him you were at lunch, but he said this was important."

"I don't suppose you wish to go and speak with him?" George said to me, hovering a bite of quiche near his lips. "I'm really quite famished."

I suggested the housekeeper bring Cadieux into the dining room. When George gave me a look, I shrugged. "Maybe he's hungry, too."

Within a matter of minutes, Cadieux was seated across the table from me, enjoying his own slice of quiche.

"I'm afraid we learned nothing remarkable from Sophie Pepin, inspector," George said. "I hope you have had more success."

Cadieux dabbed a spot of egg from his mustache. "My success is debatable. I have received a report from the officer who checked on the stationery store in Deauville. You were correct, Madame Hazelton, it was paper they produced."

"I'm delighted to hear I got something right."

"Unfortunately, it is a very popular design."

"Why doesn't that surprise me," George murmured. "They can never make it easy for us."

"Exactly," I said. "A blackmailer ought to use a very distinctive paper for his notes, don't you think? Preferably with his monogram."

"Full name and address would be even better," George agreed after washing down a bite of salad with a sip of white wine.

Cadieux shook his head and returned to his quiche.

"However, you did say they produce that paper themselves, did you not, Inspector? If that's the case, we at least know where it came from."

"That was the partial success," Cadieux said. "Whoever wrote those letters, purchased the paper from the shop in Deauville. They print the paper themselves, and they don't sell it to other shops. We have the owners reviewing their recent shipments of that style to customers outside of Deauville, and in the meantime, we need to find out if any of our suspects have visited the seaside recently."

"We know the Clements were there not long ago. They are Carlson Deaver's neighbors and were on friendly terms," I added upon seeing Cadieux's blank stare.

"Yes, you mentioned them earlier," he said. "I thought we interviewed the neighbors in the surrounding apartments. Did you find statements from them in the case file?"

"They live across the courtyard," I said. "We found no statements. It appears they were not questioned in the original investigation."

Cadieux nodded. "We may have to pay a call on them, as well."

"As well?" George asked. "Who is the primary call?"

"I wish to speak with Monsieur Deaver about a handwriting sample and wondered if you'd care to accompany me, Hazelton."

"We already saw a sample of Carlson's handwriting," I said.

"Yes, from the sister of Berthe Pepin," Cadieux said. "I saw it, too. It does not match either of the notes, but the writing on the notes don't even match each other, so I'm sure the hand is disguised. But if I am in Monsieur Deaver's office, I might be able to see if he has this Deauville paper."

"It sounds like you suspect Carlson of writing the notes," George said.

Cadieux tipped his head to the side. "He is a possible suspect."

"Why don't I go, as well," I said. "I can call on Jeanne Clement while you are obtaining your sample."

"What about your sister?" George asked, angling his head toward the salon.

"Mother and Madame Auclair have Amelia well in hand, and Lily needs her rest. With luck, perhaps they will both sleep."

The gate to the apartment building occupied by the Deavers and the Clements was open, but we stopped at the concierge's loge anyway. It was a one-room apartment with a loft overhead, likely where the woman slept.

Madame la concierge was dressed in a drab brown skirt, with a knitted shawl of the same color wrapped around her, over a white shirt. Her dark hair was sprigged with gray and worn in a knot at the back of her head. We found her standing at a table in the center of the room, sorting through the post. She glanced up as Cadieux poked his head through the open doorway.

"*Bonjour, madame*," he said, then proceeded to introduce himself as an inspector for the Sûreté.

"And what could you want with me, *monsieur l'inspecteur*?" she asked, her gaze wary as she took his measure.

Cadieux explained that the police were once again investigating the murder of Madame Deaver, which caused the woman to tut and shake her head. "Such a sad end for a kind woman." She pushed a chair toward Cadieux, though her gaze had wandered to where George and I stood in the doorway.

"These are special investigators from England who have agreed to lend us their expertise," Cadieux said. He waved us inside. "Monsieur and Madame Hazelton." There was an awkward moment when *madame la concierge* realized she had only one other chair and motioned for me to take it. Cadieux noticed and offered me his own chair so that she could use the other herself. She rewarded him with a smile that I was willing to bet showed itself rarely.

"The officers asked me what happened that night," she said. "I have already given a statement."

"If you do not mind, I would like to review those activities with you, to be sure we didn't miss anything."

Since *madame* seemed agreeable, Cadieux recited the events of that evening: Isabelle Deaver had arrived at home about half past four. She stopped at the loge and greeted the concierge. There was no further activity at the Deaver residence until Mimi Deaver arrived in her carriage to call on her daughter-in-law.

The concierge bobbed her head throughout Cadieux's summary. "I remember Isabelle arrived home early because, I was sorting the afternoon mail. Usually, by the time she comes home, I have just finished delivering it. Mimi Deaver came later, around seven o'clock."

"Then what happened?" he asked.

"The elder Madame Deaver bid me good evening and went up to the Deavers' apartment. I watched her go up the stairs. She was gone for only one or two minutes. Then I saw her rushing to me from across the courtyard, frantic. I made her sit and tell me what was wrong. She told me the apartment had been vandalized, if not robbed, and she could not find Madame Deaver. After hearing that, I called for the police. I have a telephone in here." She waved at the instrument which appeared completely out of place in her rustic lodgings.

"Thank you, *madame*," Cadieux said, his voice calm and soothing. "That agrees with our records. I understand there was no activity at the Deaver apartment between the arrivals of the two ladies, but tell me, did anyone come to call on any of your other residents during that time?"

"No one." Her tone indicated she'd been asked before and was quite certain of her answer. "Many of the residents work during the day. They returned home around that time, but they were people I recognized and expected to see." With her index finger she poked at her own chest. "I do my job, *monsieur l'inspecteur*."

"Of course you do," Cadieux said. "No one is claiming otherwise." He glanced at George and me, asking if we had questions. I did.

"I understand you must get very busy at certain times of day," I said. "When the post arrives, for example. Or when residents return from their daily work."

She gave me a cautious nod, so I continued. "So I don't suppose you'd notice when one of your residents crosses the courtyard to visit another."

She frowned and shook her head. "I am generally too busy to notice such things, *madame*."

"Madame Clement and Madame Deaver were friends," I said. "I am told they visited each other from time to time."

The concierge nodded, her gaze somewhere in the past. "Ah, yes. The Clements and the Deavers started with only a slight acquaintance. In fact, I think Madame Clement was a bit distrustful of Madame Deaver. She was so beautiful after all, and Monsieur Clement certainly noticed." The concierge narrowed one eye. "And Madame Clement noticed him noticing. Whenever her husband left the building, I could look up and be sure to see her watching out the window."

"Perhaps she missed him," I said.

She gave me a look that seemed to ask how I could be so naïve. I felt compelled to respond.

"Men," I said.

"Indeed," she continued. "But Madame Deaver was determined to befriend Madame Clement." The woman's expression grew somber. "Madame Clement had been such a cheerful, energetic young woman. A writer. She was always researching some interesting story and writing about it. Then she suffered the accident last summer. It was so disheartening to watch her struggle simply to walk. The poor dear."

I could see that George and Cadieux had begun to lose patience and were eager to redirect this conversation, but I wanted to hear more, so I spoke up first. "But she had a friend in Isabelle," I prompted. The way Jeanne had spoken up for Isabelle to Mimi led me to believe she had valued that friendship.

"Madame Deaver visited her often. She made her get out of her chair and walk, or simply sat with her on days Madame Clement was in too much pain." The concierge clutched her hands together as if she were praying. "It was so sad to see the young woman sitting at her window, watching the rest of us go about our business and wishing she could take part."

"Did she do that often?" I asked. I was getting the feeling *madame* saw much more than she let on.

"She was very sad," the woman said. "It wasn't only her injury, but she lost her baby at the same time."

"How tragic!" *Poor Jeanne.*

The concierge nodded. "You would think she would be bitter and jealous of Madame Deaver, but the two of them had the best of friendships."

That comment stopped me for a moment. "Jealous, why? Are you saying Madame Deaver was with child?" I cast a surreptitious glance at Cadieux to see that this was news to him. But then again, why would he have made such an inquiry?

"Yes," she said, glancing in confusion at our confusion.

"Are you certain of this?" Cadieux asked.

"Yes," she repeated. "Madame Deaver did not show, but I

have had four children of my own and I can tell. I asked her one day and she told me that she was indeed expecting a child." She leaned toward us as if secrecy still mattered. "She had not told Monsieur Deaver yet, so I have never said anything to him about the matter."

"Back to the evening in question," George said. Thank goodness he was still thinking, because my own mind was simply spinning with all these details. "Did you happen to notice if Madame Clement paid a call on Madame Deaver?"

"Yes." The older woman bobbed her head. "Shortly after Madame Deaver arrived home, I saw Madame Clement walking with her cane across the courtyard. I remember because I had to marvel at how well she managed the stairs up to Madame Deaver's apartment."

"You didn't mention this to the police at the time?" Cadieux asked.

"No, why would I? They were friends, after all."

"Of course," I said. "They were friends." One of whom had caught the eye of the other's husband. And if that wasn't bad enough, Isabelle was pregnant when an accident had put an end to Jeanne's pregnancy.

Chapter Sixteen

In order to call on Jeanne Clement alone, I'd had to do battle with George, who, after hearing what the concierge had to say, was newly suspicious of her. But Cadieux saw the benefit of my speaking with Jeanne on my own and defended the decision. He convinced George to wait in the courtyard below, outside the entrance. Madame la concierge would know he was there, and any casual passerby would simply think he was taking in the sun. Cadieux would go across the courtyard to interview Carlson Deaver.

Jeanne was in her salon reading when her maid showed me in. After an initial moment of surprise upon seeing me, her face brightened. She closed her book and came to her feet with open arms. "Frances," she said. "How good of you to call on me. My husband is out for the day, and I have nothing with which to occupy myself but a second reading of *Le superbe Orénoque*."

"I love Jules Verne," I said. "But I would think you'd be writing when you have some time to yourself."

She flapped a hand. "I am too dull today to put words to paper." She kissed my cheeks and, in her shuffling gait, led me to a cozy seating area. I took a chair near the coffee table.

"We shall have coffee, some pastries, and a cozy chat," she said, sending the maid off for the first two items and seating herself in the chair next to mine.

"How is your sister and her *petit bébé*?"

"Lily is asleep in a chair in my salon while Mother watches Amelia, who is teething by the way."

"We have no children of our own," she said, "but even I understand that is a difficult time for the baby."

"And for the mother," I added. "I'm not sure why Lily is so determined to take all of Ameila's care onto her own shoulders."

Jeanne looked doubtful. "You do not suppose her mother-in-law has something to do with that?"

"Maybe to a small degree. Patricia has made it clear that she thinks all child care is a mother's job, and I know Lily would like to please her, but my sister has a strong will. I can't see her bowing to someone else's, even that of her mother-in-law, particularly when it's making her own life so difficult. Our own mother is far more overbearing than Mrs. Kendrick, and Lily never gave in to her."

"I'm sure you know your sister well, and I hope she eventually does what's best for her," she said in a noncommittal way. "By the way, I read in the paper that an actress was found murdered at the Sarah Bernhardt Theater yesterday. Does that have anything to do with Isabelle's murder?"

"We don't know yet, but the police suspect it may be connected. In fact, that's why I'm here. Because you live so close to the Deavers, I wanted to ask you if you've ever seen Berthe Pepin visiting them?" Though I doubted the likelihood of such a visit, I thought it a reasonable excuse as any and gave her a brief description of Berthe.

"Is that the name of the poor victim?" Her gaze sharpened. "Are you saying Isabelle and this Berthe were acquainted with each other?"

"They worked together when Isabelle was acting." I didn't

mention Carlson's connection to Berthe. Jeanne didn't need to know everything, although as Isabelle's friend, perhaps she already did know.

"She doesn't sound familiar to me, but I understand Isabelle gave up acting when she married Carlson. I only met Isabelle last spring, so I don't know how I would have met this other actress. Unless you think she visited Isabelle. If so, I'm sure the concierge would know about it."

"I'm sure you are right." *Drat!* "I didn't think to ask when we spoke to her."

Jeanne sank back in her chair, her head slowly moving back and forth. "Now, I see. *Madame la concierge* sent you to me, didn't she? I can hear her now, telling you to check with the poor lame woman across the courtyard. Jeanne has nothing to do but gaze out the window at her neighbors and wish she could walk again. Did she also tell you I worried I'd lose my husband to Isabelle? She seemed to think that was a likely possibility even if I didn't." Jeanne slapped her palm on the arm of her chair. "How I hate being an object of pity."

I nearly blurted an apology for the situation, then bit it back, thinking that was exactly her objection—everyone feeling sorry for her. "If it makes you feel any better, I don't believe she was expressing pity but sympathy. She also expressed admiration for how far you've progressed since your injury." She hadn't said anything of the sort, but she ought to have.

Jeanne eyed me with suspicion. "You forget that I know the woman. She gives me that you-poor-dear look every time she sees me, and I hate it. I don't want to be pitied. I'd rather be thought a suspect."

If so, this was her lucky day. I lifted my hands, palms up. "Congratulations?"

Her confusion quickly turned to disbelief. "You suspect me?"

"We have not been able to strike your name from the list, but if you could answer a few questions . . ."

The maid returned at that moment with a tray of coffee and flaky pastries. Jeanne gave her a broad smile. "Did you hear that, Aimee? I am a suspect in a murder case. Can you believe it?"

The maid placed the tray on the table between Jeanne and I. "No, *madame*," she said as calmly as if Jeanne had asked her to rearrange the cups. "You would find some other way out of your problem. You would not resort to murder." She gave Jeanne a nod and stepped out of the room.

Jeanne slid forward in her seat and poured me a cup of coffee. "Well, there you have it, Frances. I'm too intelligent to be a murderer. But then, Aimee is a loyal servant. You can't believe a word she says in my defense." She handed me the cup. "You must try one of these pastries." Her words ended in a snicker. "If you dare!"

For goodness' sake, she truly did prefer to be thought a suspect. Her mood had gone from gloomy to giddy. "You are intelligent, Jeanne, but it is not murder that I suspect."

"No?" Her voice held a note of disappointment. "Then what is this about? What do you think I have done?"

"The concierge did mention seeing you looking out the window frequently." I gestured to the large window next to her desk. "It overlooks the courtyard, does it not? I assume when you work, you see everyone coming or going. It must be terribly distracting."

"Sometimes people moving about the courtyard catch my eye, but I am generally quite focused when I'm writing," she said.

"And when you aren't writing? You move around well now, and I suspect you are in far less pain than a year ago. But this past winter, sitting in a chair by the window had to be preferable to tackling the stairs and going out." I shrugged. "So, perhaps you watched the activity in the courtyard. Maybe you saw more than you are willing to admit."

She heaved a sigh. "I assume your questions are inspired by *la concierge*. How ironic of her to accuse me of spying."

"Perhaps, but isn't that part of her job? To watch out for tenants and ensure their safety?"

"Gossiping about us is not part of her job."

"We were speaking to her in an official capacity as part of our investigation of Isabelle's murder. It was not gossip."

"But you said you don't believe I murdered Isabelle."

"No, but I think you were watching Isabelle and those who came to visit her. You know something about her and her friends."

Jeanne stared at me blankly.

"Two of her friends recently received letters that suggested they'd done something horrible. Perhaps murder."

Her expression cleared. "And you think I saw something out that window and sent those letters." She shook a finger at me. "You are only the second person I know who does not underestimate me, and I appreciate that, but my life is not as interesting as you suggest. Perhaps I must rally more ambition, do you think?"

I'd been reasonably confident Jeanne hadn't killed Isabelle, but I had wondered if she was the blackmailer. Now even that was looking unlikely.

Jeanne waved a hand. "I am teasing you. There must be something about the notes that made you think of me. What can I do to prove my innocence?"

"The paper came from Deauville—pale blue with a wave motif in the upper left corner. The stationers on rue Olliffe are the only ones to sell it."

"That would be too dear for me, considering all the writing I do. If it will clear me of suspicion, please check my desk."

I had come to the conclusion that Jeanne was not the blackmailer, but I had a feeling telling her that would be more of an insult than conducting a search. I put down my cup and stepped over to the desk, opening the drawers along the left side. There was no sign of the blackmailer's paper. Nor did I see it in the center drawer or on the shelves to the side. Though I hadn't expected to find it, I was still left frustrated. I took a seat in the desk chair and gazed out the window.

"The concierge may be a gossip, but she was not wrong." Jeanne spoke in a low voice, almost as if she were speaking to herself. "I did worry about Étienne when I first saw Isabelle. She was so beautiful, so graceful. Étienne and Carlson would share a brandy or have a game of cards once or twice a month, but I never went with him. He called on them alone a few times after my accident before he suggested I come with him to meet Carlson's wife. I saw right away that Carlson didn't appreciate her. Étienne noticed, too, and he took pains to include her in the conversation and compliment her on the décor, or her clothing—whatever he could think of."

She sighed. "He was being kind. If I were a kinder person, I'd have done the same. Instead, I became jealous. Why wouldn't Étienne prefer her over me? I thought. She was the fresh bloom of spring and with my damaged leg, I was clearly autumn in decay.

"I watched them both," she continued, "believing and fearing that these two exceptional people would surely come together. But we continued to visit them once a week. I saw how Carlson discounted everything Isabelle did or said. How he belittled her and contradicted her. How she often looked like a kicked dog, curling into herself for protection."

Jeanne finally looked across the room at me. "I am speaking metaphorically of course. I have no idea if Carlson ever raised a hand to her, but he beat the spirit out of her all the same. She was a broken woman. More broken than me, and still, she tried to help me. It took me far too long—several weeks—to get over my jealousy and finally see what Étienne saw—a woman who needed my sympathy, a woman who needed a friend. I, who am so lucky to have a husband who loves me, through sickness and health, had to reach out to this poor woman who could never do anything right in the eyes of her husband."

I sat silently at the desk while Jeanne lost herself in her story.

"I tried to become a friend to her, but even though she was happy to help me physically, she never let me get close. I think Carlson made her distrust everyone but him. She didn't think she was good enough for him," Jeanne continued. "She thought they should divorce, but he wouldn't agree to it."

Interesting, this was the first I'd heard of divorce. "Do you think he murdered her?"

She shook her head. "I don't know."

"What do you think of Mimi Deaver?"

"I never met her before the luncheon at your apartment. She was a surprise." Jeanne laughed. "Well, not at first. At first, she was exactly what I expected—cruel and cutting and rather frightening."

I couldn't argue with that description.

"I don't know if Mimi spoke that way to her, but Isabelle believed Mimi didn't like her and wanted someone better for Carlson. From what I understand, Carlson didn't treat his mother much better than he did Isabelle, but Mimi didn't care. I think that meant that she knew her worth. Isabelle did not.

"At your luncheon," she continued, "once Mimi stopped flinging insults, she was less intimidating. She was human and likable. I don't know if she ever showed that side to Isabelle or if they ever warmed up to one another, but toward the end, just before Isabelle was killed, Mimi started visiting her more frequently—and always when Carlson was gone."

I rose from the desk and returned to my seat near Jeanne, absently picking up my coffee. "Would you have noticed if someone, probably two men, had slipped into the courtyard and broken into the Deavers' apartment that night?"

She gave me a mirthless smile. "Are you telling me *madame la concierge* didn't see anyone?"

"She did not, but she also stepped away from the loge to deliver the evening post."

Jeanne chewed on her lip. "I saw Isabelle come home early from her work that day. That was unusual. Because she was pregnant, I worried that something was wrong, so I went to her apartment. It took me a while to hobble over there, but she was happy to see me and hugged me. Then she very firmly sent me on my way, telling me there was nothing wrong. Her mother-in-law was coming for her soon, and she had no time to visit. I wished her a good evening and came home. By the time I climbed the stairs to my apartment, Mimi had already arrived."

I nearly choked on my coffee. "You saw her? That was about five o'clock?"

Jeanne drew back. I suppose I had pounced on her words. "About that time, yes. I saw that a cab had pulled up at the open gate. I assumed it was Mimi when I saw a woman in a red opera cape."

Right or wrong, I wanted to believe everything Jeanne told me. I hated to imagine her betraying her friendship with Isabelle, and it was difficult to conceive how she would have accomplished the murder of her friend. Though she still required the assistance of a cane, her physical condition would have been much worse eight months ago. How could she have moved Isabelle's body? How could she have caused the damage Cadieux mentioned?

She was certainly capable of the threatening letters. However, I hadn't found the writing paper in her apartment, and how would she have come into possession of Isabelle's jewelry?

We finally finished the coffee and pastry, and by the time I left Jeanne, I concluded that she must be innocent of both crimes. I headed back downstairs to the main foyer and almost screamed when George stepped up beside me. I placed one hand on my pounding heart and the other on his shoulder.

"Heavens, you startled me!"

"Sorry, darling," he said, offering his arm. "That was not my intention, but I've been waiting in that little corner for what seems like hours for you."

I'd totally forgotten that George had been waiting down here in case Jeanne had been of a murderous mind. I took his arm, and we left the building for the fresh air in the courtyard. "I'm sorry you had to wait so long, but once Jeanne had coffee brought in, it would have been rude to decline it."

"You had coffee, did you?" he said. "That's all right. I had a young lady keeping me company."

My feet froze on the gravel. George took another step before glancing at me in question. "A young lady kept you company in the foyer while you waited for me, ostensibly to save my life if necessary?"

"Uh-hum." He returned to my side and tucked my hand around his arm. "She was simply charming—laughing and dancing."

"Dancing?" I stared at him, my jaw slack.

"Yes, she was showing me a particular ballet step."

"Ballet?"

"Then her mother called her home."

"Indeed?" I studied his expression through the corner of my eye while I allowed him to lead me down the remaining steps. "How old was this young lady, George?"

"A gentleman never asks—"

"George!"

"About five or six." He flashed an innocent grin.

I shook my head. "My mother told me you were a rascal. I think she was right."

We crossed the courtyard, said goodbye to the concierge, and crossed the street where Cadieux's driver was waiting with the carriage. He scampered down without saying a word and opened the door for us.

To my surprise, Cadieux was already inside.

"Goodness," I said, climbing in across from him, "I assumed we'd be waiting for you."

"Actually, I had begun to wonder if I should come looking for the two of you."

"Don't blame me," George said, hopping in beside me. "I was just waiting outside all this time."

"Watching a young lady dance," I added.

Cadieux looked confused. "What?"

"Nothing," we both said at once.

He clucked his tongue. "At least, tell me you have the case solved by now."

"I do not." Goodness, men were demanding. "Jeanne and I had a long conversation, and she made me understand Isabelle a little more, but I don't believe Jeanne is our culprit, and she had no suspicions as to who was." I explained that Jeanne's injury had been far worse nine months ago and that she would have had a difficult time overwhelming Isabelle, not to mention moving her body. "Besides, I believe their friendship was genuine and close. I don't think Jeanne would have hurt Isabelle."

"That's unfortunate, we were pinning all our hopes on you," George said. "Now I suppose we'll have to do it ourselves, eh, Cadieux?"

"It always seems to work that way," the inspector said. "Did you learn anything new, *madame*?"

"Jeanne confirmed that Isabelle really did come home early after working at the Daughters of Charity on the day of her murder," I said. "Jeanne saw her arrive, and fearing something wrong with Isabelle or the baby, called on her. They spoke briefly, then Isabelle sent Jeanne away, saying Mimi would be around soon. It took her some time to walk back to her own apartment, and before she made it inside, a cab had arrived at the gate. She saw a woman in an opera cape step out and assumed it was Mimi."

"Is she certain about the time," Cadieux asked.

"She thought it was about five o'clock when she saw the cab stop at the gate," I said. "The concierge said Isabelle arrived home about half-past four, so Jeanne's story rings true. I find it strange that Mimi would take a cab rather than her own carriage, but someone else in an opera cape is too much of a coincidence."

"The concierge told us Mimi arrived later than that," George said.

"Yes, but this earlier time would have been when the concierge was delivering the mail," Cadieux said. "If it was Mimi Deaver, she could have entered the building unseen. I must have another conversation with Madame Deaver." Cadieux jotted a note to himself, then glanced at me. "I don't suppose Madame Clement had any information about the letters?"

"She denied writing them, of course," I said. "And I did not find the paper we're looking for in her apartment."

"In that, I am equally empty-handed," Cadieux said. "Monsieur Deaver told me he hadn't been to Deauville in years, and I've yet to find any reason for him to want both his wife and mistress dead. When I questioned him about any enemies of his who might have harmed them, he was shocked at the very idea and denied that he had any enemies. He still thinks we should be pressing Madame Bernhardt more."

Cadieux sighed and pulled a folded sheet of paper from his pocket. "I did, however, acquire a handwriting sample," he said. "So even though I couldn't find the paper, we can do a comparison to the threatening letters, not that I think it will help us much."

"That's something, I suppose," I said. "Is that all we have?"

"No," George said with a snap of his fingers. "We have the wealth of social information your mother managed to obtain from New York, the former home of the Deavers. I'd forgotten to mention that."

Cadieux looked quite interested in this information until I informed him that George meant gossip.

"It sounded quite credible to me," he countered. "Though it really leads to even more questions." He proceeded to tell Cadieux of the late Mr. Deaver's violent temper, which may have led Mimi to leave him and ultimately follow her son to Paris.

"I thought the upper classes were too genteel for such behavior," Cadieux said.

"Not at all. They just don't call in the police," I said. "The volatility of their former homelife might explain why Mimi is so protective of her son and unwilling to give him up to a wife."

Cadieux made a face of disgust. "Do you think it possible that she murdered his wife and mistress?"

"Isabelle was expecting her that evening," I said. "Someone arrived at the gate in a cab around five o'clock, far earlier than necessary to depart for the opera. Even if Jeanne is mistaken, and it wasn't Mimi, would a burglar have a cab drop him off?"

"If it was a typical house breaker, no," Cadieux said. "But just because we believed they didn't expect to find Madame Deaver at home, doesn't mean we were right. They may always have intended to abduct her." He opened his hands in a who knows? gesture. "It's also possible it was simply another resident arriving home."

"Wearing an opera cape?" I asked.

"Even if it wasn't Mimi who arrived earlier," George said, "she must still be a suspect. It's possible she arrived at seven, as the concierge stated, murdered Isabelle, made a mess of the house, then ran back to the concierge to send for the police."

"That would give her a short amount of time to hide the body," Cadieux mused. "But she knew the apartment well, I suppose it's not impossible."

"She disapproved of her son's marriage to Isabelle, and it's possible she thought Carlson was on the verge of offering marriage to Berthe," George said. "That could be motive for both murders. One of the chefs at the charity where Isabelle volunteered recognized a photograph of Mimi, and Isabelle's body was found near there."

"I think we may have neglected to mention that," I added.

"I believe you did, but now that you have, I think it's time I had a talk with Madame Deaver." He glanced at the two of us. "Do you care to join me?"

"We wouldn't miss it."

Chapter Seventeen

George and I had considered Mimi a potential suspect since we first began to work on this case. She certainly had the opportunity. As for motive, if she was trying to protect her son, that would serve both for Isabelle and Berthe, but try as I might, something kept me from believing it.

And I was beginning to feel that Inspector Cadieux was more determined than confident that Mimi was the culprit. This was an old case. Our list of suspects was dwindling. Evidence was scarce, and memories were fading. If no arrest was ever made, a shadow of doubt would always linger over Carlson Deaver—and possibly over Sarah Bernhardt, too.

But Mimi? Though I felt she knew more than she was willing to tell the police, I couldn't see her as a murderer. Perhaps Cadieux's questions would force her to reveal something.

The driver stopped the cab outside the walled garden surrounding the house she shared with the *comte*. It was accessed by a gate, which was unlocked. George and I stood aside while Cadieux rang the bell, then spoke to the maid who answered the door. She would have left us to wait on the stoop had he not insisted she let us inside while she checked to see if *madame* was at home.

"Well done, inspector," I murmured as I stepped past him to follow the maid. "I never made it past the foyer when I last called here."

It was quite eye-opening to see the luxury in which Mimi lived. We trailed the maid down the marble-floored hallway, partially covered with sumptuous rugs, past the dimly lit salon, and into a miniscule office where she left us while she went to see about her mistress. I knew how much the upkeep on such a house could cost, not to mention the furnishings. If rumors about Henri's lack of fortune were true, Mimi was spending a great deal of hers on this place.

George looked around at what was little more than a closet. "Out of all the rooms we just walked past, she brings us here?"

"One might think we were unwelcome," I said. "There's barely space in here for the three of us."

"Actually, this could be fortuitous." George rounded the desk, picking up odd papers and opening drawers. "Inspector, you may wish to look the other way."

I took the papers from George's hand and placed them back on the desktop. "Stop it, George. There's no room for him to turn the other way, and I don't feel comfortable snooping through Mimi's things."

"Odd, it doesn't bother me a bit." George slid open the top drawer and glanced up. "There's a window right there, inspector. Damn fine view I'd wager."

"Indeed," Cadieux said, facing the window.

"Honestly, the two of you are incorrigible. What if she comes in here and sees you going through her things?"

George straightened, holding a sheet of paper—a very familiar sheet of paper with a blue wave motif. Unlike the threatening notes, it held a great deal more writing. "Then I'd ask her to explain this," he said.

I bit my lip. Perhaps I ought not defend Mimi.

Cadieux turned from the window just as the door opened. The sharpening of his gaze told me he recognized the paper and the blackmailer's scrawl.

Still trying to collect my wits, I stepped aside to allow Mimi to enter the room, which she did with all the dignity of a queen, her jade silk skirt swished against the doorframe. Though I had considered her a suspect for Isabelle's murder, it was with a growing reluctance. The thought of her as the blackmailer, never entered my mind, but I had to wonder—was she the recipient or sender of that letter?

Mimi's hand rose to the many ropes of pearls around her neck as she eyed us from the threshold. I spared a glance for George, whose hands were miraculously empty, then turned back to our unwitting hostess.

"Good afternoon, Mimi," I said. "I hope you can forgive us for dropping in on you like this."

"So good of you to see us," George added.

"How could I not?" she said. "My maid tells me you have brought a police officer with you, and I am bursting with curiosity." Though she sounded calm, Mimi's tone was less than pleasant.

"Inspector Cadieux of the Sûreté," George said. "He has some questions we hope you will be willing to answer."

Mimi gave George an assessing look. "And the two of you?"

"We are assisting the investigation."

"Indeed? Then I suggest we move to the salon. I think we'll be far more comfortable in there." She led us a short way down the hall to the far more spacious room. Still, the word comfortable didn't come to mind upon viewing the highly formal salon, where the sound of our footsteps echoed off all the marble—floors, fireplace, and Grecian style columns. Except for the furnishings, which were modern, the room seemed to be from a much earlier age. The north-facing windows left the room gloomy.

Mimi drew us to an area arranged for conversation, and we all took seats. "Now, how can I help you?" she asked.

Cadieux explained that the police were once again looking into the murder of her daughter-in-law. "My son told me as much," she said. "It seems a note has surfaced that you feel is related to poor Isabelle."

"Yes, that has prompted us to review the old evidence and question witnesses again, such as yourself." Cadieux's tone was gentle, inviting confidence.

"Indeed? Am I a witness?"

"You were the first to note her disappearance and, of course, the state of her apartment," he replied. "Would you mind if I asked you about that night again?"

Mimi compressed her lips but gave him a nod to go ahead.

Cadieux pulled a note pad from his pocket and flipped the pages until he found what he was looking for. "What time did you arrive at your son's apartment?" he asked.

"I don't recall the exact time, but we were to attend the opera together, so I suppose I arrived about seven o'clock."

"In your carriage?"

"Of course."

"Did you send your driver or attendant up to escort Madame Deaver back to the carriage?"

"I did not bring an attendant, and the horses were a bit jumpy, so I left the driver to deal with them and went to fetch Isabelle myself."

"At about seven o'clock?"

"As I stated."

Mimi's composure was faltering. Having a police inspector in one's home asking questions is unsettling enough. When those questions are about murder, it becomes significantly worse. Mimi was no longer meeting Cadieux's gaze, and her hands would not lay still in her lap. Perhaps I was wrong about her.

"Obviously, Madame Deaver did not answer your knock," Cadieux continued. "What made you go inside, and what did you see?"

"The apartment door was ajar, which struck me as odd, since it was the middle of January. I didn't knock, I pushed it open." She paused and ran a hand across her eyes. "The place was a shambles—glassware broken on the floor, a potted palm knocked over, the soil strewn over the carpet. Carlson had a cabinet in the salon that held glasses and bottles of spirits and wine. The doors were thrown open, and much of the contents lay broken on the floor."

Mimi rubbed her hands over her arms as if the memory chilled her. "After taking a few steps past the door, I stopped. It looked as though the damage had just happened, and I feared that whoever had done this was still in the apartment. I hurried back to the gate and had the concierge telephone the police. Then I went back to the carriage and waited for them to arrive."

"You never looked for your daughter-in-law?"

"No, I told you, I feared the perpetrators were still inside. I'm ashamed to say I didn't even call out to her."

Cadieux cocked his head. "Did you hear crashing sounds or footsteps?" He waved a hand. "General sounds of intruders?"

Mimi folded her hands in her lap and straightened her back. "No, nothing like that. I cannot explain my fear, I can only tell you that it existed. I later learned of course, that they were no longer there." She sniffed. "Nor was Isabelle."

"Then you returned to your carriage to wait?"

"I did."

Cadieux cocked his head. "Why were you and Isabelle going to the opera?"

Mimi blinked. "I beg your pardon?"

"Why were you going to the opera, or anywhere for that matter, with your daughter-in-law? The general consensus is that you despised her. Why would you choose to spend an evening in her company?"

I was beginning to feel nervous for Mimi. I caught George's eye, and he shook his head. The message was clear—do not interfere.

Mimi leaned forward, her hands gripping the arms of her chair. "And who makes up this general consensus? The local gossips? Women who had tried to lead my son to the altar but failed?"

"The opinions came from people close to Isabelle, neighbors, friends, even your son believed you disapproved of his choice." Cadieux's gaze was unwavering. "Why the sudden change of heart?"

"I was surprised by my son's choice, and I admit that I was not particularly welcoming when I first met Isabelle." Mimi sat back, stroking her pearls between her fingers. "However, I felt she deserved a chance, and over time our relationship became at first cordial and then warm. Now, I would like to know what is prompting this inquisition. I have answered these questions before. If you are accusing me of something, I'd like to know what it is. If not, then you should leave and stop wasting my time."

"Very well," the inspector said. "We have a witness who claims you arrived at your son's apartment two hours before the time you claim to have arrived. More than enough time for you to have murdered Isabelle."

I saw a flash of fear in her eyes before her jaw tightened. "Your witness is mistaken. It was January after all. Evening comes early at that time of year. It may well be that they simply recall my arriving after dark."

But it hadn't been after dark. Jeanne remembered a woman in a red opera cape. Was it Mimi? It would be quite a coincidence if two women dressed for the opera showed up at the Deaver apartment that evening. This time Cadieux caught my eye. I had been the one to interview the neighbor after all. I couldn't forget that Jeanne had said Isabelle and Mimi had come to terms with one another. Though I couldn't see Mimi murdering Isabelle, Cadieux was waiting for an answer.

"It wasn't yet dark when a woman in a red opera cape was seen arriving in a cab at the apartment building."

Mimi stared at me, aghast. "Frances, you don't know what you're saying. It wasn't me. I did not kill Isabelle." Her eyes filled with panic and the sight tore at my heart. "For heaven's sake, I haven't the skills even to defend myself. How could I have done what was done to that girl?"

That girl. Her words sent a jolt through me. Not Isabelle, but *that girl*. She didn't do it. I had sensed it, but I couldn't explain why until now, and the explanation was so diabolical I found it hard to believe myself. I had no idea how I'd convince George and Cadieux. Before I could say anything, George stood up and held out the note.

"Perhaps you can explain this," he said.

Mimi looked at the note without touching it, then gave George a challenging look. "I don't know what you mean."

Cadieux stepped up and took the letter from George, looking it over casually as if he already knew what it said. "More than one note on this paper has found its way into our hands. 'I know what you did' was all they said." He showed her the letter. "Now this one is demanding payment. Somebody knows what you did and means to make you pay. Or are you the blackmailer?"

Mimi sighed and hung her head.

Cadieux came to his feet and took a step toward her. "Which is it, Madame Deaver? Either you murdered Isabelle Deaver or you know who did."

"I didn't kill her," Mimi sobbed, but she gazed at Cadieux as if she knew this was the end.

"She didn't," I said. I didn't even recall moving but found

myself standing beside Cadieux. "And I don't think she is the blackmailer, either."

George squinted at me. "Are you defending her?"

"I think there is more to this than meets the eye." I turned to face Mimi. "During this investigation, we have learned a few things about your past. One of those things was that you were a victim of your husband's temper."

Mimi dropped her gaze to her hands once more.

"As Mimi stated," I continued, "she couldn't defend herself, but she could run away. She put an ocean between herself and her husband. I'm fairly sure she didn't murder Isabelle." I bent down and met Mimi's gaze as she lifted her head. "I think I know what happened that night, at least generally," I said. "But you must explain it to them."

She lifted her hands to her eyes as her tears began to flow. "My intentions were good," she said between sobs.

George stepped beside me and placed his arm around my shoulders. "Frances, I think it's quite clear that she is our murderer."

"No, George—"

"Think of it," he said. "She was in the apartment alone with Isabelle. Berthe had one of those notes when her body was found. It looks like Mimi sent her the note. And she very likely killed her. She could easily have slipped backstage after the performance."

"That is a good point," Cadieux said. "Can anyone verify your whereabouts Thursday night, *madame*? Friends? Servants?"

"No," she said without lifting her head.

"I suspect Mimi is covering for the blackmailer," I said. "The only person who had a grudge against Berthe."

I never took my gaze off Mimi, waiting for some confirmation from her that I'd gotten this right. Finally, she raised her gaze to meet mine. The fear in her eyes pushed me on. "Mimi, are you willing to go to prison for her?"

She released a heavy sigh, gave me an almost imperceptible nod. "I was not at the theater on Thursday. I was here. With Isabelle," she whispered.

"Isabelle?" Cadieux echoed. "You misspoke, Madame. You said the victim's name. Who did you mean to name?"

"She meant Isabelle," I said. "I believe she was a victim in one sense, but Mimi didn't kill her. In fact, she isn't dead. Is she, Mimi?"

Mimi paused, then her voice shook as she said, "No."

Cadieux tilted his head in confusion, while George's eyes grew wide. I continued: "However, I do think Isabelle wrote the threatening letters. She is the blackmailer, and I think she may have killed Berthe."

"No!"

A second voice had echoed Mimi's shout. We all turned to see that a panel in the wall next to the bookshelf was open, revealing a tall but oddly fragile-looking woman, her lovely face surrounded by a cloud of dark curls.

"Gentlemen," I said. "I give you the late Isabelle Deaver."

I love it when I'm right.

Chapter Eighteen

George and Cadieux goggled at the new arrival. Understandably, I suppose. After all, they hadn't had enough time to fully take in what I'd said, so they likely thought they were seeing a ghost. I was still amazed that my guess was correct.

Isabelle, clearly alive, rushed across the room to Mimi, who had come to her feet and opened her arms to her daughter-in-law. She shook her head as Isabelle stepped into her embrace.

"You shouldn't have come out," Mimi said.

"I could hardly watch him take you away for murdering me."

Mimi turned to face the three of us, drawing a deep breath as if to brace herself. "As you see, Isabelle is not dead, so I'd like you to leave us now. You can have nothing more to discuss with me."

Cadieux's expression was tight with anger. "You are very much mistaken, *madame*. We have a great deal to discuss with both of you." His tone was sharp as he pointed a finger at Isabelle, causing her to shrink into Mimi. "Not the least of which is who is buried in your grave?"

I took a step back when he turned his angry gaze to me. "And I would like also to know how you knew what these two were up to. And why you did not share your knowledge of their deception?"

He waved a hand at the group of us. "All of you take a seat," he ordered. Sitting down himself, he picked up his note pad from the coffee table, slapped it on his knee, and glared at us one at a time.

When his gaze landed on me, I protested. "I don't know how I've managed to anger you, inspector. It's not as if I've known the answer all along. When Mimi referred to the dead woman as 'that girl,' it just came to me—everything started adding up. Jeanne told me Carlson wouldn't agree to a divorce. The concierge told us Isabelle was with child. We suspected Carlson was violent—as they say, like father, like son—and she needed to get away from him. Running away was her only option, but Carlson had enough money to search for her for years, if he wanted to. Isabelle needed to give him a reason not to search. Therefore, nobody killed Isabelle, and Isabelle killed Berthe."

"I did no such thing," Isabelle said.

"How did you come to that conclusion?" Mimi looked shocked.

George and Cadieux waited attentively.

"Well, it's obvious, isn't it?"

Cadieux leaned back in his seat, crossing his arms.

George raised his hands helplessly. "Apparently, not, my dear. Do you care to enlighten us?"

Well, not as obvious as I'd thought. "Berthe was Carlson's mistress. Isabelle was the only one with a motive to kill her."

I turned when Isabelle gasped.

"So, now that we know Isabelle is alive—"

"I didn't kill Berthe," she insisted.

"Actually, prior to suspecting Mimi, I thought we suspected

the blackmailer for that crime," George said, "—that he confronted Berthe after the performance at the theater."

"Yes," I said. "I assume that also would have been Isabelle's doing."

"Just what kind of a person do you think I am?" Isabelle looked horrified.

Mimi patted her daughter-in-law's hand. "If it had been Isabelle, why would she have sent a note to Sarah Bernhardt?"

"And this note." Cadieux raised the letter we'd found in Mimi's office.

Mimi lifted her hands helplessly. "Neither of us can imagine who might have sent it."

That's right, I'd concocted this theory about Isabelle as the blackmailer before I knew Mimi had helped her. When Mimi had said she couldn't have done what had been done to "*that girl*," rather than to Isabelle, it had confirmed my suspicion that Isabelle was still alive. Perhaps my excitement had caused me to act hastily. I glanced around at my audience, embarrassed and contrite. "I see that I must retract my statement. I do not know who murdered Berthe."

"Thank you for that small concession." Mimi's voice was heavy with sarcasm. Unnecessary, in my opinion. Anyone might have made the same mistake.

Cadieux leaned forward, resting his forearms on his knees and eyeing the two Deaver women. "We will return to this blackmail letter in a moment. Right now, let us begin at the beginning," he said. "Why did you start this pretense, and how did you manage it?"

Mimi and Isabelle shared a look, then Mimi sighed. "I'll start," she said. "My husband, Carlson's father, had a nasty temper, though he managed it well enough in public. I'm not sure how you knew"—Mimi glanced my way—"but it's true. It was the kind of trait one doesn't discover until one comes to know a man well. I won't delve into the details of our life together, but after twenty-five years of trying and failing to get away from him, I finally stumbled over the perfect opportunity.

"I had proof that he managed a business deal unethically,"—she shrugged—"perhaps even illegally. I placed that proof in a sealed envelope and gave it to a friend, with instructions to send it to the *New York Times* in the event of my death or absence from public life."

"Carlson had already left on his European tour, so I packed up my daughter and our things, and I moved out. I told my husband I wouldn't seek a divorce, but I wanted a settlement all the same, and I never wanted to see him again." She grimaced. "He was angry. There was a great deal of back-and-forth between our lawyers, but in the end, he agreed, and I was free."

Cadieux, who had listened patiently to her story, spoke up in the silence that followed it. "Am I to understand that your son inherited some of his father's traits?"

"I fear that he inherited them. It was also the behavior he'd been exposed to all his life. I don't think he was as bad as his father," Mimi added, to which Isabelle scoffed.

"Perhaps he was," Mimi amended. "It came as no surprise that Carlson had no respect for the fair sex. I tried to break up any connections he made that might have led to marriage, but I couldn't be everywhere, and he never told me about Isabelle. They were already married by the time I met her. She was so gentle, and quiet, and deferential." Mimi shook her head sadly. "I knew she wouldn't be safe."

"Carlson changed completely once we were married," Isabelle said, her gaze distant. "I kept telling myself that if I tried harder to make him happy, we would be fine. Eventually, I gave up and suggested we divorce." Isabelle took a deep breath and let it out. "That was a mistake. We had a violent fight. Not only would he not agree to a divorce," she said. "He threatened that if I ever left him, he'd find me and make me regret my actions."

"I had that experience with Carlson's father," Mimi added. "When Isabelle came to me one day and told me she was with child and feared Carlson would harm the baby, I decided we had to get her out of that marriage. After hearing about Carlson's threats, I thought the only way we could succeed was if Carlson thought she was dead."

"I assume he still believes you to be dead?" George asked Isabelle.

Isabelle shrank into her chair. "He still believes I'm dead, and I would dearly like to keep it that way."

"So, the two of you put your heads together and devised a plan to fake your death?" Cadieux asked.

"New Year's Day," Mimi said. "It was a couple of weeks before we could execute it, but even the planning gave us both hope."

Isabelle nodded in agreement. "I was more than three months' pregnant, so we had to do something quickly, yet we needed the right opportunity. When I found out about Carlson's card game, I knew it would go on all night. It was perfect. We had only a light staff of three. I told them that morning that I'd be gone, so they could have the afternoon and evening off. I left the Daughters of Charity early that day. When I came home, I packed up my jewelry and anything else of value that I thought a thief might steal, and of course that I could eventually sell. Mimi provided for my immediate needs."

"I understand Jeanne Clement called on you when you arrived at home," I said.

"That's right, she did." Isabelle blinked a few times and sighed. "It was so difficult to send her away, because I knew that would be the last time I'd see her. I nearly cried, but I sent her on her way with a promise to call on her the next day. When Mimi arrived, we knocked things over, pulled the contents from the drawers, anything we thought a thief might do in search of something to steal. Then we gathered up my things and left in the cab Mimi had waiting."

"A cab," I echoed. "Of course, you wouldn't have wanted Mimi's staff to witness your departure when they were meant to witness Mimi not finding you at home later that same evening."

"Except for my maid, who helped me slip out of this house, my staff all thought I was in my bedchamber, napping or getting dressed for the evening. This was life-or-death," Mimi said. "We were very careful."

"The cab dropped us a block away from the Daughters of Charity." Isabelle continued the story. "It was shortly after six o'clock by then, and the office was closed, but throughout the month, I had been bringing clothing from home. I told anyone who inquired they were donations for the poor, but in truth, I had been packing for my departure. My bags were hidden in an unused cabinet in the kitchen. Mimi dismissed the cab that brought us, we collected my bag, and then hired another cab to take us to the train station."

Mimi squeezed her daughter-in-law's hand. "I saw Isabelle onto the train, we said our farewells, then I hired a third cab to take me home. My maid was waiting by a side door to slip me back into the house. I arrived with barely enough time to pretend I was going to the opera."

"I assume everything you did after that, matches the statement you gave to the police," Cadieux said. "At least for that night."

Mimi agreed and gave him a brief summary of her evening's activities. To the best of my recollection, they did indeed match the police report. "Where did the train take you?" I asked Isabelle, thinking I might already know the answer.

"Deauville," she said. "An old friend I knew from the theater had moved there to take care of her mother, who lived just outside of town. We had kept up a correspondence, and when she told me her mother had died, I asked if I could move in with her and share the costs. I took another name, assumed a different appearance, and gave birth to my son. Fortunately, I had her to help me with him." She smiled. "I had escaped to something of a perfect life."

Cadieux turned back to Mimi with a weary air. "The morning after the young Madame Deaver's disappearance, you came to the morgue and identified a woman's body as belonging to her. Why did you do that, and who was that woman?"

Mimi glanced at Isabelle so briefly, I wondered if I'd imagined it. "I don't know who she was," she said. "I was at Carlson's house when a police officer came by to say they had an unknown woman at the morgue. She was about Isabelle's age with dark hair and fair skin. They thought she might be Isabelle and wanted someone to come in and identify her."

She twined her fingers together as she gazed at Cadieux. "I truly thought it would be much better if Carlson believed Isabelle was dead rather than missing. Obviously, I couldn't allow him to go. Carlson had been drinking—a lot. On top of that, I had just given him some drops to make him sleep, so I volunteered to go immediately and identify her myself."

"Perhaps you aren't aware, but that in itself is a crime," Cadieux said. "What of the family of that poor unknown woman? They've no idea what happened to her."

"We do know who she was, inspector," Isabelle said, shaking her head when Mimi started protesting. "Mimi doesn't want to tell you that I had some assistance from a friend at the Daughters of Charity. He was the one who hid my bags for me, and he contacted Mimi when a woman who came to us for meals was found dead in the café across the square. He thought she looked enough like me to pass. She had come to the charity a few times. She would never accept assistance and refused to give her name, or even speak with one of us. Had your officers known that, would they have worked any harder to find her killers?"

"That's not the point," Cadieux began.

"I think it is. You asked what of her family? If she had any family, where were they while she wandered the streets, being chased away from one corner to the next? Tell me the police wouldn't simply have considered her another unfortunate soul without a name."

Cadieux frowned, possibly because she was right. "Nevertheless, you had no right to make that decision."

"She would have been buried in a pauper's grave, with no name," Isabelle said. "Is that so much different than being buried with the wrong name?"

"Again, that was not your decision to make."

"We did it to save the life of my grandson," Mimi said. "Carlson had to believe Isabelle was dead, or he'd go looking for her. If he found her, the law would give him custody of the boy. I was desperate. When I was given this opportunity to convince him, I couldn't refuse it. In fact, when I was told about the woman, I rushed to Carlson's apartment so that I would be there in case the police contacted him. If I could identify the woman as Isabelle, he'd have no reason to look for her."

"Is that why there wasn't a funeral?" I asked. "So that no one who knew Isabelle could deny that was her body? How did you fool Carlson?"

"He never looked." Mimi shook her head. "Carlson had always been fascinated with Isabelle's beauty. When I told him her face was cut and bruised and she had marks on her neck, he said he wanted to remember her as she was."

"That was quite a risk to take," I said.

Mimi nodded. "I was counting on Carlson's desire to remember Isabelle as fresh and pretty, but the woman did resemble Isabelle in enough ways that while he might not have been fooled had he seen her, he'd simply believe I was mistaken rather than deliberately lying to him. Considering what was at stake, it was a risk worth taking."

Cadieux gave me an impatient glare. I suppose we had wandered away from the point. "Who is the person that alerted you?" he asked.

"I won't tell you unless you can assure me you will not charge him with a crime," Mimi stated.

Cadieux bristled at her audacity. "What gives you the idea that you have any negotiating power in this matter?"

"Come now, inspector," George said "Whoever alerted them to the woman's death, did nothing more than everyone else in the area who went home and told their families about it."

Cadieux arched a brow. "Whose side are you working for, Hazelton?"

"I'm only pointing out the truth. You don't need the person's name."

For my part, I was quite sure the person was Victor Garaud, and I truly hoped that Cadieux wouldn't pursue it further.

"Has it occurred to either of you"—Cadieux paused and glanced at me, then George—"or any of the four of you, for that matter, that your friend at the charity could be the blackmailer?"

It hadn't.

All right, I suppose Cadieux should pursue this. "The notes read, 'I know what you did,'" I said to Isabelle and Mimi. "Your friend at the charity does know what you did, or at least knows some of it."

Mimi looked aghast, but seemed to be considering the possibility. Isabelle clearly disagreed. "He could not have done it, though I am pleased you seem to have given up the idea that I was blackmailing everyone. It would be difficult after all to blackmail myself."

"You received one of the letters?" Cadieux asked.

"Yes, I suspect I received the first of them. It was posted to me in Deauville. Whoever it is found out where I live. My letter did not say, 'I know what you did,' but, 'I know who and where you are.' It threatened to tell Carlson if I didn't pay a sum of money—a sum I didn't have."

"Do you still have the letter?" Cadieux asked.

Mimi gestured to the letter Cadieux held. "It is in your hand."

Cadieux took a longer look at the letter. "There is no salutation. I assumed it was sent to you," he said to Mimi.

"It was sent to Isabelle," Mimi said. "She brought it here to me."

"How long ago did you receive the letter?" Cadieux asked Isabelle.

"Last month," she said. "On the eighteenth."

"Do you recognize the hand?" I asked.

"No, it's not even writing at all, is it? It's just a scrawled printing. I don't know anyone who writes that way."

Cadieux nodded as he read the letter. "Your instructions were to deliver the money here in Paris," he observed. "Did you?"

"Not exactly. As I said, I didn't have such a sum"—she gestured to the letter in Cadieux's hand—"but I did have my jewelry. I didn't dare let go of all of it, but I thought the earrings alone would be worth more than he asked for. There was no way to communicate with him, so I put the earrings in an envelope and brought it to Paris—to the place in the instructions—and hoped it would be enough."

"Did you consider what might happen if the blackmailer attempted to sell them?" I asked. "The police might still have been waiting for your jewelry to show up at a pawnbroker or jewelry store."

"I didn't think of that until it was too late. Mimi and I had kept up a sparse correspondence, and I told her what I'd done. We thought if anyone did recognize my jewelry, he'd be thought a murderer rather than a blackmailer, so we hoped the man was smart enough to hold on to the earrings."

"Apparently, he wasn't that smart," George said. "He sent one of them on to Madame Bernhardt. And you were right to worry, she recognized it as yours."

"I don't understand why he sent her that letter. Or Berthe for that matter. He didn't even ask them for any money."

"I think the culprit knew you couldn't have managed to fake your death on your own," George said, "so he was making contact with other people in your life. Once he sent them the letters, he could observe how they reacted and determine which of them might have assisted you."

"I assume he didn't count on Sarah going to the police," I said. "Then things got out of hand."

"Well, that proves it couldn't have been my friend from the Daughters of Charity," Isabelle said. "He already knew that it was Mimi helping me."

"Just because the blackmailer was fishing for more accomplices, doesn't mean he didn't know about your mother-in-law," Cadieux said.

Isabelle looked uncomfortable, worrying the end of her shawl. "It was not my friend. He wouldn't do that to me. It doesn't make any sense. Why would he help me only to turn on me?"

"I'm afraid we'll have to ask him that," Cadieux said. "I'm going to need his name, *madame*. I suspect he's the blackmailer."

Cadieux stopped his accusations there, but I knew that he believed the blackmailer was also the person who killed Berthe. I think we all believed that, even if it wasn't clear why Berthe was killed, she had the threatening note.

"I promised him no harm would come to him for helping me." Isabelle shook her head. "I don't want to give you his name."

Mimi placed a hand on Isabelle's shoulder. "I understand your loyalty and desire to protect him, but if he is involved in this blackmail, he is hurting you."

Isabelle simply shook her head.

I glanced at the letter in Cadieux's hands. "It's the same paper as the other notes," I said. "The paper from the Deauville shop. I still think the blackmailer is someone who saw Isabelle in Deauville, discovered where she is living now, and purchased the paper there."

"That doesn't exclude her friend from the charity," Cadieux said. "Does he know where you live? Has he visited you there?"

Isabelle chewed her lower lip and watched Cadieux warily.

"Madame Deaver," Cadieux said with great patience. "I'm afraid you must come to terms with the possibility that the person blackmailing you and your friends is someone you knew and trusted. We know this paper comes from Deauville. You were hiding in Deauville. If your friend knew this, he is likely the blackmailer."

"I noticed nothing special about the paper." Mimi leaned over Cadieux's shoulder to get a look at the letters. "It is not so unusual. I have a supply of it and I don't recall going to Deauville to purchase it. It must be available locally."

"My officers have looked into this," Cadieux said. "If you didn't go there to buy it, perhaps it was given to you as a gift?"

She looked flummoxed. "I can't think who."

"Wherever the paper came from, the blackmailer had to be someone who knew where Isabelle was living," I said.

"Well, I hope you don't think it was me," Mimi said. "I went to far too much effort to make sure Isabelle had a safe place to hide to ever consider compromising it." She pressed a hand to her forehead and let out a *tsk*. "But you haven't seen the second letter," she said. "Isabelle is here now because the fiend is asking for another payment." She glanced at Cadieux's shocked face. "Maybe you could follow Isabelle and set some sort of trap for him?"

I almost thought I saw steam coming from Cadieux's ears. To his credit, he drew a calming breath before speaking to Mimi. "Madame, may I see that letter, please?"

Isabelle pulled a sheet of paper from her pocket and handed it over. Cadieux unfolded the page and skimmed it quickly. "*Mon Dieu!* This says you are supposed to make the payment tonight!"

Chapter Nineteen

Cadieux took a turn about the room as if composing himself. Or perhaps he simply thought better on his feet. When he returned, it was clear he'd made a decision, his forehead was no longer furrowed, and his bearing was confident as he picked up both the letters Isabelle had received and sat down next to her on the velvet settee, placing the letters side by side on the coffee table.

"Madame," he said to her, "what happened the first time you paid this person?"

"You can see the instructions." She gestured to the letter. "I went to the Tuileries Garden at the appointed time."

"That would have been right around dusk," Cadieux said, as if to himself.

"Yes," she replied. "It was just starting to grow dark. I found the bench he told me to look for and left the envelope with the earrings."

"And then what?" the inspector asked.

Isabelle looked confused. "And then I left."

Cadieux narrowed his eyes. "You didn't linger to see who picked up the package?"

"I followed the instructions to the letter. I was afraid to do anything else."

Cadieux bent forward to study the blackmail letters. George, Mimi, and I hovered behind him and Isabelle, attempting to read over their shoulders until Cadieux turned around and waved us back to our seats.

"This time he has changed the location to Luxembourg Gardens, just before they close. Madame Deaver is to leave an envelope with three thousand francs on a very specific bench in relation to the back gate."

"The garden closes at sundown, and the gates are locked," I said. "He must expect to be in the park, near enough to that bench to retrieve the envelope before anyone else does."

"And still be outside the gate before it's closed," George added. "What do you intend to do, inspector? Have some officers positioned in the garden?"

"Exactly."

"But won't that frighten him away?" Isabelle asked, twisting her fingers in her lap.

"They will not be in uniform, so he should not notice them at all," Cadieux replied. "They will appear to be enjoying the park, like everyone else."

"It is, after all, the police who close the garden and send everyone off," George said. "If he was concerned about their presence, he would have chosen a different location."

"Yes, I suppose that's true," she said. "But I don't want him frightened away."

Cadieux crossed his arms and eyed Isabelle. "You seem quite concerned about the blackmailer's welfare, *madame*. Are you certain he is not your friend?"

"I am concerned, because if I do not pay him then he will tell Carlson I am alive and where to find me. If the police arrest him, he has no reason to keep my secret."

It must not have occurred to Isabelle that Cadieux would

have to expose her secret. Perhaps not immediately, but sooner or later, he would have to write a report, closing her case, since she had not been murdered, after all. That information would work its way to Carlson quickly, considering how frequently he contacted the police.

Behind Isabelle, Mimi stood, wringing her hands. Apparently, the thought of Carlson finding them out had occurred to her.

George gave Isabelle a sympathetic look. "The only thing keeping the blackmailer from informing your husband of your whereabouts is the expectation that you will continue to pay him what he asks, whenever he asks. At some point, you will run out of funds, will you not? Then your husband will learn how to find you at a time when you are without money and least prepared to escape him. Better to deal with this threat to your security now, when you still have resources, than later, when the blackmailer has wrung you dry."

"*Mon Dieu!*" Isabelle lifted shaking hands to her cheeks.

"I am confident that we will not frighten him off, *madame*," Cadieux said. "In fact, we will catch him."

"He won't have a chance to hurt Isabelle, will he?" Mimi asked the inspector.

"Not even the smallest chance," he replied turning to Isabelle. "Because you will not be there. We will have someone else pose as you and drop off the payment."

"What?" Isabelle stared at Cadieux in disbelief. "He will certainly know it isn't me. No, I do not like this idea at all."

I could understand her concern. She was not only hiding from Carlson. She was hiding his child as well. At this point, she was willing to give the blackmailer anything he wanted, so long as he kept her secret. The only reason she revealed herself to Cadieux was to keep Mimi from being arrested for murder. With that single action, all the decisions had been taken from her hands. She had no control. The secrecy Isabelle worked so hard for was about to be destroyed, one way or another, along with her peace of mind. Still, I couldn't help agreeing with George, better now than later.

"We will have a woman portraying you." Cadieux spoke over Isabelle's pleas. "We will make sure she appears as much like you as possible. It will be dusk by then. He shouldn't notice the difference." He held up a hand to stop her protest. "This is a dangerous situation, and I cannot have you there."

"So Mimi and I are to wait here for someone to tell us you've caught the man or for my husband to come and demand custody of my son, is that it?" Her eyes had taken on the fear I assumed she felt every day while living with Carlson.

Cadieux faced her, his eyes gentle. "I have had a few exchanges with your husband, *madame*, and they have not left me with a good impression. I also have no patience for men who prey on those they see as weaker than them. I can make you no promises except that I will do my best to keep your husband at bay until you have managed to lose yourself again."

Like a balloon that had deflated, Isabelle sunk into a chair. "If he knows I am alive—if he finds out about my son—he won't rest until he finds me."

"It occurs to me," George said, "that Carlson Deaver is the type of man who would not want it known that his wife was so desperate to get away from him that she faked her death."

Cadieux lifted one shoulder in a casual shrug. "If it becomes necessary, I will make it clear to him that word will get out."

Mimi smiled. "You most definitely have his measure, gentlemen. He will not like that at all." She rested a hand on Isabelle's shoulder. "I can hire a good *avocat*, my dear. We will fight him in court if need be."

Cadieux consulted a watch he'd pulled from his pocket. "I shall post an officer here to wait with you in case our plan goes awry." He put away the watch and straightened his coat as if he were ready to leave.

Isabelle touched his sleeve to stop him. "You think this blackmailer also killed Berthe, don't you?"

"Mademoiselle Pepin had the note in her possession when we found her, so we know she was a target. The blackmailer would have to have told her something convincing enough that she agreed to meet him after the performance in Madame Bernhardt's dressing room." Cadieux turned his hands palms up. "For some reason, he felt he had to kill her."

"But why blackmail Berthe?" Isabelle asked. "I would never have asked her to help me."

"As I said earlier, I believe the man was guessing at who might have assisted you. She was someone you knew from the theater. It's possible he thought she would be happy to help you get away from your husband, so she could have him for herself."

His theory had also been mine and had made perfect sense to me up to this moment, but that was when I thought Isabelle, herself was the letter writer. The more I learned about Isabelle and her experience, the less inclined I was to agree with Cadieux.

"I'm not so sure it does make sense that the blackmailer killed Berthe," I said. "Isn't part of blackmail not knowing who is doing it? Why would he want to meet face to face with Berthe and allow her to see him? Particularly if he was simply guessing at her role in Isabelle's disappearance. She easily could have reported him to the police."

"And now that you mention it," George said, "he didn't ask for a meeting with Sarah Bernhardt or Isabelle. In fact, he's going to great lengths to keep Isabelle from seeing him."

Cadieux raised his hands defensively. "I admit there are many flaws with this theory and so many ways in which I could be wrong. If so, we will find out soon enough. But right now, we have an opportunity to catch the blackmailer and the fact that Mademoiselle Pepin had the threatening letter leads me to believe her murderer has something to do with the blackmail."

He focused his gaze on Isabelle. "If the blackmailer is your friend from the charity—"

"Which it isn't," Isabelle was quick to add.

"—or someone like him, then he is not a professional criminal. I can't say why he chose to meet Berthe in person. Perhaps Berthe already knew or suspected who was responsible for the letter she received and asked him to meet her with a plan to confront him. We will find out one way or the other when we catch the man."

He waited until we all agreed that was so. "Then I expect the two of you to wait here and trust us to get on with our business."

Cadieux turned back to George and me, and raised a hand as if to show us out. "Shall we?"

The inspector directed the driver to take us back to the Sûreté, and once inside the cab, we began to plan. "Madame Hazelton," he said, "is there any chance I can count on you to deliver the payment?"

A thrill washed over me. I had considered offering to take on the task but thought George would hate the very thought of it. "I was hoping you'd ask," I said, just as George raised a loud objection.

"One of your officers should do that," he said, his dark brows drawn together as he glared at Cadieux. "Don't put Frances in that dangerous position."

"I would never endanger Madame Hazelton." Cadieux was clearly insulted. "She will be as safe as if she were sitting in her salon at home."

George scowled. "We may have had some unusual guests in our salon, but they have yet to include a blackmailer who might also be a killer. Besides, back at the house, you said it was far too dangerous to allow Isabelle to do it."

"That was for the *mesdames* benefit. As much as I sympathize with them, I still don't quite trust Isabelle Deaver." Cadieux flapped a dismissive hand. "And you underestimate Madame Hazelton. She knows how to handle herself in uncertain circumstances."

Did I? I glanced at Cadieux with some surprise. "I think you may overestimate my abilities."

"This is no professional criminal," Cadieux said. "This is an opportunist. I am willing to wager a month's wages it is this man from the Daughters of Charity."

"That would be Monsieur Garaud," I said. "We spoke with him yesterday, and while I do not see him blackmailing her, I suspect he has feelings for Isabelle which may complicate matters as far as her husband is concerned."

"Leave the husband to me," Cadieux said with a note of disgust. "With regard to Garaud, perhaps you could render some assistance, Hazelton."

"You mean there's a task you can't hand off to Frances?" At Cadieux's laugh, George relaxed. "What do you have in mind?"

"I'd like you to go over to the charity as soon as possible and keep an eye on Monsieur Garaud. Follow him when he leaves, and if Isabelle Deaver should happen to show up, bring her back to her mother-in-law's home before she gets a chance to speak with him. I don't want Garaud to be forewarned. When we get back to the Sûreté, I'll assign an officer to assist you in case you have to split up."

"I'm eager to get back in the field again, but I'd rather be assisting Frances. How many men will you be able to place in the park?"

"As many as I can find," Cadieux said. "Madame Hazelton will enter and leave through the gate on rue Auguste Comte, the opposite side of the park from the Senate. There, I will have two men inside the gate and two outside."

George studied me, looking for any sign that I was reluctant to agree to the inspector's plan. "What say you, Frances? Will you be all right on your own?"

"I don't think I'll be alone," I said. "Aside from Cadieux, it sounds as though I'll have a bevy of officers watching over me. How could I be safer?"

Both men scowled at me. "Careful with talk like that," George said. "You are tempting fate."

I rolled my eyes. "Fine, I feel a modicum of confidence that the police will do their utmost to protect me, how is that? Besides, I agree with the inspector: This is someone who happened to be in Deauville and recognized a woman they thought to be dead. An opportunist, as he said. I don't think I'm in grave—"

"Don't say it!"

Both men had spoken as one. Goodness they were superstitious. "I shall take great care," I said.

By this point, we had arrived at the Sûreté. We had the cab wait for us then followed Cadieux to his office. A uniformed officer hailed him as we mounted the stairs. We all turned to see Carlson Deaver barreling toward us with determination and a full head of steam. The officer put out an arm to stop Carlson, until Cadieux waved him off.

George and I waited at the stairway when Cadieux stepped toward Carlson and walked him away from the stairs. "What can I do for you, Monsieur Deaver?"

Carlson's expression was twisted with rage. "What can you do? You can arrest that woman, that murderer. That's what you can do!"

"We have been over this, *monsieur*. There is no evidence that Madame Bernhardt had anything to do with your wife's death. You would do well to stop shouting about her far and wide. She is well within her rights to sue you for damages to her reputation."

"I am shouting because the police won't do anything about

her. She had that mob come down here to protest for her, and the police look the other way. What about Berthe Pepin's murder? Are you going to insist that the Divine Sarah Bernhardt had nothing to do with that, either?"

"At this moment we have no reason to believe she did. The investigation is still ongoing, and the police are not swayed either by protestors or grieving husbands." He put a hand on Carlson's arm and lost the hard edge in his voice. "I know as well as you that such an investigation can seem endless, but we have new leads, and we are starting to see our way to the end. You will let us do our jobs, yes? And soon we will have justice for your wife and Berthe Pepin."

Carlson ran a hand down his face. His expression softened. "What are your new leads?" He glanced past Cadieux and saw us on the stairs as if for the first time. "Is that the Hazeltons? What are you doing here? Surely, you're not involved in this?"

Cadieux patted Carlson's arm to regain his attention. "Go home, my friend. We will have some information for you soon." With that, Cadieux signaled the uniformed officer to take custody of Carlson. Without waiting to see how that ended up, Cadieux turned and ushered us up the stairs.

"You handled that much better than I would have, inspector," I said. We had reached the third floor and were headed toward Cadieux's office. "After what we learned about Carlson today, I had difficulty even looking at him."

"It comes with the job," he replied with a flap of his hand. "Most of my conversations do not take place with the kind and softhearted of society, you must understand. Generally, they are very unpleasant individuals." He shrugged. "But they deserve justice too, yes?"

"Unfortunately, men like Carlson Deaver rarely receive the justice they actually deserve," George grumbled.

"We shall see," Cadieux said. He stopped two officers walking toward us in the hallway. "I need to recruit some men for an assignment this evening," he told them. "See who is on the roster and bring me a list of those available."

The officers responded with "*Oui, chef*," and headed for the stairs. Cadieux waved us into his office. His eyes seemed to sparkle. Clearly, he was eager for the chase. "Now, before I let you go to prepare," he said, "we have about thirty minutes to devise a plan for this evening. It must work perfectly. Tonight, we catch a blackmailer."

"And possibly a murderer," George added.

Chapter Twenty

Thirty minutes later, I was back in a cab, heading to our apartment. Cadieux arranged everything with great efficiency. He paired George up with one of his officers. They were on their way to the Daughters of Charity to keep an eye on Monsieur Garaud. He sent me home with orders to change into plainer clothing, then wait for him to call for me at six-fifteen to take me to Luxembourg Gardens. I was to drop off the money exactly at seven—two hours from now. I hadn't thought to ask what he planned to do for money.

I hoped he didn't expect me to bring it.

It was a relief to be back home again. When Madame Auclair met me in the foyer, I asked about my mother. Catching sight of the clock, I realized I'd left her alone, and with a baby, for the entire afternoon. What a terrible hostess I was.

"She is in the salon, *madame*."

Good, that must mean Lily had returned to the Kendricks' apartment. Not that I didn't want to see my sister, but at least I knew Mother wasn't still caring for little Amelia.

"Are you expecting Monsieur Hazelton for dinner?" the housekeeper asked.

Good question. In fact, I had to wonder if either of us would be home for dinner. "You should count on my mother only for dinner tonight, but if something could be made available for a late supper when we return home, Monsieur Hazelton and I would be very grateful."

"Of course, *madame*."

Once again, I blessed our landlord, for having such a hectic schedule. The staff was remarkably comfortable adapting to odd hours.

Madame Auclair left for the kitchen, and I headed for the salon to see Mother. I found her writing a letter at the desk against the far wall and sank into a nearby chair. "I'm so sorry to have left you to your own devices all day, Mother. Did Lily sleep for long? Did you find something to occupy your time?"

She turned in her chair to face me, a look of mischief in her eyes. "Of course I managed to occupy myself," she said. "Lily was dead to the world for at least three hours after lunch"—she lifted her gaze to the ceiling for a moment—"and—how shall I phrase this?—during that time, Amelia and I worked out a few problems with the help of Madame Auclair."

I toyed with the idea of not even asking what she'd done. If I didn't know, I couldn't be considered complicit in whatever havoc she was about to wreak. Curiosity won out. "Why does the word *uh-oh* come to mind?"

"I have no idea whatsoever," she said airily. "Nor do I believe that even is a word. You may speak French, my dear, but your English vocabulary is atrocious."

"Nevertheless, I'm certain you know what I mean. Come now, you sound far too innocent to actually *be* innocent. What sort of devilment have you been up to?"

"I hired a nurserymaid for Amelia."

She had spoken the words so quickly they ran together. It took a moment to realize what she'd said. I gasped. "You didn't! While Lily was sleeping?"

Mother looked surprised by the question. "Of course. Had she been awake, she would have tried to stop me. However, she did wake up for the final bit, and the three of them went home together, so I'd have to call that agreement. I know it wasn't what Lily wanted, but she was too worn out to argue with me about it. By the time she is feeling refreshed again, she will realize what an advantage a nurserymaid can provide."

"Good for you," I said. "How did you find someone so quickly?"

"I asked your housekeeper. As it happens, she has a niece who is just the right age, and as the eldest of six children she has relatively good experience. Madame produced her within an hour, and after a short interview, we agreed that she would take the position while Lily remained in Paris. If Celia, that's the maid, does not wish to leave Paris when Lily is ready, or if Lily chooses to let her go when she returns home, Lily will still write her a reference. Thus, they both gain something from the experience."

"It sounds like an excellent arrangement to me, but I don't know what Patricia Kendrick will say about it."

Mother drew in a deep breath. "I am dining at her apartment this evening and bracing myself for that conversation. I'll make it clear that it was my idea and I insisted my poor tired daughter needed some help. How was Lily to refuse me? I will also remind Patricia of how much work is involved in caring for an infant. Our memories can paint those early months as all roses and sunshine, and forget about the diapers and crying."

Mother crossed her arms over her chest. "I refuse to allow her to make Lily feel bad about accepting help. If Patricia disapproves of the nurserymaid, she can take it up with me. If she dares."

I'd certainly never have the nerve to take it up with Mother. Which reminded me, I now had to inform Madame Auclair that none of us would be here for dinner tonight.

I took care of that task, then headed upstairs to my room to ring for Bridget, marveling that the world had gone about its business while I'd been occupied. Mother stepped in to help Lily, and as a result, I was free to continue our investigation.

While I waited for Bridget, I searched my wardrobe for an appropriate gown to change into. It should be something in a muted color, with little or no embellishment to draw attention to me. I needed to blend in. I found a jacket and skirt in a medium gray summer wool that looked quite businesslike. It would serve admirably. By the time Bridget arrived, I had managed to unbutton my skirt but not the blouse. Buttons down the back were the most foolish invention.

"Let me help you, ma'am." Bridget came to my rescue, as usual, and had the blouse undone in a trice. "I didn't know you were going out this evening or I'd have had something ready for you."

"Not to worry, Bridget. This came up rather at the last minute, and that outfit will do perfectly."

She wrinkled her nose. "Are you certain? It's rather plain."

"That's exactly what I'm after tonight. Mr. Hazelton and I are assisting Inspector Cadieux with a case, and I am hoping to fade into the background." When Bridget helped me step into the gray skirt, I caught sight of myself in the dressing table mirror. My hairstyle was a bit too complicated to pass for Isabelle who was also shorter than me. A simpler style would be better. Once I had the jacket on and was buttoning it up, I took a seat at the dressing table.

"I need to look a few inches shorter, Bridget. What do you think of a simple knot at the back of my head?"

Bridget focused her blue, suspicious eyes on me, one hand on her hip, the other holding the hairbrush. "So short and dowdy is what you're after, is it?" She began the dismantling of my hair style, watching me in the mirror. "It won't be particularly flattering, ma'am."

"That won't be a problem, Bridget. I'm attempting to look like someone else, and I only need to fool one person, hopefully from a distance. My height is the biggest difference between us." And my eyes, I thought. Isabelle had large brown eyes, but if I kept mine downcast, the blackmailer would be unlikely to notice they were blue. I glanced into the mirror to see Bridget frowning at me. "What is it?"

"This sounds like something dangerous."

"It shouldn't be," I said. "I shall be surrounded by policemen, and my task should only take a moment or two. Inspector Cadieux assures me I will be fine."

She sighed, but returned to the task of my hair. "Let's hope he's right."

Cadieux arrived promptly, as I'd expected. He approved my outfit with the exception of my hat. He preferred the one he brought with him—a monstrosity I'd never wear under normal circumstances. It was black straw with a short veil, which I had to admit would detract from the color of my eyes. The crown was low and the brim flat. "This really doesn't suit me at all," I said, watching myself in the wall mirror in the foyer as I attempted to adjust the hat.

"Good," he said. "It is meant to be something Isabelle Deaver would wear, so the less it suits you, the better." He cast a single glance at my reflection in the mirror and gave me a nod. "It will do."

"Fine." I moved away from the mirror and faced him. "Are we ready, then?"

He opened the door and gestured for me to precede him. Taking a deep breath to calm my nerves, I swept out the door and down the stairs to the gate, where Cadieux had a carriage waiting.

Once we were off to our destination, Cadieux handed me a small paper-wrapped parcel. I weighed it in my hands. "I assume this isn't really money, is it?"

He gawked. "Definitely not. On the unlikely chance the blackmailer eludes us, I have no intention of rewarding him."

"But then won't he immediately share Isabelle's whereabouts with Carlson?"

"It's just as likely that he will give Isabelle another chance," Cadieux said. "This secret is all the leverage he has. Once he tells it, he loses his power over her and no longer has any chance of turning that power into profit."

"I hadn't thought of that. Telling Carlson is probably the last thing he would want to do."

"That doesn't mean he won't, but we will be prepared for that possibility, too."

Really? "How can you stop someone from passing on information?"

"He is not likely to visit Monsieur Deaver in person, but in case he does, we have someone watching the apartment. That person will also monitor Deaver's mail and any messages that might be hand delivered."

"You've replaced the concierge, haven't you? How very resourceful."

"I have my moments of inspiration," he said. "Besides, the woman deserves a rest. The only thing we have little control of is the newspapers. If the blackmailer tells them, and they print the story, we can no longer keep Monsieur Deaver in the dark. But let us be positive, shall we? This exchange may go off without a hitch."

"Yes," I said, forcing my fingers away from each other as I noticed I was actually wringing my hands. "Let us hope."

Catching sight of the movement, he frowned at me. "You seem nervous, Madame Hazelton. I am surprised. Are you usually afflicted with nerves before you swoop in and confront the villain in your cases?"

"To be honest, I don't know. I've never knowingly done so. I tend to be in the middle of such a confrontation before I realize I'm in the presence of the villain." I glanced up at him as I pondered the notion. "There was that one time when my mother was with me, but by that point I was so angry I forgot to be nervous."

Cadieux observed me with surprise. "Your mother? Someday, I must meet that woman, but for tonight, you should not expect any confrontation. We will stay with the carriage down the street from the park until just before the appointed time. You will walk a block to the gate, all the while knowing I have officers on the street watching you. When you have left the package on the bench, you will return here."

"Will you be waiting here?"

"I am afraid not, but the driver is also an officer. He will not let anyone but you into the carriage. You will be safe."

"Yes, yes. I'm sure I will be." I wished I were as confident as I sounded.

"Are you sure?" Cadieux stilled my shaking hands with one of his own. It was warm and somehow, conveyed his confidence in me.

I met his gaze. "Yes, I am."

He withdrew his hand to reach into his pocket for his watch. "That is good, because I believe it is time."

So soon? I glanced out the window of the carriage to see the sun was touching the horizon. How long had we been waiting here? Up the street, the gates of Luxembourg Garden loomed.

"All right, then. I'm off." I adjusted the veil over my eyes, opened the door, and slipped down to the pavement.

"*Bonne chance*," Cadieux said, giving me a smile before he closed the door behind me.

I set off, moving with the foot traffic along rue Auguste Comte, the lingering sun warming the black hat I wore. Luxembourg Garden was a beautiful place to rest from the toil of the day, take a seat in one of the many chairs scattered along the paths, lounge on a blanket in the grass, even have a picnic lunch or supper. Few passersby could resist stepping inside the tall gates, if only for one refreshing moment.

Indeed, several people entered along with me, even though it was very close to closing time. I checked the watch pinned to my lapel. I was a few minutes early. I pretended to admire the fountain in the distance through the soldier-straight rows of plane trees while I looked for the correct bench. There, the second one from the rear gate.

It was occupied by a couple deep in conversation.

Stay calm, I admonished myself. I was meant to wait until the police blew their whistles, the signal that the park was closing. The couple would undoubtedly leave the bench at that point, wouldn't they? I squeezed my arm against my side to ensure myself that the parcel was still in my pocket. It was.

I walked a few yards past the bench, stopped and watched the picnickers on the broad expanse of grass. Then turned back. Suddenly I realized why I was so nervous. I wasn't afraid for my life—this was a simple operation, and the police were scattered about to protect me.

No, the problem was that I feared I'd fail them. That somehow, I'd make a mistake or be too obvious—or worse, that the blackmailer would recognize me and leave without picking up the package. I was worried that I'd ruin the whole plan.

I startled at the shriek of the first whistle. Deep in my thoughts, I'd lost track of the time. Glancing around, I saw the couple had already left the bench. I strolled in that direction. Those enjoying a leisurely afternoon had already packed up their baskets of food, their books and newspapers, and had headed toward one gate or another. No one seemed to be looking my way, but I placed myself in front of the bench before dropping off my parcel. Then I stepped around to the path and headed toward the gate and the street beyond, forcing myself to keep my gaze forward—until I'd passed through the gate.

At that point, I couldn't resist. Tucked away behind one of

the wide stone posts that framed the gate, I watched as people drifted past the bench and out to the street. The package remained in its spot.

Until it didn't.

I blinked. Yes, it really was gone, but who had it? I never saw anyone pick it up or even walk close enough to the bench to do so. But someone had. I examined everyone who moved toward the gate as if they were insects under a microscope. The woman coming toward me couldn't possibly have the package hidden anywhere on her person. Her clothing fit tightly to her body, but she held the hand of a little boy carrying a small boat. He adjusted his jacket. Goodness, would a blackmailer use a child like that?

Then I saw him. A man wearing a fedora pulled down over his brow and an overcoat—on a fine day like this, when there was absolutely no need of an extra layer. He approached the gate at a normal pace. Where were the police? Had they missed him completely? Would he get away?

At the very moment I decided I would have to stop him myself, I spied another man, also wearing an unnecessary overcoat, oddly combined with a straw boater. His coat was open and flapping as he quickly caught up with the man I'd been watching. The problem was that I didn't know where the second man had come from. Could he have picked up the package? Was he one of Cadieux's men? Would they be dressed so conspicuously?

Both men were coming closer. Another few steps and the first man would pass by me. Then what? Surely, the police had an eye on him. Another breath and he was almost beside me. Just as the first mysterious man passed through the gate, the second one caught him by the arm. Relief coursed through me. Surely, the second man was a police officer intent on apprehending the blackmailer.

Unfortunately, the blackmailer was larger and shook him off.

I did the only thing I could think of and barreled into the first man. At the same time, the smaller man tackled him from behind. All three of us ended up on the pavement in the center of the gate, each of us struggling to get away and at the same time determined to hold on to one of the others.

A few people stopped to watch. Others sidestepped so as not to trip over us. A pair of hands grabbed me under my arms and pulled me up. I struggled against them until I saw that a group of police officers had both of the mysterious men on their feet. I glanced at the ground to see the package between them.

But which one of them had picked it up?

"Madame Hazelton." I heard the words growled near my ear. It was Cadieux who had me. He let me go and turned me around to face him. "I thought you understood your directions," he said.

"But, but," I sputtered. "He was getting away."

"Madame Hazelton?"

I turned at the sound of my name and looked into the incredulous face of the first mysterious man.

"Henri?" Could the *comte* really be the blackmailer?

The other man had lost his hat in the struggle. As soon as he glanced my way, I recognized him, too.

Monsieur Garaud.

Chapter Twenty-one

"Ah! You have him." George ran up to the gate and stopped to take in the chaotic scene before him. Monsieur Garaud struggled while two officers fastened handcuffs on his wrists. Henri, who was already secured, shouted that he'd have all of their jobs once he lodged his complaint with the *préfet de police*, the mayor, and other officials whose names I didn't recognize. I brushed bits of grass and dirt from my clothes, Cadieux shouted orders, and the blackmail payment still lay on the ground.

George glanced from me to Cadieux. "What exactly is going on here?"

The inspector held up a hand, signaling that George should wait, then swept up the package and gave orders to his officers for the removal of the detainees to the Sûreté. He would meet them there.

At his request, George and I followed the inspector to the carriage that still waited for him a block away. None of us spoke until we were inside and on our way. "I take it you followed Monsieur Garaud from the charity to the park?" Cadieux said to George.

"In a manner of speaking, we did. When he hailed a taxi, it became clear he wasn't going to his usual spot for dinner nor to his home. Your officer and I decided he must be coming here or paying a call on Isabelle. We split up. I chose the park. It seems I arrived several minutes behind him. Is he our man?" His brow furrowed. "And what was the *comte* doing there? And why do you have bits of grass on your skirt, Frances?"

Pity. I'd thought I'd brushed away the evidence of my failure to follow Cadieux's instructions. Rather than upset George with the truth, I focused on more important matters. "I think Henri is the blackmailer."

"Did you see him pick up the package?" Cadieux asked.

I heaved a sigh. "No. The package was on the bench, then it was missing, and Henri was walking toward the exit."

"Did you see him with the package?" George asked.

"No."

Cadieux waved a hand. "My officers were better positioned to see which one of those two picked it up. We will find out soon enough."

"If Victor Garaud had already picked up the package, why would he attack Henri?" I asked. "Wouldn't he have simply scurried away?"

George looked confused. "Garaud attacked the *comte*?"

"Yes," I said. "I saw him from the corner of my eye as I was running at Henri. We both landed on him at about the same time."

"You ran at him?" George's dark brows drew together.

Oops.

"Did I miss the part of your assignment that had you apprehending the blackmailer singlehandedly?" George asked. "What were you thinking?"

"That he was getting away," I replied—quite reasonably, I thought.

"We had him in our sights the whole time," Cadieux said.

I knew he made the comment as a rebuttal to mine, but it served my purposes as a way to console George. "You see," I said. "If the police had Henri in their sight the whole time, then they also had an eye on me. Therefore, I was never in any danger."

Both men stared at me while they tried to untangle my logic. In this case, I thought it better to keep them baffled. "In any event, I am safe, and both men are in custody, so all's well that ends well, don't you think?"

Cadieux shook his head and gave George a look of sympathy. "Just agree with her, *mon ami*, it will save us all time. As for ending well, we have yet to reach the end and may have a long way to go."

The officers had already returned to the Sûreté with Victor and Henri, by the time the three of us arrived. George was working to convince the inspector to let us sit in, or listen in, to his questioning of the suspects, claiming that information we'd gathered during our investigation could be valuable in determining if the men were lying.

Cadieux remained doubtful but led us down a hallway to an interrogation room with a battered table and four wooden chairs. "You may wait here while I check on the suspects. Under interrogation, I expect each of them to point a finger at the other, but it is possible one of them may give himself away through a hasty comment."

When Cadieux left the room, George turned a smoldering glare on me. He was clearly still angry. I suppose I ought to have trusted the police to do their jobs, but instinct had taken over. With a wary smile, I took a seat at the table and patted the chair next to me. Rather than sit, George swooped me up from my seat and hugged me against his chest.

"Don't ever do anything like that again," he murmured close to my ear. When he released me, he cupped my face in his hands, his eyes gazing into mine. "Ever," he repeated. "What if he'd had a weapon?"

I hadn't thought of that. Frankly, I hadn't thought at all. "I won't, dear. Or at least I'll try not to." I took his hand in both of mine. "I was worried the whole time that something would go wrong." I hated to admit it, but George deserved to know.

"Ahem."

We both glanced over at the door to see Cadieux waiting patiently, leaning against the frame. "Whenever you are ready?" He motioned to the table.

"Ah, yes," George said. We released each other and joined the inspector at the table.

"What comes next?" I asked.

"Two of my officers saw *monsieur le comte* remove the package from the bench."

"Henri is the blackmailer." Though I had suspected as much, it was still a shock to have it confirmed.

"We shall see," Cadieux said. "I am still very interested in why Monsieur Garaud was in the park and why he lunged at the *comte*." He shrugged. "Perhaps to get the package, yes? We shall speak with him first."

"Why him when it was Henri who picked up the payment?" I asked.

"*Monsieur le comte* presents a dilemma," Cadieux said. "He picked up the package, this we know. But do you remember why Madame Deaver was paying the blackmailer?"

"Of course," I said. "To keep him from revealing to her husband that she was still alive."

"*Exactement!*" Cadieux laced his fingers together and leaned toward us. "Even if Monsieur Garaud is not the blackmailer, because he alerted the Mesdames Deaver to the body the police found, we know already that he is aware that Isabelle Deaver was not murdered that night. Questioning him should be quite straightforward."

"I see," George said. "If Henri is the blackmailer, then he knows Isabelle is alive. If not, he should be under the impression that Isabelle was murdered back in January."

"Questioning him will take a bit more finesse." Cadieux stood at the sound of movement in the hallway outside the door. "That will be our first suspect." He pointed out some grillework near the ceiling on the back wall. "We'll be right next door. You should be able to hear everything."

George and I agreed with the arrangement as Cadieux headed for the door. "Be sure to keep your voices down. I'd rather that no one know I've left you here, so if you are discovered, I shall have to ask you to leave."

George and I settled in when Cadieux left us. We heard footsteps and shuffling in the hallway outside, Cadieux giving instruction to another officer as they entered the room next door. Finally, Victor's voice and the closing of the outer door indicated that everyone was assembled. I assumed the interrogation room was similar to ours—dull beige walls, scarred wooden table, and a mismatched selection of chairs.

"Victor Garaud, have you been told that you may have an *avocat* present to advise you, if you so wish?" Cadieux asked.

Victor muttered something I didn't quite hear, but since Cadieux continued with his questions, I assumed he denied any need of legal counsel.

"Why were you in the park today?" Cadieux asked.

Victor cleared his throat. "As I said. I have nothing to say to the police."

"This could be short," I whispered. George replied with a grimace.

"Do you know why we have detained you?" Cadieux continued.

"I assume for fighting with that man."

"Fighting, you call it?" Cadieux asked. "It looked more like assault. Were you waiting for *monsieur le comte*?"

"*Monsieur le comte?*" Victor's voice was little more than a squeak. I could picture his foot shaking as it had done when George and I had questioned him.

"Yes." Cadieux's voice again. "Do you mean to say you did not know the man you attacked?"

"I-I—" Victor cleared his throat. "I have nothing to say."

The young man's voice shook. He was a bundle of nerves, and I had a feeling I knew why. I moved around to the other side of the table where I knew a drawer was placed. I found a pencil inside then dug into my bag for something to write on, ultimately finding one of my calling cards.

"What are you doing?" George whispered.

"He's afraid to answer Cadieux's questions," I whispered back.

"Obviously, but why does that have you scrambling about?"

"Because of why he's afraid." I'd written a note on the card and handed it to George. "Cadieux has to ask about her."

"I'm not—"

"Hush," I whispered. "Read it."

George glanced at the card in his hand. His brows shot up as he read it. When his gaze returned to me, he was nodding. "You could be right, but what am I to do with this? Slide it under the door?"

"Yes, that would work." I swept my hand in a go-ahead motion.

With a shrug, George slipped quietly from the room, returning immediately, with a gesture that said it was out of our hands now.

"What is that?" I heard the inspector ask. Then, "Let me see it."

There was a pause where I heard only footsteps, perhaps, Cadieux's? Then a long-suffering sigh—definitely from Cadieux. "All right, Monsieur Garaud, you visited the park this evening and for some reason, you attacked another man. Why? Did Isabelle Deaver ask you to go there and wait for him?"

"No!"

That was the loudest comment we'd heard from Victor.

"She had nothing to do with it. She asked me to stay away."

George gave me a wink that made me grin.

In the other room, Cadieux tutted. "Did she? How long have you been in communication with Madame Deaver?"

"I—of course, I haven't spoken with her. She was killed."

"We know she is alive, Monsieur Garaud, and we know you are aware of it. Now, with that out of the way, what were you doing in the park today?" There was silence for a few minutes before Cadieux spoke again—in a kinder tone this time. "There is no reason to protect her secret any longer."

"Isabelle has been paying someone to keep that secret," Victor said at last. "When I met with her yesterday, she told me that she was to make another payment today. I saw the letter he sent her and noted the details. Then I went to the park this evening and waited." There was another pause. Then Victor sighed. "I-I thought I could stop him."

"How?"

"How?"

"Yes," Cadieux snapped. "How did you plan to stop him? Did you plan to murder him? Threaten him?"

"I-I wanted to find out who he was. Then, yes, perhaps threaten him. He had to stop. Isabelle has suffered enough."

For a few moments all we could hear was a murmured conversation, which I assumed was between Cadieux and his officers.

"Isabelle Deaver is very dear to you, is she not, *monsieur*?"

"Through our work together, we came to be friends. I care about her welfare."

"Yes, I believe you do. You helped her to plan her disappearance." Cadieux's tone was friendly, jovial. "You even alerted Mimi Deaver to the body of an unknown woman so that she could identify that body as Isabelle. I can think of no one who would go to such lengths for me."

The officers in the room chuckled and joined Cadieux in

marveling at all Victor had done for Isabelle. "Yours must be a very rare friendship, indeed."

"I believe it is," Victor said cautiously.

"Tell me," Cadieux continued, "how long ago did you become lovers?"

"We are not—"

"You insult my intelligence with your denial, *monsieur*." Cadieux spoke dismissively. The table squeaked, and I pictured the inspector leaning over it, face to face with Victor. "This evening you confronted a man you believe to be blackmailing Madame Deaver. You helped her escape her husband. Those are the actions of a man in love. You did those things to save the one you love—or maybe two loved ones?"

I smothered a gasp and gaped at George. I hadn't seen this coming.

"He wouldn't give her a divorce," Victor said after a long pause. "This was the only way I could conceive to protect Isabelle and our son."

Chapter Twenty-two

Cadieux asked Victor a few more questions, this time related to Berthe's murder. Victor provided an alibi and wrote down the names of the people he'd been with. A few minutes later the officers took him away, and Cadieux was back in our interrogation room, seated across the table from us.

"It appears there are a couple of points Isabelle Deaver neglected to mention," George said.

"Rather important ones," I agreed. "I had assumed her child was Carlson's. I suppose she was trying to protect the baby, and Victor."

Cadieux nodded. "I'm inclined to believe he's been truthful and was in the park to confront the blackmailer. A foolish effort, but assault is neither blackmail nor murder. We'll hold him until we check his alibi for the night of Berthe's murder and settle the matter of *monsieur le comte*."

"Yes, what about Henri?" I asked.

"The man we know picked up the blackmail payment," George added.

"He lives with Mimi Deaver," I continued, "who was involved in the plot to make Isabelle disappear. She also has a supply of the paper the blackmail notes were written on." Cadieux frowned at me, probably for pointing out details we all knew, so I moved on. "He could easily have overheard a discussion between Mimi and Isabelle, or read their correspondence. I think he's a likely suspect."

"I agree with you there," Cadieux said. "The problem will be in proving it."

"Will you mention Isabelle?"

At the sound of people moving through the hallway outside the door, Cadieux came to his feet and straightened his coat. "My hope is that he will be the one to mention her, but do feel free to send me a note if you'd like to give me some pointers." With a chilly smile, he left us to join Henri in the next room.

"I have a feeling he didn't appreciate my nudge," I said.

George grinned and bumped my shoulder with his own. "Perhaps he's miffed he didn't think of it first."

"You're probably right," I said, settling myself comfortably for the next round of questions.

Cadieux didn't make us wait long. "*Monsieur le comte*," he said upon entering the room next door, "have you been told that you may have an *avocat* present if you so wish?"

"I have no need of one, do I?" Henri's tone was relaxed, filled with goodwill. "I have committed no crime."

A shoe scuffed the floor, probably Cadieux moving about the room. "Indeed?" he said. "Why do you think we have detained you?"

"I assume it has to do with the little scuffle in the park, but I assure you I was simply defending myself. The other man attacked me."

"The other man?" Cadieux said. "You are not acquainted with him then?"

"Never saw him before in my life."

"Odd that a stranger would attack you for no reason."

"I can't argue with that, it was very odd."

"Perhaps it was the package he wanted."

"Package?"

"The package you removed from the bench, *monsieur le comte*. These officers saw you pick it up and tuck it into your coat."

"Ah, yes, that. I suppose it might belong to the other gentleman. As to my actions, I assumed someone had forgotten it. I simply hoped to return it to its owner."

"By hiding it in your coat, then leaving the park?"

"See here, just what are you suggesting?"

"That package was a blackmail payment, *monsieur*. We had officers stationed throughout the park. They saw you enter the park and walk directly to the bench. Then you retrieved the parcel, and hid it in your coat."

"This is absolutely fascinating." Henri did indeed sound interested, and totally innocent. "I bet someone came to you claiming to be threatened with something—perhaps exposure of a scandal—if they didn't pay up, this very day, at the park. Your bevy of officers were meant to catch the villain, weren't they? Then I blundered into the park and ruined your operation." He let out a series of *tsks*. "Such a shame."

"Not necessarily," Cadieux said. "We did catch you."

"Surely, you don't believe I am the culprit?" Henri's tone of bonhomie faltered.

"You did pick up the package."

"But I told you why I did that." There was a long pause where I imagined Cadieux simply staring at Henri, willing him to speak. "What about the man who attacked me? How do you know he isn't the blackmailer?" Henri's voice had taken on a rough edge.

Cadieux chuckled. "That man is one of my officers. He was simply doing his job—apprehending a criminal."

"You dare to call me a criminal? You dare to accuse me of blackmail?"

"*Quoi? Ah, oui.* Allow me to correct myself," Slow footsteps made me think Cadieux was casually walking about the room. "You are *suspected* of blackmail—and possibly murder."

"Murder? What are you talking about?"

"We believe this blackmailer may also have committed murder."

"Surely you don't believe I murdered that actress?"

The footsteps stopped. "Which actress, *monsieur*?"

"I assume you are investigating the murder of the actress a day or two ago," Henri said, his voice agitated.

"Do you mean Berthe Pepin?"

"Yes, her. I had nothing to do with that."

"Are you saying you did not go backstage to meet with her that night?"

"I am saying exactly that." Henri's tone held a note of panic. "I didn't meet with her, speak with her, or touch her. In fact, I was at a reception all night—well into the morning. There are witnesses. You can verify it."

"We will, *monsieur*. You may depend upon it." There was a pause after Cadieux spoke, and I pictured Henri breaking into a cold sweat as he came to the realization that he was in a great deal of trouble. His next words confirmed it.

"I want my *avocat*."

"I believe that is the first good decision you've made in a long time." I imagined Cadieux wearing a self-satisfied smile as he said this.

There was a plop, like something hitting the table. "Write down the location of this reception, and the names of the people you were with." There were more footfalls as Cadieux moved. "When he's done, officers, you may take him back downstairs."

* * *

It was a few moments before Cadieux popped his head into our room and signaled for us to follow him up the open winding staircase to his office on the third floor. Once inside, we all took seats, Cadieux behind his desk, George and I facing him.

"I assume you heard the interview?" Cadieux asked.

George nodded. "It was interesting, to say the least. I was particularly impressed by how quickly you managed to hire Victor Garaud and make him an officer."

"When you mentioned the murdered actress, I was waiting for Henri to blurt out that Isabelle wasn't dead." I sighed. "Unfortunately, he wasn't that foolish."

"Both tactics were worth a try," Cadieux said. "Once le Comte de Beaulieu speaks to his *avocat*, it is unlikely he will speak with us again. I hope to obtain a warrant to search his home. The fact that he showed up at the park and picked up the blackmail payment isn't very strong evidence, but should be enough for a warrant. The problem will be conducting a search before he is released."

"How long can you hold him?" George asked.

"Twenty-four hours. I can request another day if we find more evidence, but *monsieur le comte* has connections and will be pushing for release."

"Once he's released, he can hide or dispose of any evidence at his home," George said. "And go directly to Carlson Deaver to tell him his wife is still alive." He glanced at me. "That means Isabelle will be in danger."

"But if Henri admits he knows Isabelle is alive, wouldn't that make him more likely to be the blackmailer?" I asked. "Would he risk that?"

George scoffed. "I'm certain Henri could get Carlson to agree not to reveal who provided that information. In fact, if the world continues to believe Isabelle is dead, Carlson can treat her any way he likes and no one would know."

A chill overtook me at the thought. "Then you must get your warrant quickly," I said to the inspector.

"That will not ensure Madame Deaver's safety," Cadieux said. "Even if the prosecutor files charges, *monsieur le comte* will be released on pretrial bail."

"What do you mean, *if* he files charges?" I asked.

Cadieux swiped a hand through his hair. "*Mon Dieu, madame*, the elements of the case alone could be enough to put a prosecutor off."

I turned to George, still not understanding the problem.

"Isabelle has been officially pronounced dead," George said. "Henri will be accused of blackmailing a dead woman until that bit of bureaucratic paperwork can be dispensed with, along with the embarrassment to the police. Deaver might file a civil suit against his wife for illegally withholding custody of his child, unless, of course, she confesses that the child isn't his. Not to mention that Mimi might be charged with intentionally misidentifying a body." George shrugged. "With all that legal chaos going on in the background, it's quite possible the prosecutor will choose not to bother with an aristocrat dabbling in blackmail."

"That is all before the prosecutor takes into consideration that the Comte de Beaulieu is a rather important personage and one who can afford a very good *avocat*." Cadieux sighed, spreading his hands wide.

I supposed that was true. Mimi reportedly funded their lifestyle, but there was a family house in the country. Henri must have some assets to sell. And many connections, people who would gladly do him a favor.

"I am confident he is our blackmailer," Cadieux continued. "If I manage to obtain the warrant to search his premises before he is set free, perhaps I can find the jewelry Madame Deaver already gave him and make a better case. I don't have a strong one at the moment."

"Henri might go free?" I couldn't believe it. "Because the circumstances are so convoluted?" Perhaps I did believe it. Who would want to explain this mess to a judge?

Cadieux raised his hands palm out. "It is difficult to predict, though if I had more evidence, and Madame Deaver's status were cleared up legally, I would feel more confident."

George cleared his throat. "But the question remains, did he murder Berthe?"

Cadieux released a heavy sigh. "We will of course check *monsieur le comte*'s alibi, but I have a feeling he is telling the truth."

"Without Henri, I believe we are out of suspects," George said.

"Someone called on Berthe backstage after the performance," I said. "It's likely whoever that was is the person who killed her."

Cadieux pulled out the file pertaining to Berthe's murder and spread the papers across his desk. George and I moved our chairs forward to get a better look. I picked up a page that noted the times. "The performance ended at ten," I read. "Everyone was gone from the theater and the doors locked by eleven. But what about the people who do the cleaning? Does it take only an hour to clean a theater?"

"It doesn't matter," George said. "They don't clean it until the following morning."

I returned to the paperwork with a frown. "Then the theater was empty by eleven that night. Was it the cleaning people who found her in the morning?"

"It was Madame Bernhardt," George said. "The cleaners don't bother with her dressing rooms. She has staff for that. So, since Berthe was found in Sarah's dressing room, that was almost certainly where she was murdered, and it would have to have been after Sarah left for the evening."

"She said she left the theater quickly to get home to her son." I scanned the witness statements. "The police note she left around half past ten, along with several other actors." I continued to leaf through the statements. Something was missing. "Didn't anyone speak to Carlson Deaver about Berthe's murder?"

"Yes, of course," said Cadieux. He took the file and flipped through a few loose pages until he found what he was looking for. "Here it is." He frowned. "But this must be wrong."

George and I rounded the desk to look over Cadieux's shoulder. "What is it?" George asked.

"Monsieur Deaver was informed about Berthe Pepin's murder—indeed, he was already at the Sûreté, complaining about our failure to arrest Madame Bernhardt." Cadieux glanced upward and shook his head. "However, it looks as though no one has questioned Monsieur Deaver in relation to Berthe's murder."

"Seriously?" I stared at Cadieux. "Sophie Pepin told us he dined at her home that night. She said he left about nine to go home. He had time to get to the theater, but he left that note to Berthe." I glanced at George. "We assumed the police would verify his whereabouts."

Cadieux came to his feet, causing George and me to take a step back. "I will remedy that oversight right now."

"Are you going to question him?" George asked.

"Yes, though I don't feel a great deal of confidence. The only motive I can imagine is a lover's spat. And even if he did murder the woman, I have no evidence that points to him. I can only hope for a confession from a guilty mind." He frowned. "Afterward, I should let Isabelle Deaver know we have her blackmailer, even if we can't prove it. What will the two of you be doing?"

"We may also find ourselves at Mimi Deaver's home," George said. "We can deliver that message to Isabelle for you. After all, they may wish to find another residence once they know what Henri has been up to."

"And I want to speak with Mimi," I said. "I have an idea of something George and I can do to assist in moving Henri's case along."

Cadieux gave me a wary glance. "Tell the officer I left there he may take a dinner break," he said. "I have a feeling your idea is something the police would rather not know about."

I smiled. "It will be much better if you don't."

Chapter Twenty-three

"And you are sure it was Henri?"

It was heart-wrenching to deliver the news about Henri's misdeeds to Mimi, even worse to do so in her gloomy salon. Every lamp, sconce, and the chandeliers overhead were glowing, but it was still so dark in there one would think we were in the midst of a storm.

"There is no doubt it was Henri," I told her. "More than one officer observed him pick up the payment." Best not to mention that I'd tackled him myself.

Mimi was seated on the sofa next to Isabelle. She took her daughter-in-law's hand in her own. "I'm so sorry, my dear. Clearly neither of us is a good judge of men."

"I'm sorry, too," Isabelle said. "I know you care a great deal about him." She glanced from George to me. "What will happen when he is arrested? Will my story become public?"

"There might be a small problem with that," George said. "Even though we caught him picking up the package, he denies knowing that it was a payment from you. Instead, he claims he simply picked up a package he found by chance. We have nothing else that ties him to the blackmail."

"Are you saying he may go free?" Mimi choked out the words.

"The police can hold him for forty-eight hours at most," George said. "Inspector Cadieux will request a warrant to search this house for further evidence, but time is not on our side. He may not receive it until after Henri is free."

"But don't the police think he also murdered Berthe?" Isabelle's eyes were wide with astonishment.

Mimi gasped. "Heavens, I'd forgotten about that. Is Henri a murderer?"

George and I exchanged a look. "We don't think he killed Berthe. The police will check his alibi, but for now they are looking elsewhere."

Mimi dropped her gaze to her hands. "By 'elsewhere,' do you mean my son?"

"Do you think he murdered Berthe?" I asked.

"I don't know," she said, her voice barely a whisper. "I can't believe I'm saying this. I did fear for Isabelle, but now, I don't know if he is capable of such a thing." She lifted her gaze to mine. "If he is, I would want to know. I am tired of keeping my head in the sand."

"Speaking of Carlson," Isabelle said. "Will Henri tell the world that I am alive?"

"Unless he returns home to find you here, I doubt he will make any sort of public statement," I said. "To admit he knows you are alive would only give the police that much more ammunition in their case against him."

George cleared his throat. "That doesn't mean he won't anonymously reveal your address in Deauville to your husband or try once more to blackmail you."

Isabelle covered her face with her hands while Mimi tried to comfort her. "We cannot have that," Mimi said. "Is there nothing to be done?"

"Well, if we had more evidence, that would help," I said. "If, for example, you found something that might relate to his blackmail, it might be enough to charge Henri with the crime."

She gave me a hard look. "By something, do you perhaps mean the jewelry Isabelle gave him in exchange for his silence?"

"That would be perfect," I agreed.

Mimi let her gaze linger on each of us in turn, then came to her feet. "Since the police have custody of Henri for such a short time, I suggest we begin our search right now."

In France, the term *hôtel* can mean an actual hotel for travelers, a municipal building, or a grand house. The hôtel de Beulieu, Henri's family home, was the latter, and grand was an understatement. We might need more than the forty-eight hours the police could hold him to conduct this search.

We started in Henri's library, which he also used as an office. The room was the size of our drawing room at home, filled with furnishings both old and contemporary. George and Isabelle scoured the bookshelves that lined two of the walls for a hiding place suitable for a small piece of jewelry. Mimi and I took the desk. Well, I took it. Mimi fretted and paced about the room.

I seated myself at the desk and tried to get a sense of Henri's style of organization. The surface was clear of any clutter or dust. It held only a leather desk pad, a perpetual calendar in brass, a pen holder, and a desk lamp. Not much to learn from this except that Henri was neat. I scooted the chair back to open the center drawer.

"Unlocked," I said, sliding it open. "That's a happy surprise."

"Henri's servants have been with him for years," Mimi said. "He trusts them to respect his privacy. I suppose he trusts me, too."

I heard the despair in her voice and paused in my snooping to face her. We only had a short time to find the evidence. Mimi's resolve could not waver. "As you trusted him."

"I did," she said. "And then he blackmailed a member of my family. Pursing her lips, she flapped her hand. "Carry on."

"I'm surprised by how modern the furnishings are in this house," I said, thinking it best to keep her talking. "You mentioned his servants being with him for years. I would have expected the house to be full of antiques."

"That was the case when I first moved here," she said. "Every room was furnished in the heavy old style." She wrinkled her nose. "It was decades old and uncared for. Much of it was worm-eaten, threadbare, and odorous. Anything salvageable we sent to the Beaulieu château somewhere in Brittany, and good riddance. I spent my first six months in Paris furnishing this house."

I let her reminisce, while I returned to my task. Over an hour later, I joined George and Isabelle in searching the bookshelves, and we still found nothing incriminating in the library. That is to say, nothing that incriminated him in a blackmail scheme. On the other hand, I had found plenty of notes from lady friends, many of them quite recent. Henri was generous when it came to wining, dining, and gifting. I thought about Carlson's comment to George that Mimi supported the *comte*. Did she also pay for his gifts to these other women?

What was I thinking? Of course she did, just as my dowry had paid for my husband's gifts to his lady friends. Would there ever come a time when that thought didn't make me grind my teeth?

I put my past aside and gave Mimi a sympathetic smile. To the group at large, I said, "I think we are ready to move on to another room."

"We've gone through everything here," George agreed.

"His private chambers would be the next likely place for him to hide something," Mimi said. "His bedroom, dressing room, and private salon. They are on the next floor."

"I don't think it's necessary for you to accompany us, if you'd rather not," I told the older woman. She had seen every one of those love notes I'd found. Learning how often her beloved had strayed must be agonizing.

"I am definitely coming," she said, and led the way to the stairs.

Mimi enlisted the aid of her maid, and we spent another hour combing through Henri's personal effects. I had learned far more than I ever wanted to know about the man. The maid and I had gone through his dressing room while George and Isabelle took on the bedroom, then the five of us trudged, heads down, into Henri's private salon. "I feel that this is an insurmountable task," Isabelle said, taking a seat on a slipper chair. "If we don't find the other earring in Henri's private rooms, must we search the whole house?"

"I don't know that we have the time," George said. "It has taken almost three hours for the four of us to search the three rooms we've managed to cover." He took a seat and rested his arm on a tiny side table that moved under its weight. I heard a jingle as he pulled away from it. "A rather delicate thing," he said.

Less interested in the furniture than the noise, I swooped down next to the table and found a small pull for a flat narrow drawer. I put my index finger into the loop and pulled open the drawer, exposing one glittering earring resting on several folded sheets of blue paper.

"Aha!" George grinned for all he was worth. "Finally."

"You mean you found it?" Isabelle and Mimi both rushed over. "That's it," Isabelle said. "I gave him two earrings from that set. The other one he gave to Sarah."

"And here is the paper he used for the notes," George said. "Perhaps he took it from your supply, Mimi."

She confirmed it was the same. "I believe that paper has been in my office since I've been in this house. Henri probably left it for me."

Relief flooded through me. The longer our search had taken, the more I had begun to believe Henri would get away with his crime. Then I glanced at Mimi who stood next to the little table, crying into a handkerchief George had just handed her. I tapped his shoulder and the two of us stepped aside.

"Are we putting an end to their problems," I whispered, "or simply exchanging them for new ones?"

"The latter, I suspect," George replied. "You and I are not used to working by the book, but when it comes to filing charges, there are rules to follow and chains of custody for evidence. We may have mucked that up."

"Then perhaps we should let them decide what to do."

With his agreement, we returned to Mimi and Isabelle. "We may have acted a bit hastily," I said. Asking them to take seats, I looked to George to explain.

"Frances and I are working with the police," he said. "If we turn over that jewelry to Cadieux, it would be subject to many questions. Why were we searching the house in the first place? Is it possible that we didn't actually find the earring here but brought it into the house ourselves? That question is particularly likely since Isabelle is here, too.

"Nevertheless," George continued, "it ought to be enough to charge Henri with blackmail, but chances are that would expose Isabelle's secret, and I'm not sure where that would leave you in the whole scheme of things. In contrast, if he is not charged, but the possibility he could be in the future remains, he might not tell Carlson the secret. That way, the police wouldn't learn he knew Isabelle was alive. I believe Henri would be eager to protect himself."

"You may want to think about this before we take any action," I said. "As much as I want Henri to pay for his crime, I would not want to see him cause you more harm."

Mimi nodded and dried her eyes. "I understand what you are saying. I want Henri to pay, too, but there may be another way. I would like to give this some thought as you say. For now, why don't we go downstairs and have a bracing cup of tea?"

We had just reached the first floor when the butler found us. A case of lucky timing for us, as it would have been difficult to explain to one of Henri's faithful servants why we were all in his private quarters.

"What is it, François?" Mimi asked.

"An Inspector Cadieux is here to see you, *madame*," he said. "I have put him in the salon."

"Very good," Mimi said. "We will join him there. Please send in tea and coffee for all of us."

Cadieux got up from the rose velvet armchair when the four of us entered the salon. His mouth curled in a grimace. "I assume I don't want to know how the four of you have passed your evening, do I?"

"Not yet, inspector," Mimi said, indicating he should return to his seat, then took the chair next to his. The rest of us pulled up chairs nearby. "I wonder, inspector, if I even want to know the details of how you have passed your evening?" Mimi said. "I understand it was spent in the company of my son."

Cadieux nodded. "Madame, I have had the kind of day no policeman should have. We have in custody a blackmailer. I am confident of that, and I will take that case to the prosecutor, but he is unlikely to prove it in a court of law. I have just left Carlson Deaver,"—his gaze softened—"your son, *madame*. I am sorry. He has an unfortunate temper. His wife will attest, I am sure, that he is capable of causing bodily harm. He cannot account for his whereabouts on the night of Bertha Pepin's murder from the time he parted company with Sophia Pepin until he returned to his apartment."

He lifted his shoulders in a shrug. "I would be willing to bet Carlson Deaver killed Berthe Pepin, but I cannot find one witness or piece of evidence that is irrefutable, so he, too, will likely walk free."

A gasp escaped Isabelle's lips which she quickly muffled with her hand.

"I am sorry, inspector," Mimi said. "Carlson is my son, and I love him, but I know what his father was. If Carlson is like him, I wish I could give you that evidence. If Carlson is like his father, he should be in prison."

"I assume this talk of Carlson means Henri is no longer under suspicion for that crime?" I asked.

"He was at the reception, as he claimed until at least two o'clock in the morning," Cadieux said. "When pushed, the medical examiner estimates that Berthe was killed earlier than two, possibly even before everyone had left the theater, allowing her killer to simply walk out with the others."

Cadieux glanced at Isabelle. "And your friend has also been cleared of any suspicion."

"My friend?" The look of confusion on Isabelle's face reminded me that we had neglected to inform her about Victor Garaud's role in the day's proceedings. Cadieux corrected that omission.

"You arrested him?" she asked, when he had finished, her tone bordering on outrage.

"He placed himself in that situation," Cadieux said, with some asperity, and explained how Garaud tried to stop Henri from walking off with the blackmail payment I'd left on the park bench. "At the time we did not know the motive for his actions. If you had told us the nature of your relationship with him, we might have prevented his arrest."

"She has become accustomed to keeping secrets, inspector." I had never heard Mimi speak so gently. She put an arm around Isabelle's shoulder. "I'm sure you can understand why her trust is hard-won."

Cadieux lifted a hand to stop her. "Monsieur Garaud has been released, *madame*. I'm sure he is eager to tell you all about it."

"Again," George said, "that leaves us with only one suspect."

Mimi seemed to be holding back tears. "Isn't it possible the actress had another lover?"

"She lived with her sister," I said. "Sophie said there was not another man, and she was confident she would know."

"At this point, the only way we can charge your son is if he confesses," Cadieux said.

Despite what she'd said about providing evidence, Mimi's heart must have been torn in two. She wanted to protect Isabelle, but she also loved her son. "I think I might be able to arrange a confession, inspector," I said. "I'd need Mimi and Isabelle's help to bring it about, but if Carlson is guilty, I think my plan could work."

"I am willing to help," Mimi said, "But what if he is innocent?"

"Then there will be nothing for him to confess."

Cadieux leaned forward in his seat. "Let us hear this plan of yours, Madame Hazelton."

Chapter Twenty-four

The following afternoon, George and I were in a cab headed to Henri's home, to pay a call on Mimi and set my plan in motion. "What if this doesn't work?" I said for what had to be the hundredth time.

"It's far too late to turn back now," George said. "If it doesn't work, we are no worse off than we were yesterday."

"Isabelle could be significantly worse off."

He squeezed my hand. "She is willing to take the risk. Besides, I think it will work, and quite frankly, I'm looking forward to it."

I drew in a calming breath. George was right. We'd all contributed to my initial plan until it was the closest thing to perfect that I could imagine. Everyone knew their roles. We were about to set the trap, and all we could do now was hope that Carlson walked into it.

The cab stopped in front of the house and let us off. We paid the driver, walked up the path and knocked on the door. All our motions felt sped up to me. The butler answered far too quickly and didn't have us wait while he checked to see if Mimi was at home, but instead showed us to the dreary salon, where a maid was delivering tea to Mimi and Carlson. With the chandelier overhead unlit, the room was even darker than usual. That would help.

They were seated in the conversation area opposite the door and across the room. Carlson stood when George and I were announced. Mimi reached out a hand. "How lovely to see you," she said. "Will you join us for tea?"

"Yes, please do," Carlson said. "Henri is out socializing again, and I am dismal company for Mother at present."

I bit back a laugh. Carlson would have no idea that Henri was still being held at the Sûreté. Mimi had arranged the seating so that hers was the only chair on her side of the coffee table: She faced the wall behind us, while we looked out to the room. I sat beside Carlson on the settee, and George took a chair next to me. The first thing I noticed was that Carlson did not look well. His eyes were puffy and shadowed, as if he had not been sleeping. If that was due to a guilty conscience, we were about to put it at ease.

"I was surprised to see the two of you at the Sûreté yesterday," Carlson said as he took a cup of tea from Mimi. "As I'm sure you noted, I was far too angry to greet you properly. The police have been absolutely infuriating."

"Yes, you did seem rather out of sorts," George said. "Completely understandable, of course. You'd like to know the status of your late wife's investigation, and sometimes it can seem like the police move at a glacial pace."

"I understand that you've been concerned about the note Sarah Bernhardt received and that the police have not acted on it," I said with as much sympathy in my voice as I could muster.

"They have done nothing," he said. "What more do they need, I ask you? That note says it all—someone knows what she did! As for the jewelry being sent with the note, I don't believe that for a moment. If the police searched Madame Bernhardt's home, they'd likely find the rest of Isabelle's jewelry. She stole it when she killed my wife."

"Unfortunately, she isn't the only one who received such a note," George said.

Carlson furrowed his brow. "She isn't? How do you know that? What is your interest in this investigation?" He returned his cup to the table and gazed at us as if we were strangers. "Why were you both at the Sûreté yesterday?"

"We have been working with the police on this case," George said. "They really are doing their best to see justice done. A careful investigation can take quite some time."

He looked doubtful. "Indeed?"

"I think it's time for a change of subject," Mimi said. "Frances, I believe you are familiar with the young lady Carlson has been escorting lately?"

Carlson had opened his mouth to comment when his body jerked and his expression changed from confused to horrified. He'd been reaching for his cup and had instead knocked it to the floor.

"Carlson," I said, relieved he hadn't dropped the tea on my side, "are you well?" I did my best to ignore the specter Carlson was gaping at—Isabelle, who seemed to float in from the window where she'd been hiding behind the draperies. She wore theatrical makeup that made her look positively ghoulish. Carlson may have missed his wife, but he certainly didn't want a visit from beyond the grave.

Mimi looked at her son with some concern. "My dear, what is wrong?"

Behind Mimi, on the other side of the room, Isabelle stared into the distance and reached out a hand toward her husband. Her expression gave me shivers—and I knew she was no ghost, so I could imagine how Carlson must have felt.

"Gah!" Carlson jumped to his feet and quickly put the settee between him and the apparition moving toward us. Isabelle hovered just far enough behind Mimi's chair to retain her ghostly appearance. Carlson glanced at George and me, still seated and staring at him. "What is wrong with you?" he asked. "Don't you see her?"

We all craned our necks, glancing around the room, then did our best to look confused. "See who?" George asked.

Carlson thrust out his hand. "Her! Isabelle, or her ghost!"

George rounded the settee to Carlson's side. He was assigned to keep Carlson from getting too close to the "ghost." With an arm across his shoulder, he guided the frightened, shaking man back to his seat. "There's nobody there, old man," he said gently.

"My dear, you're shaking," Mimi said with genuine distress. Still, she gave nothing away. "Frances, pour him another cup of tea. That should settle your nerves, dear."

"Carlson, you hurt me," Isabelle intoned, making Carlson pull his feet up as if he were trying to climb up the back of the settee. Isabelle was a better actor than I had imagined. She'd made her voice sound as if it had come from far away—another room, or perhaps another world.

The color drained from Carlson's face until he was whiter than Isabelle's makeup. "Do you hear that? She's talking to me."

"Drink your tea, Carlson," Mimi said. "You begin to worry me."

"Can't you hear her?" Perspiration beaded on his forehead. Clearly, Isabelle's visit from the hereafter was not a happy occasion.

"Are you saying you hear Isabelle?" I put my hand to my chest. "Carlson, that is so touching."

The look he sent me said otherwise. "There is nothing touching about it." He pointed to Isabelle. "That creature is angry with me. My Isabelle adored me."

"I know better now, Carlson. You never cared about me. You simply wanted me to idolize you."

"That—that's not true."

"Sadly, it is true," she said.

Carlson slammed his palm on the table. "Why are you here, dammit? Why can't they see you?"

"I have a message for you," Isabelle said, while George snapped his fingers at Carlson's face. "Clear your conscience," she said. "I know what you did." She thrust her finger in his direction with her last words, and that was as much as Carlson could take. He shot off the settee and ran for the door.

"Carlson!" Mimi still feigned ignorance of this charade. "Where are you going?"

George caught Carlson before he reached the door to the salon. "Come, man, you must sit down." As George spoke, the door opened, seemingly of its own accord, and revealed another specter out in the hallway.

Carlson let out a high-pitched scream and scrambled across the room, away from what appeared to be the spirit of Berthe who wafted into the room, light as a ballerina.

"Berthe!" he shouted.

Mimi, George, and I didn't even bother to question him, but sat mesmerized by the performance of the amazing Sarah Bernhardt. If Isabelle had been convincing as a deceased version of herself, Sarah had us all believing she was indeed the ghost of Berthe, making the most of their similarities and hiding their differences with a filmy white veil and a loose billowy tea gown. The traces of gray in Sarah's hair were gone, leaving light red waves, falling across her shoulders.

"Carlson." She said his name as if she were deeply disappointed with him. As she took one step inside the room, Carlson shrank against the wall.

"Berthe, I didn't mean to hurt you," he stammered.

George and I exchanged a look. Was that a confession?

"Hurt me? Or kill me?"

Sarah had the tone and cadence of Berthe's voice down pat, but where Carlson would have been used to Berthe speaking in

English, Sarah spoke in French to cover any slight difference he might pick up, knowing Berthe so well. She took care to speak slowly so that he'd understand.

"I didn't mean to kill you," he replied in English. "I lost my temper." Carlson sidestepped into a table, knocked it over and tumbled to the floor. He never took his eyes off the apparition of Berthe, who slowly shook her head. "I'm sorry, Berthe, I'm so sorry."

"Why did you do it?" she asked, her expression sad and confused.

"You had that note. I found it when I visited your house." He buried his face in his hands. "I thought you were involved in Isabelle's murder."

"You didn't love Isabelle."

"I cared for her. She was biddable, trainable. She would have been the perfect wife." He spoke the last word on a sob.

"But you loved me."

"You are my very heart."

"Why did you kill me?"

"Because you took something from me!" Carlson, still on his knees, slammed his fist into the floor. "I could not let a woman get the better of me."

The spirit of Berthe put her fist on her hip and sneered at Carlson. "You were angry with me, not because you think I took your toy away, but because I wouldn't take her place. I wouldn't be subservient. You couldn't control me. What kind of man needs to have such control over his wife?"

"How—how dare you speak to me like that?"

"I am not afraid of you, Carlson. What will you do, kill me again?"

Sarah pushed her hair over her shoulder and took in the room. "How much more of this must we endure," she asked, speaking in her own voice, while gesturing to Carlson on the floor against the wall. "He has confessed to murdering Berthe, are we not done here?"

The panel next to the bookshelf opened and Inspector Cadieux and another officer stepped out. Cadieux gestured to Carlson, and the officer strode over and took hold of Carlson's arm. As the officer drew him to his feet, Carlson glanced around blankly, as if he'd just woken from a sound sleep.

"What is happening?" he asked.

Cadieux stepped forward. "You are under arrest, *monsieur*, for the murder of Berthe Pepin." Turning to Sarah he bowed. "Forgive our delay, Madame Bernhardt. We were simply entranced by your performance. I only wish I had flowers to throw at your feet."

Sarah placed a hand over her heart. "I am touched, *monsieur l'inspecteur*."

"Indeed, you were inspired, *madame*," I said. George, Mimi, Isabelle, and I had joined them across the room.

"*Brava!*" George chimed in.

"I am only pleased that I inspired this one to a confession." Sarah gestured to Carlson.

It appeared that Carlson was slowly coming to realize the woman standing in front of him was not Berthe. And when his expression changed from confusion to outrage, I assumed he also realized that he had indeed confessed.

"This was all a trick." He turned his rather stunned gaze to Cadieux. "You can't use my words against me. You tricked me into confessing."

"Me? I had nothing to do with this," Cadieux said. "I was simply asked to be here at a certain time. As for your confession, it sounded freely given to me. No one threatened you or used violence. Your own conscience made you confess."

I wasn't sure if Carlson even heard the inspector, for he was seemingly enthralled with Sarah. "You," he pointed a shaky finger at her. "She is the one you should arrest. She killed my wife."

"Don't be ridiculous, man," George said. "No one killed your wife. She's standing right behind you."

The expression on Carlson's face might have been comical, if not for the fact that Isabelle flinched when he turned around. Mimi noticed and wrapped an arm around her. Carlson's lips parted, but in his bewilderment, he had no words.

"You went too far, son," Mimi said. "Isabelle had to run from you, the same way I had to run from your father. And poor Berthe didn't get a chance to run."

"You pretended to be dead?" Carlson breathed, clearly astonished. "This is your fault. I killed Berthe, because I thought she murdered you. I was avenging your death—or what I thought was your death. Arrest her," he said, turning to Cadieux. "What she did cannot be legal."

Cadieux shrugged. "There was no insurance paid out, so she didn't defraud anyone. From what I understand, she only took from the house items you had given her, so she didn't steal anything, either. There is the matter of the wrong person being interred, but that was the other Madame Deaver's doing." He appeared perplexed. "On the whole, I can't think of a crime Isabelle Deaver has committed.

"You on the other hand," Cadieux continued, "have committed murder. In fact, you've just admitted it again." He nodded to the other officer. "Take him away."

Mimi shed a few tears when the officer led an angry and cursing Carlson from the room. Isabelle did her best to comfort her and led her back to the settee.

"It would seem your plan worked, Madame Hazelton," Cadieux said. "Though I am surprised Madame Deaver went along with it. This cannot be easy for her to see her own son arrested for murder."

"I think it would have been harder for her to know her son committed murder and remained free," I said. "And it sounded like the only way to prove his guilt was if he confessed."

"I think that is true," he said. "I only wish we could work on the conscience of our blackmailer, but I believe *monsieur le comte* does not feel any guilt for his actions. We will have to let him go tomorrow. Will Madame Deaver welcome him back home?"

I smiled. "I think Madame Deaver has a plan for Henri, too. I shouldn't worry that he will go unpunished, inspector. I have a feeling he will not appreciate his homecoming."

Chapter Twenty-five

The following day was a busy one! First of all, it was the day of the women's golf tournament. Mother had put some sort of bug in Patricia Kendrick's ear that had her not only attending the tournament but also caddying for her daughter. I happily ceded the position to her.

"That's as it should be," Mother said, never letting on that she had anything to do with this turn of events.

It wasn't yet fully dawn when we arrived at the Kendricks' apartment ready to transport everyone to Compiègne in the motorcar. When Patricia came downstairs to join us in the foyer, I was delighted to see Lily right behind her.

I greeted her with a hug. "Are you coming, as well?"

She beamed at me. "I certainly am," she said. "The nurserymaid is working out splendidly, and I think it important that we are all there to support Anne as she wins the Olympic tournament."

"Lily is far more optimistic than I," Anne said. "I just hope to put in a good effort on behalf of England."

Patricia hugged Anne to her side. "You will do England and all of us proud, my dear."

"Not if we don't get you there on time," Mother said.

"Yes," I agreed, climbing into the driver's seat. "If we are all ready, we should be off."

Though I was not as adept at driving as George, we encountered no difficulties with either the route or the motorcar on the road to Compiègne. In fact, we made a merry party. Mother sat up front with me. The three ladies managed to fit in back with Anne's golf bag across the floor at their feet. The day was fine, and I honestly don't know what more we could have asked for.

Well, a win would have been nice. Our parasols aloft, the three of us followed Anne and Patricia from hole to hole, an easy feat, as there were only ten contestants. By the sixth hole, however, it became clear that the Americans were likely to capture the first, second, and third places. Anne had played well, but was still four strokes behind the player in third place.

By the end of the tournament, she had not caught up, but she had played a good round and come in fourth. Patricia beamed with pride for her daughter. "Did you know," she said to me, "that the winner, Miss Margaret Abbott's mother was also competing?"

"I did hear that," I said. "I believe she placed seventh."

"But as far as I know," Lily said. "You are the only mother who caddied for her daughter."

"Fortunately, the bag was light, and I was not expected to offer my opinion on strategy." Patricia said with a laugh. "Nevertheless, I can't recall when I last enjoyed myself so immensely."

"As did I," Anne said.

"As did we," Lily agreed. "However, shouldn't we be on our way to your celebratory dinner?"

"I think you are just eager to see Amelia," I teased. "But you are right, we should be going. I'm sorry to say, I shan't be able to stay for the dinner. I have another obligation I must attend to."

Mother raised a brow. "Has this something to do with Mimi Deaver?"

"It does," I said. "I am to act as moral support as another mother and daughter team go to battle." In truth, they were mother and daughter-in-law, but that didn't have the same ring to it. "Alicia Stoke-Whitney and her daughter, Harriet, will be joining you for dinner, though, so you won't feel the odd man out." Alicia had not been pleased to hear that Carlson had officially been charged with murder but was greatly relieved that Harriet was safe.

Mother gave me a smile. "Her company is welcome, but I will miss you, nonetheless."

Her words warmed me and made me wish Rose were here. In the midst of all the mother and daughter relations, I missed her terribly. Instead, I hugged my mother. "I am pleased to hear that," I said, tipping my head to the ladies climbing into the back seat, "because I don't think the three Kendrick ladies will even notice I'm gone."

After dropping everyone at the Kendrick apartment, I drove back to ours. I'd rather drive from one corner of France to the other than through Paris traffic. I had so many close calls I feared I was sucking all the air out of the city one gasp at a time. Fortunately, George was prepared to take up the task of driving me to Henri's home, where we were to meet Mimi. We both fell back against our seats once we pulled up outside the house.

"I truly believe a cab is a much better way to get around Paris," I said, still breathless from the drive.

"Much better on the nerves," George said. He turned to face me. "Are you certain you don't want me to come in with you?"

"I am quite sure Mimi doesn't want you to come in. She wants to prove to herself that she can do this." I gave him a level look. "However, if you hear me scream, you must come to our rescue immediately."

He grinned. "You may count on me."

"I do," I said, placing my hand on his arm. "And I thank heaven that I can."

George leaned as close to me as the motorcar would allow. When that proved to be not enough, he cupped my cheek with his hand. "You know I feel the same."

"Yes, but it's always good to hear you say it." I turned and let myself out of the motorcar. "This shouldn't take long."

"Then Henri should be here soon. I'll wait down the street until he arrives."

Mimi and Isabelle were waiting in the foyer when I walked up. "Thank you for coming, Frances," Mimi said, waving me inside. "I don't feel quite as nervous as I'd expected, but I'm glad to have you here, in case I forget to mention something."

"It is also smart to have a witness." I took in the foyer and what I could see of the salon through the open door. "You worked very quickly."

She shrugged. "Movers can be very cooperative when a bonus is offered. Every stick of furniture I brought into this house has been moved to storage. When I settle somewhere, I'll send for it."

"I hope you won't go too far away," Isabelle said. "Once I am divorced and Victor has saved enough money for us to marry, I hope to settle near you. I still think of you as my family, you know."

Mimi smiled and patted her arm. "You are the only good that's come of this disaster."

Carlson had been charged with murder, and with a confession, Cadieux was certain he would be in prison for a long time.

Isabelle peered out the side light. "I think he's here," she said.

"Where is the butler?" I asked.

"Funny thing," Mimi said. "The servants seem to have become accustomed to being paid. When I told them I was leaving, and they saw the first of the furnishings being moved out, they packed their bags and left."

Isabelle took a step away from the door when Henri pushed it open. He glanced around, noting the absence of, well, any creature comforts.

"Mimi? What is going on?"

"Henri," Mimi said. "I've been waiting for you."

"So I see." Henri's bluff, cheerful manner was tempered with caution. "But this is hardly the greeting I was expecting. He cast a glance at Isabelle and stepped back in what appeared to be genuine surprise. "Isabelle? You are alive!"

"Stop it, Henri!" Mimi allowed her disgust to come through in her tone. "You have been aware that Isabelle was alive for some time."

Still, he feigned confusion. "Why are these ladies here, Mimi?" He peeked into the salon. "*Mon Dieu!* What have you done with everything?"

"It's all gone," she said. "You will find a few family pieces here and there, but everything that is mine is gone. As I will be, too. I'm leaving with Isabelle. You are on your own."

"Darling, don't act in haste. Let us talk about this." He reached out to embrace her, but she slipped away from his hand.

"You wish to talk, Henri? Why don't we talk about how I've been supporting you for the last year and more while you take up with your mistresses and leave me alone. Now that I think about it, I was supporting them, too, wasn't I? If that wasn't bad enough, you blackmailed Isabelle."

"No—"

"Don't bother denying it." She raised her hand palm out. "I've finally come to my senses, Henri, and I see that I gain no benefit from our association." She shrugged. "So, I'm leaving."

Henri's brows lowered. He wagged his finger at Mimi. "Do not shut me out, Mimi," he said. "I can still make trouble for the late Madame Deaver, you know." He cast a glare at Isabelle.

Mimi reached into her pocket and held up an earring. Isabelle's earring. "I think this should keep you at bay, Henri. This is the jewelry you extorted from Isabelle. I have witnesses who will happily tell the police exactly where it was found. And I will happily tell them about your trip to Deauville at the beginning of August."

"I never told you—" he began.

"Of course you didn't," Mimi continued. "It was on your calendar, which is also in my possession. Now, you will stay away from Isabelle and me, because if I ever see your face again, I will turn both items over to the police, and they will charge you with blackmail."

Henri could not have looked more astonished if she had doused him with a bucket of water. "*Mon Dieu*, Mimi! When did you become so hard?"

"Not hard, Henri, wise. And it's about time." Mimi's gaze took in Isabelle and me. "And I think I'm done talking with you now. Ladies, are you ready to go?"

Isabelle and I each took one arm and guided Mimi through the door while Henri stared in disbelief. Though she had appeared fearless, I could feel her shaking as we moved down the path to the street where George waited.

Once we were all settled in the motorcar, I looked at the two stronger, wiser women in the backseat.

"Henri is standing at the door as if he doesn't know what to do with himself," George observed as he pulled into the street.

"He had better figure it out soon," Mimi said. "I canceled my account with the city, too, so he has no electricity or water. He is facing a cold, dark night ahead."

"With no furnishings," I added.

"And no servants," Isabelle said with a smile. "You really are wise, Mimi."

George started the motorcar and pulled into the street. "Where are we taking you ladies?" he asked.

"The Ritz," Mimi said. "Isabelle's young man is waiting there for her, as is their little baby."

"We are all staying in Paris for Berthe's funeral tomorrow," Isabelle said. "Sarah kindly offered to pay the expenses, and Mimi and I intend to help Sophie financially, if she will allow us."

"It seems the least I can do for her," Mimi added. "After the funeral, Victor and Isabelle will travel to Deauville. As for me, I thought a little luxury might be nice while I decide what to do with myself. I've considered paying a visit to Lottie."

"I'm sure she'd be delighted to see you," I said.

Mimi frowned. "I worry that she thinks I've neglected her. I haven't seen her since I came to France. Now that she's married, I'd like to assure myself that she chose wisely and is happy."

"This brings to mind that old saying," I said.

George glanced at me. "Don't interfere with your child's marriage?" he guessed.

I laughed and patted his cheek. "A mother's work is never done."

Acknowledgments

My books would never have made it into your hands without the assistance and support of the people noted below.

Many thanks to David Anstett of Alliance Française de Detroit for introducing me to your friends and colleagues. To Anne Deguy for taking the time to meet with me in Paris. Our conversation gave me a greater understanding of Parisians of any era.

A big thank you to Cara Black for pointing me in the right direction regarding French law and to the most beautiful library I've ever seen. I'm also grateful to the Richelieu Library for the wealth of information, photographs, and film on the Sarah Bernhardt Theater.

Writing is so much more fun with writer friends, and I'm so grateful to Mary Keliikoa, my wonderful critique partner, Barb Goffman, my editor, and all my agency siblings, particularly Sierra Godfrey and Melissa Liebling-Goldberg. Thank you for your invaluable feedback.

Thanks so much to my editor John Scognamiglio and the team at Kensington who work so hard to make the Countess of Harleigh series a success. Thank you to the booksellers and librarians who champion my books and recommend them to readers.

My family is such a wonderful support. I'm so grateful for all of you. And a special thanks to my husband, Dan, love of my life and greatest support of all.